BY LAND

where tombstones mark the way and corpses litter the route;

BY SEA

where bubbles signal the last gasps of victims;

BY AIR

where vultures lazily flap awaiting the certain sight of their next meal—

Wherever you travel in Hitchcock territory, you can be sure of a first-class ticket to terror.

SLAY RIDE

"The horrifying malignance of John Wyndham's full-length novel is alone worth the price!"
—Chattanooga Times

ALFRED HITCHCOCK PRESENTS

SLAY RIDE

More tales from
Stories That Scared Even Me

Alfred Hitchcock, Editor

A DELL BOOK

ACKNOWLEDGMENTS

MEN WITHOUT BONES, by Gerald Kersh. Reprinted by permission of Joan Daves. Originally appeared in *Esquire*. Copyright, 1954, by Gerald Kersh.

NOT WITH A BANG, by Damon Knight. Reprinted by permission of the author. From *Far Out,* by Damon Knight. Originally appeared in *Magazine of Fantasy and Science Fiction*. Copyright, 1949, by Mercury Press, Inc.

PARTY GAMES, by John Burke. Reprinted by permission of the author and London Authors. Copyright © 1965, by John Burke.

X MARKS THE PEDWALK, by Fritz Leiber. Reprinted by permission of the author and the author's agent, Robert P. Mills. Copyright © 1963, by The Barmaray Co., Inc.

CURIOUS ADVENTURE OF MR. BOND, by Nugent Barker. Reprinted from *Best Tales of Terror* (No. 2), Faber and Faber.

TWO SPINSTERS, by E. Phillips Oppenheim. Reprinted by permission of Peter Janson-Smith Ltd., London. Copyright, 1926, by the Executors of E. Phillips Oppenheim deceased.

THE CAGE, by Ray Russell. Reprinted by permission of the author and his agents, Scott Meredith Literary Agency, Inc. Copyright © 1959, by Ray Russell.

OUT OF THE DEEPS, by John Wyndham. Reprinted by permission of the author and the author's agents, Scott Meredith Literary Agency, Inc., and Michael Joseph, Ltd., London. Published in England as *The Kraken Wakes*. Copyright, 1953, by John Wyndham.

*The editor gratefully acknowledges
the invaluable assistance of Robert Arthur
in the preparation of this volume*

CONTENTS

AHEM!
IF I MAY
HAVE A MOMENT—

I hope no one will construe the title of this tome as a challenge. It is—in case you were so eager to get to the stories that you didn't notice—*Stories That Scared Even Me*. This is meant as a simple statement of fact, not as a summons for you to cry in ringing tones that some of the stories didn't scare *you*. Why the word *Even* is in there I don't know. I proposed to call the book, in a simple and dignified manner, *Stories That Scared Me*. I was overruled. It seems that *Stories That Scared Even Me* has more swing to it. And this is, obviously, the day of the swinger.

For myself, I do no more than affirm that the stories in this book all gave me one or more of the pleasurable sensations associated with fear. Some quite terrified me. Some profoundly disturbed me and left me with a sense of deep uneasiness. Others prickled my nerve ends pleasurably, touched my spine with chills, or made me swallow hard as I registered their impact. Some did several of these things at once.

On that basis I offer them to you, trusting you will share with me these emotions, so enjoyable when they can be experienced in the snug embrace of an easy chair in the comfort of one's home.

And now I relinquish the screen to the main feature.

ALFRED J. HITCHCOCK

MEN
WITHOUT
BONES

Gerald Kersh

We were loading bananas into the *Claire Dodge* at Puerto Pobre, when a feverish little fellow came aboard. Everyone stepped aside to let him pass—even the soldiers who guard the port with nickel-plated Remington rifles, and who go barefoot but wear polished leather leggings. They stood back from him because they believed that he was afflicted-of-God, mad; harmless but dangerous; best left alone.

All the time the naphtha flares were hissing, and from the hold came the reverberation of the roaring voice of the foreman of the gang down below crying: "Fruta! Fruta! *FRUTA!*" The leader of the dock gang bellowed the same cry, throwing down stem after stem of brilliant green bananas. The occasion would be memorable for this, if for nothing else—the magnificence of the night, the bronze of the Negro foreman shining under the flares, the jade green of that fruit, and the mixed odors of the waterfront. Out of one stem of bananas ran a hairy grey spider, which frightened the crew and broke the banana-chain, until a Nicaraguan boy, with a laugh, killed it with his foot. It was harmless, he said.

It was about then that the madman came aboard, unhindered, and asked me: "Bound for where?"

He spoke quietly and in a carefully modulated voice; but there was a certain blank, lost look in his eyes that suggested to me that I keep within ducking distance of his restless hands which, now that I think of them, put me in mind of the gray, hairy, bird-eating spider.

"Mobile, Alabama," I said.

"Take me along?" he asked.

"None of my affair. Sorry. Passenger myself," I said. "The skipper's ashore. Better wait for him on the wharf. He's the boss."

"Would you happen, by any chance, to have a drink about you?"

Giving him some rum, I asked: "How come they let you aboard?"

"I'm not crazy," he said. "Not actually . . . a little fever, nothing more. Malaria, dengue fever, jungle fever, rat-bite fever. Feverish country, this, and others of the same nature. Allow me to introduce myself. My name is Goodbody, Doctor of Science of Osbaldeston University. Does it convey nothing to you? No? Well then; I was assistant to Professor Yeoward. Does *that* convey anything to you?"

I said: "Yeoward, Professor Yeoward? Oh yes. He was lost, wasn't he, somewhere in the upland jungle beyond the source of the Amer River?"

"Correct!" cried the little man who called himself Goodbody. "I saw him get lost."

Fruta!—Fruta!—Fruta!—Fruta! came the voices of the men in the hold. There was rivalry between their leader and the big black stevedore ashore. The flares spluttered. The green bananas came down. And a kind of sickly sigh came out of the jungle, off the rotting river—not a wind, not a breeze—something like the foul breath of high fever.

Trembling with eagerness and, at the same time, shaking with fever chills, so that he had to use two hands to raise his glass to his lips—even so, he spilled most of the rum— Doctor Goodbody said: "For God's sake, get me out of this country—take me to Mobile—hide me in your cabin!"

"I have no authority," I said, "but you are an American citizen; you can identify yourself; the Consul will send you home."

"No doubt. But that would take time. The Consul thinks I am crazy too. And if I don't get away, I fear that I really will go out of my mind. Can't you help me? I'm afraid."

"Come on, now," I said. "No one shall hurt you while I'm around. What are you afraid of?"

"Men without bones," he said, and there was something in his voice that stirred the hairs on the back of my neck. "Little fat men without bones!"

I wrapped him in a blanket, gave him some quinine, and let him sweat and shiver for a while, before I asked, humoring him: "What men without bones?"

He talked in fits and starts in his fever, his reason staggering just this side of delirium:

". . . What men without bones? . . . They are nothing to be afraid of, actually. It is they who are afraid of you. You can kill them with your boot, or with a stick. . . . They are something like jelly. No, it is not really fear—it is the nausea, the disgust they inspire. It overwhelms. It paralyses! I have seen a jaguar, I tell you—a full-grown jaguar—stand frozen, while they clung to him, in hundreds, and ate him up alive! Believe me, I saw it. Perhaps it is some oil they secrete, some odor they give out . . . I don't know . . ."

Then, weeping, Doctor Goodbody said: "Oh, nightmare —nightmare—nightmare! To think of the depths to which a noble creature can be degraded by hunger! Horrible, horrible!"

"Some debased form of life that you found in the jungle above the source of the Amer?" I suggested. "Some degenerate kind of anthropoid?"

"No, no, no. *Men!* Now surely you remember Professor Yeoward's ethnological expedition?"

"It was lost," I said.

"All but me," he said. ". . . We had bad luck. At the Anaña Rapids we lost two canoes, half our supplies and most of our instruments. And also Doctor Terry, and Jack Lambert, and eight of our carriers . . .

"Then we were in Ahu territory where the Indians use poison darts, but we made friends with them and bribed them to carry our stuff westward through the jungle . . . because, you see, all science starts with a guess, a rumor, an old wives' tale; and the object of Professor Yeoward's expedition was to investigate a series of Indian folk tales that tallied. Legends of a race of gods that came down from the sky in a great flame when the world was very young. . . .

"Line by criss-cross line, and circle by concentric circle, Yeoward localized the place in which these tales had their root—an unexplored place that has no name because the

Indians refuse to give it a name, it being what they call a 'bad place'."

His chills subsiding and his fever abating, Doctor Goodbody spoke calmly and rationally now. He said, with a short laugh: "I don't know why, whenever I get a touch of fever, the memory of those boneless men comes back in a nightmare to give me the horrors. . . .

"So, we went to look for the place where the gods came down in flame out of the night. The little tattooed Indians took us to the edge of the Ahu territory and then put down their packs and asked for their pay, and no consideration would induce them to go further. We were going, they said, to a very bad place. Their chief, who had been a great man in his day, sign-writing with a twig, told us that he had strayed there once, and drew a picture of something with an oval body and four limbs, at which he spat before rubbing it out with his foot in the dirt. Spiders? we asked. Crabs? What?

"So we were forced to leave what we could not carry with the old chief against our return, and go on unaccompanied, Yeoward and I, through thirty miles of the rottenest jungle in the world. We made about a quarter of a mile in a day . . . a pestilential place! When that stinking wind blows out of the jungle, I smell nothing but death, and panic. . . .

"But, at last, we cut our way to the plateau and climbed the slope, and there we saw something marvelous. It was something that had been a gigantic machine. Originally it must have been a pear-shaped thing, at least a thousand feet long and, in its widest part, six hundred feet in diameter. I don't know of what metal it had been made, because there was only a dusty outline of a hull and certain ghostly remains of unbelievably intricate mechanisms to prove that it had ever been. We could not guess from where it had come; but the impact of its landing had made a great valley in the middle of the plateau.

"It was the discovery of the age! It proved that countless ages ago, this planet had been visited by people from the stars! Wild with excitement, Yeoward and I plunged into this fabulous ruin. But whatever we touched fell away to fine powder.

"At last, on the third day, Yeoward found a semicircular plate of some extraordinarily hard metal, which was covered with the most maddeningly familiar diagrams. We cleaned it, and for twenty-four hours, scarcely pausing to eat and drink, Yeoward studied it. And, then, before the dawn of the fifth day he awoke me, with a great cry, and said: 'It's a map, a map of the heavens, and a chart of a course from Mars to Earth!'

"And he showed me how those ancient explorers of space had proceeded from Mars to Earth, via the Moon. . . . 'To crash on this naked plateau in this green hell of a jungle?' I wondered. 'Ah, but was it a jungle then?' said Yeoward. 'This may have happened five million years ago!'

"I said: 'Oh, but surely! it took only a few hundred years to bury Rome. How could this thing have stayed above ground for five thousand years, let alone five million?' Yeoward said: 'It didn't. The earth swallows things and regurgitates them. This is a volcanic region. One little upheaval can swallow a city, and one tiny peristalsis in the bowels of the earth can bring its remains to light again a million years later. So it must have been with the machine from Mars . . .'

" 'I wonder who was inside it,' I said. Yeoward replied: 'Very likely some utterly alien creatures that couldn't tolerate the Earth, and died, or else were killed in the crash. No skeleton could survive such a space of time.'

"So, we built up the fire, and Yeoward went to sleep. Having slept, I watched. Watched for what? I didn't know. Jaguars, peccaries, snakes? None of these beasts climbed up to the plateau; there was nothing for them up there. Still, unaccountably, I was afraid.

"There was the weight of ages on the place. *Respect old age,* one is told. . . . The greater the age, the deeper the respect, you might say. But it is not respect; it is dread, it is fear of time and death, sir! . . . I must have dozed, because the fire was burning low—I had been most careful to keep it alive and bright—when I caught my first glimpse of the boneless men.

"Starting up, I saw, at the rim of the plateau, a pair of eyes that picked up luminosity from the fading light of the fire. *A jaguar,* I thought, and took up my rifle. But it could not have been a jaguar because, when I looked left, and right I saw that the plateau was ringed with pairs of shining eyes . . . as it might be, a collar of opals; and there came to my nostrils an odor of God knows what.

"Fear has its smell as an animal-trainer will tell you. Sickness has its smell—ask any nurse. These smells compel healthy animals to fight or to run away. This was a combination of the two, plus a stink of vegetation gone bad. I fired at the pair of eyes I had first seen. Then, all the eyes disappeared while, from the jungle, there came a chattering and a twittering of monkeys and birds, as the echoes of the shot went flapping away.

"And then, thank God, the dawn came. I should not have liked to see by artificial light the thing I had shot between the eyes.

"It was grey and, in texture, tough and gelatinous. Yet in form, externally, it was not unlike a human being. It had eyes, and there were either vestiges—or rudiments—of head, and neck, and a kind of limbs.

"Yeoward told me that I must pull myself together; overcome my 'childish revulsion,' he called it; and look into the nature of the beast. I may say that he kept a long way away from it when I opened it. It was my job as zoologist of the expedition, and I had to do it. Microscopes and other delicate instruments had been lost with the canoes. I worked with a knife and forceps. And found? Nothing: a kind of digestive system enclosed in very tough jelly, a rudimentary nervous system, and a brain about the size of a walnut. The entire creature, stretched out, measured four feet.

"In a laboratory I could tell you, perhaps, something about it . . . with an assistant or two, to keep me company. As it was, I did what I could with a hunting-knife and forceps, without dyes or microscope, swallowing my nausea—it was a nauseating thing!—memorizing what I found. But, as the sun rose higher, the thing liquefied, melted, until by nine o'clock there was nothing but a glutinous gray puddle, with two green eyes swimming in it. . . . And these eyes—I can see them now—burst with a thick *pop*, making a detestable sticky ripple in that puddle of corruption. . . .

"After that, I went away for a while. When I came back, the sun had burned it all away, and there was nothing but something like what you see after a dead jellyfish has evaporated on a hot beach. Slime. Yeoward had a white face when he asked me: 'What the devil is it?' I told him that I didn't know, that it was something outside my experience, and that although I pretended to be a man of science with a detached mind, nothing would induce me ever to touch one of the things again.

"Yeoward said: 'You're getting hysterical, Goodbody. Adopt the proper attitude. God knows, we are not here for the good of our health. Science, man, science! Not a day passes but some doctor pokes his fingers into fouler things than that!' I said: 'Don't you believe it. Professor Yeoward, I have handled and dissected some pretty queer things in my time, but this is something repulsive. I have nerves, I dare say. Maybe we should have brought a psychiatrist. . . . I notice, by the way, that you aren't too anxious to come close to me after I've tampered with that thing. I'll shoot one with pleasure, but if you want to investigate it, try it yourself and see!'

"Yeoward said that he was deeply occupied with his metal plate. There was no doubt, he told me, that this machine that had been had come from Mars. But, evidently, he preferred to keep the fire between himself and me, after I had touched that abomination of hard jelly.

"Yeoward kept himself to himself, rummaging in the ruin. I went about my business, which was to investigate forms of animal life. I do not know what I might have found, if I had had—I don't say the courage, because I didn't lack that—if I had had some company. Alone, my nerve broke.

"It happened one morning. I went into the jungle that surrounded us, trying to swallow the fear that choked me, and drive away the sense of revulsion that not only made me want to turn and run, but made me afraid to turn my back even to get away. You may or may not know that, of all the beasts that live in that jungle, the most impregnable is the sloth. He finds a stout limb, climbs out on it, and hangs from it by his twelve steely claws; a tardigrade that lives on leaves. Your tardigrade is so tenacious that even in death, shot through the heart, it will hang on to its branch. It has an immensely tough hide covered by an impenetrable coat of coarse, matted hair. A panther or a jaguar is helpless against the passive resistance of such a creature. It finds itself a tree, which it does not leave until it has eaten every leaf, and chooses for a sleeping place a branch exactly strong enough to bear its weight.

"In this detestable jungle, on one of my brief expeditions —brief, because I was alone and afraid—I stopped to watch a giant sloth hanging motionless from the largest bough of a half-denuded tree, asleep, impervious, indifferent. Then, out of that stinking green twilight came a horde of those jellyfish things. They *poured up* the tree, and writhed along the branch.

"Even the sloth, which generally knows no fear, was afraid. It tried to run away, hooked itself on to a thinner part of the branch, which broke. It fell, and at once was covered with a shuddering mass of jelly. Those boneless men do not bite: they suck. And, as they suck, their color changes from gray to pink and then to brown.

"But they are afraid of us. There is race-memory involved here. We repel them, and they repel us. When they became aware of my presence, they—I was going to say, ran away—they slid away, dissolved into the shadows that kept dancing and dancing and dancing under the trees. And the horror came upon me, so that I ran away, and arrived back at our camp, bloody about the face with thorns, and utterly exhausted.

"Yeoward was lancing a place in his ankle. A tourniquet was tied under his knee. Near-by lay a dead snake. He had broken its back with that same metal plate, but it had bitten him first. He said: 'What kind of a snake do you call this? I'm afraid it is venomous. I feel a numbness in my cheeks and around my heart, and I cannot feel my hands.'

"I said: 'Oh my God! You've been bitten by a jarajaca!'

"'And we have lost our medical supplies,' he said, with regret. 'And there is so much work left to do. Oh, dear me, dear me! . . . Whatever happens, my dear fellow, take *this* and get back.'

"And he gave me that semi-circle of unknown metal as a sacred trust. Two hours later, he died. That night the circle of glowing eyes grew narrower. I emptied my rifle at it, time and again. At dawn, the boneless men disappeared.

"I heaped rocks on the body of Yeoward. I made a

pylon, so that the men without bones could not get at him. Then—oh, so dreadfully lonely and afraid!—I shouldered my pack and took my rifle and my machete, and ran away, down the trail we had covered. But I lost my way.

"Can by can of food, I shed weight. Then my rifle went, and my ammunition. After that, I threw away even my machete. A long time later, that semi-circular plate became too heavy for me, so I tied it to a tree with liana-vine, and went on.

"So I reached the Ahu territory, where the tattooed men nursed me and were kind to me. The women chewed my food for me, before they fed me, until I was strong again. Of the stores we had left there, I took only as much as I might need, leaving the rest as payment for guides and men to man the canoe down the river. And so I got back out of the jungle. . . .

"Please give me a little more rum." His hand was steady, now, as he drank, and his eyes were clear.

I said to him: "Assuming that what you say is true: these 'boneless men'—they were, I presume, the Martians? Yet it sounds unlikely, surely? Do invertebrates smelt hard metals and——"

"Who said anything about Martians?" cried Doctor Goodbody. "No, no, no! The Martians came here, adapted themselves to new conditions of life. Poor fellows, they changed, sank low; went through a whole new process—a painful process of evolution. What I'm trying to tell you, you fool, is that Yeoward and I did *not* discover Martians. Idiot, don't you see? *Those boneless things are men. We are Martians!*"

NOT WITH
A BANG

Damon Knight

Ten months after the last plane passed over, Rolf Smith knew beyond doubt that only one other human being had survived. Her name was Louise Oliver, and he was sitting opposite her in a department-store café in Salt Lake City. They were eating canned Vienna sausages and drinking coffee.

Sunlight struck through a broken pane like a judgment. Inside and outside, there was no sound; only a stifling rumor of absence. The clatter of dishware in the kitchen, the heavy rumble of streetcars: never again. There was sunlight; and silence; and the watery, astonished eyes of Louise Oliver.

He leaned forward, trying to capture the attention of those fishlike eyes for a second. "Darling," he said, "I respect your views, naturally. But I've got to make you see that they're impractical."

She looked at him with faint surprise, then away again. Her head shook slightly. *No. No, Rolf, I will not live with you in sin.*

Smith thought of the women of France, of Russia, of Mexico, of the South Seas. He had spent three months in the ruined studios of a radio station in Rochester, listening to the voices until they stopped. There had been a large colony in Sweden, including an English cabinet minister. They reported that Europe was gone. Simply gone; there was not an acre that had not been swept clean by radioactive dust. They had two planes and enough fuel to take them anywhere on the Continent; but there was nowhere to go. Three of them had the plague; then eleven; then all.

There was a bomber pilot who had fallen near a government radio station in Palestine. He did not last long, because he had broken some bones in the crash; but he had seen the vacant waters where the Pacific Islands should have been. It was his guess that the Arctic ice fields had been bombed.

There were no reports from Washington, from New York, from London, Paris, Moscow, Chungking, Sydney. You could not tell who had been destroyed by disease, who by the dust, who by bombs.

Smith himself had been a laboratory assistant in a team that was trying to find an antibiotic for the plague. His superiors had found one that worked sometimes, but it was a little too late.When he left, Smith took along with him all there was of it—forty ampoules, enough to last him for years.

Louise had been a nurse in a genteel hospital near Denver. According to her, something rather odd had happened to the hospital as she was approaching it the morning of the attack. She was quite calm when she said this, but a vague look came into her eyes and her shattered expression seemed to slip a little more. Smith did not press her for an explanation.

Like himself, she had found a radio station which still functioned, and when Smith discovered that she had not contracted the plague, he agreed to meet her. She was, apparently, naturally immune. There must have been others, a few at least; but the bombs and the dust had not spared them.

It seemed very awkward to Louise that not one Protestant minister was left alive.

The trouble was, she really meant it. It had taken Smith a long time to believe it, but it was true. She would not sleep in the same hotel with him, either; she expected and received, the utmost courtesy and decorum. Smith had learned his lesson. He walked on the outside of the rubble-heaped sidewalks; he opened doors for her, when there were still doors; he held her chair; he refrained from swearing. He courted her.

Louise was forty or thereabout, at least five years older than Smith. He often wondered how old she thought she was. The shock of seeing whatever it was that had happened to the hospital, the patients she had cared for, had sent her mind scuttling back to her childhood. She tacitly admitted that everyone else in the world was dead, but she seemed to regard it as something one did not mention.

A hundred times in the last three weeks, Smith had felt an almost irresistible impulse to break her thin neck and go his own way. But there was no help for it; she was the only woman in the world, and he needed her. If she died, or left him, he died. Old bitch! he thought to himself furiously, and carefully kept the thought from showing on his face.

"Louise, honey," he told her gently, "I want to spare your feelings as much as I can. You know that."

"Yes, Rolf," she said, staring at him with the face of a hypnotized chicken.

Smith forced himself to go on. "We've got to face the facts, unpleasant as they may be. Honey, we're the only man and the only woman there are. We're like Adam and Eve in the Garden of Eden."

Louise's face took on a slightly disgusted expression. She was obviously thinking of fig leaves.

"Think of the generations unborn," Smith told her, with a tremor in his voice. Think about me for once. Maybe you're good for another ten years, maybe not. Shuddering, he thought of the second stage of the disease—the helpless rigidity, striking without warning. He'd had one such attack already, and Louise had helped him out of it. Without her, he would have stayed like that till he died, the hypodermic that would save him within inches of his rigid hand. He thought desperately, If I'm lucky, I'll get at least two kids out of you before you croak. Then I'll be safe.

He went on, "God didn't mean for the human race to end like this. He spared us, you and me, to—" he paused; how could he say it without offending her? "parents" wouldn't do—too suggestive "—to carry on the torch of life," he ended. There. That was sticky enough.

Louise was staring vaguely over his shoulder. Her eyelids blinked regularly, and her mouth made little rabbitlike motions in the same rhythm.

Smith looked down at his wasted thighs under the tabletop. I'm not strong enough to force her, he thought. Christ, if I were strong enough!

He felt the futile rage again, and stifled it. He had to

keep his head, because this might be his last chance. Louise
had been talking lately, in the cloudy language she used
about everything, of going up in the mountains to pray for
guidance. She had not said "alone," but it was easy enough
to see that she pictured it that way. He had to argue her
around before her resolve stiffened. He concentrated furiously and tried once more.

The pattern of words went by like a distant rumbling.
Louise heard a phrase here and there; each of them
fathered chains of thought, binding her reverie tighter.
"Our duty to humanity . . ." Mama had often said—that
was in the old house on Waterbury Street, of course,
before Mama had taken sick—she had said, "Child, your
duty is to be clean, polite, and God-fearing. Pretty doesn't
matter. There's plenty of plain women that have got themselves good, Christian husbands."

Husbands . . . To have and to hold . . . Orange blos-
soms, and the bridesmaids; the organ music. Through the
haze, she saw Rolf's lean, wolfish face. Of course, he was
the only one she'd ever get; *she* knew that well enough.
Gracious, when a girl was past twenty-five, she had to take
what she could get.

But I sometimes wonder if he's really a nice man, she
thought.

". . . in the eyes of God . . ." She remembered the
stained-glass windows in the old First Episcopalian
Church, and how she always thought God was looking
down at her through the brilliant transparency. Perhaps
He was still looking at her, though it seemed sometimes
that He had forgotten. Well, of course she realized that
marriage customs changed, and if you couldn't have a regular minister . . . But it was really a shame, an outrage
almost, that if she were actually going to marry this man,
she couldn't have all those nice things. . . . There wouldn't
even be any wedding presents. Not even that. But of course
Rolf would give her anything she wanted. She saw his face
again, noticed the narrow black eyes staring at her with
ferocious purpose, the thin mouth that jerked in a slow,
regular tic, the hairy lobes of the ears below the tangle of
black hair.

He oughtn't to let his hair grow so long, she thought. It

isn't quite decent. Well, she could change all that. If she did marry him, she'd certainly make him change his ways. It was no more than her duty.

He was talking now about a farm he'd seen outside town —a good big house and a barn. There was no stock, he said, but they could get some later. And they'd plant things, and have their own food to eat, not go to restaurants all the time.

She felt a touch on her hand, lying pale before her on the table. Rolf's brown, stubby fingers, black-haired above and below the knuckles, were touching hers. He had stopped talking for a moment, but now he was speaking again, still more urgently. She drew her hand away.

He was saying, ". . . and you'll have the finest wedding dress you ever saw, with a bouquet. Everything you want, Louise, everything . . ."

A wedding dress! And flowers, even if there couldn't be any minister! Well, why hadn't the fool said so before?

Rolf stopped halfway through a sentence, aware that Louise had said quite clearly, "Yes, Rolf, I will marry you if you wish."

Stunned, he wanted her to repeat it but dared not ask, "What did you say?" for fear of getting some fantastic answer, or none at all. He breathed deeply. He said, "Today, Louise?"

She said, "Well, *today* . . . I don't know quite . . . Of course if you think you can make all the arrangements in time, but it does seem . . ."

Triumph surged through Smith's body. He had the advantage now, and he'd ride it. "Say you will, dear," he urged her. "Say yes, and make me the happiest man . . ."

Even then, his tongue balked at the rest of it; but it didn't matter. She nodded submissively. "Whatever you think best, Rolf."

He rose, and she allowed him to kiss her pale, sapless cheek. "We'll leave right away," he said. "If you'll excuse me for just a minute, dear?"

He waited for her "Of course" and then left, making footprints in the furred carpet of dust down toward the end of the room. Just a few more hours he'd have to speak to her like that, and then, in her eyes, she'd be committed to him forever. Afterward, he could do with her as he liked—beat her when he pleased, submit her to any proof of his scorn and revulsion, use her. Then it would not be too bad, being the last man on earth—not bad at all. She might even have a daughter. . . .

He found the washroom door and entered. He took a step inside, and froze, balanced by a trick of motion, upright but helpless. Panic struck at his throat as he tried to turn his head and failed; tried to scream, and failed. Behind him, he was aware of a tiny click as the door, cushioned by the hydraulic check, shut forever. It was not locked; but its other side bore the warning MEN.

PARTY GAMES

John Burke

The moment Alice Jarman opened the front door and saw Simon Potter on the step she knew that there would be trouble.

Behind her the party was growing noisy. Already a fight had broken out. Two boys were shouting at each other and there was an occasional thump as one or other of them was thrown heavily against the wall. But it was the usual sort of fight. A party at which small boys didn't fight wasn't much of a party.

Simon Potter said: "Good afternoon, Mrs. Jarman."

He was eight years of age and he was not the kind of boy who would become involved in a fight. He was polite, neat, quiet, and clever; and he was unpopular. His unpopularity was such as to keep him out of a scuffle rather than bring one down upon him. He was a cold little boy. Even as he stood there with his deferential smile he gave Alice the shivers.

He wore a new raincoat, his shoes were highly polished —probably by himself, she thought—and his pallid brown hair was sleeked back. He carried a neatly wrapped present.

Alice stepped back. Simon came on into the hall.

At the same moment the door of the sitting-room was flung back and Ronnie came pounding out. He stopped when he saw Simon. He said what Alice had been sure he would say.

"I didn't invite *him*."

"Now, Ronnie—"

"Many happy returns, Ronnie," said Simon, holding out the package.

Ronnie could not help looking at it. He could not help the instinctive movement of his hand towards it. Then he shook his head and looked up at Alice.

"But, mum . . ."

She smoothed it over—or, rather, blurred it over. The noise and exuberance from the sitting-room helped. Ronnie was unable to concentrate. He wanted to stay and argue, wanted to accept the present, and wanted to get back into the uproar. The three things bubbled up and blended in his mind. Alice took Simon's coat and steered him toward the gaiety. He didn't need to be told to wipe his feet; he added nothing to the muddy treads which some of them had left. Ronnie tried to say something, but somehow he was holding the package and then he began to unwrap it as he followed Simon into the room.

Alice stood by the door for a minute or two and looked in.

"Hey . . . look . . . super!"

Ronnie tossed shreds of paper aside and opened the box within. He took out a model crane and held it up.

"It's battery operated," said Simon quietly.

It was a simple statement, but it wiped the pleasure off Ronnie's face. The others, who had crowded closer, edged back and turned to stare at Simon. His present was more expensive than any which they had brought. He had done the wrong thing. He was always doing the wrong thing. The fact that he did a thing made it wrong.

A large boy with carroty hair pushed Ronnie. Ronnie put the crane on a chair and pushed him back. A girl with a blue hair-ribbon said, "Oh, don't start that again," and stepped to one side. She found herself close to Simon. He smiled. He looked at her and then at another girl a few feet away as though to draw them both nearer to him. "Always talking to girls," Ronnie had once said of Simon to his mother. Alice watched. Yes, she could see that he was a boy who would talk to girls because he had nothing to say to boys. But the girls were not flattered. Instead of listening to him they giggled and made eyes at each other and then scurried away, looking back and still giggling.

Alice went towards the kitchen and drew the curtains. It would soon be quite dark outside. In summer they could have had the party in the garden; but Ronnie had elected to be born in the winter, so most of his celebrations had been accompanied by a trampling of wet feet into the house and a great fussing over scarves and gloves and rain hoods and mackintoshes when the guests left.

Tom would be home in another twenty minutes or so. She would be glad to see him. Even though the din would not diminish, it would somehow be more tolerable when shared. Tom would organize games, jolly them all along, and make the little girls in particular shriek with laughter. Until he came she couldn't concentrate on the food or on anything else. She had to keep dashing back to the sitting-room to make sure that nobody was really getting hurt and nobody was being neglected. She had started them off on a game of musical chairs, but her piano playing was pretty terrible, and while she was at the keyboard there had been chaos behind her. Then she had suggested a treasure hunt, only to realize that she had done nothing about hiding the treasure before the party started.

She was not very good at organizing parties. The sheer pressure of the children's excitement overpowered her. No matter how much trouble she took in the days beforehand, when the birthday itself came she was never ready for it.

Not that it mattered, Tom assured her. Just open the door, let 'em in, and leave 'em to it. When there were signs of the furniture cracking up under the strain, bring on the sandwiches and jelly and cake and ice cream.

It was all very well for Tom. He did not get home until after she had taken the first shock of the impact. Twenty children together were not just twenty separate children added together, one plus one and so on: they combined into something larger and more terrifying. There was no telling what they might do if the circumstances were right . . . or wrong, depending on the way you looked at it.

There was a howl of derision from the sitting-room. Alice nerved herself to go and make another inspection.

By the time she got there it was impossible to tell what the cause of the howl had been. Simon Potter was backed against a wall, while Ronnie and his best friend grinned and bobbed their heads with a lunatic merriment, exaggerating the movement, slapping their sides like bad actors in a school play.

Ronnie saw his mother watching him. His grin became genuine and affectionate. Then, before she could frown or ask him a silent question, he swung round and gathered up an armful of his presents.

"Come and look! Look what my Dad gave me!"

Somebody groaned theatrically; a boy with pimples blew a loud raspberry. But they all gathered obediently round. It was the accepted thing to do. This was Ronnie's party and Ronnie's birthday, and at some stage it was only fair that he should insist on their inspecting his trophies.

"My Dad gave me this." Alice felt soft inside at the sound of adoration in his voice. "And this. My Dad gave me this as well." It would have been just the same if Tom had given him a cheap scribbling pad or a box of crayons: the devotion would have been there, unwavering. She loved him for loving so intensely.

Simon was watching gravely. He showed neither excitement nor boredom. He did not make approving noises; and he did not exchange glances of sly boredom with anyone. He was remote, dispassionate, unmoved.

Yet somewhere behind that bleak little face there must be envy or, at the very least, sadness. Simon's father had died years ago. His mother had brought him up with a single-minded fervour that allowed him no relaxation and little contact with other children, even though he spent so many hours and days and weeks at school with them. She worked hard in a solicitor's office and managed to run the home as well, determined that the boy should not feel the loss of his father too deeply. Each afternoon he stayed on at school for an hour in a class set aside for children with difficult journeys, difficult home backgrounds, or with working parents who could not leave their jobs in time to meet their children. By the time he did get home Mrs. Potter was in the house waiting for him, ready to devote herself to him. She was proud of the life they made together, proud of their home, and proud of Simon's unfailing neatness and politeness and cleverness.

Alice saw him clear his throat. She saw it rather than heard it—the way he ducked his chin and gulped. He edged forward. She thought for a moment that he was going to ask if he could have a closer look at one of Ronnie's presents. Then he said:

"What about a game?"

The heads turned. They stared at him. It was a little girl who broke the sudden silence. She seemed glad of the diversion.

"Yes. Let's do something. What shall we play?"

"If we could get some pieces of paper"—Simon glanced swiftly at Alice and she realized that all along he must have been aware of her scrutiny—"we could put someone's name on it and—"

"Oh, *paper* games," groaned someone.

"Choose a name," Simon persisted, "and write it down one side of the paper. Then divide the paper up into squares, and have, say, flowers and trees and the names of —well, footballers if you like—and they have to begin with the letters of the name."

The boy who specialized in blowing raspberries blew another. "What's he talking about?" said the girl with the blue hair-ribbon.

"It's easy." Simon's voice rose pleadingly. "You write the name down one side of the paper. Then you write the things you're going to have across the top—that is, I mean, the categories you've chosen. And—"

"Oh, *paper* games."

Alice intervened. It was time for an adult to take control and tell them what to do. She walked into the room and tried desperately to recall the games they had played when she was a child. Her mind refused to render up its memories. All she could remember was a girl going through the seat of a chair and screaming, and a squat little boy who had gathered an audience around him while he practised spitting into the fire.

She said: "Now, everybody." They turned thankfully towards her. "What about Postman's Knock?" she ventured.

There were shrugs and hisses and moans; but the girls squealed hopefully and nudged one another, and in no time at all they were playing Postman's Knock. Alice retreated again, leaving them to it. From the kitchen door she glanced occasionally across the hall and then felt absurdly like a voyeur. Some of the boys behaved with a flamboyant confidence that indicated a prolonged study of films which they ought never to have been allowed to see. Some of the girls wriggled, others relaxed and enjoyed themselves. It was frightening to see in these children of eight and nine years of age the pattern of what they would be as adults— patterns already forming, some already established.

And there was Simon outside the door, waiting. He knocked. The girl who came looked at him warily, prepared to be haughty or coquettish. After they had kissed she wiped her lips with the back of her hand. Simon went back into the room. The girl looked up at the ceiling, and said, loudly enough for him and the others inside to hear: "Ugh!"

They soon tired—the boys sooner than the girls.

"Murder. Let's play murder!"

As the door opened and Ronnie came racing out, Alice tried to assemble good reasons why they should not play murder. She was not quick enough. Already they were racing upstairs. Two boys came into the kitchen, making for the back door, and stopped when they saw her.

"Not outside," said Alice quickly. This, at any rate, she could prevent. "It's too muddy in the back garden. You've got to stay indoors."

They turned and dashed away. She heard footsteps pounding overhead. There was a distant slamming of doors. Lights were switched off. Ronnie appeared suddenly in the splash of brightness thrown out from the kitchen. He and the pimply boy were grinning and whispering. Simon Potter passed them on his way towards the stairs. As he went they clutched each other conspiratorially.

Before Alice could make a move, Ronnie swung towards her. "Don't mind if we close the door, Mum?" He did not wait for an answer, but closed it quietly and made her a prisoner. She knew there would be yells of protest if she opened it again.

There was a full minute of uneasy silence. In her head it was incongruously noisier than the last hour had been. In the hush a tension was building up. Something was going to snap.

A muffled thump came from upstairs. It was repeated. It might have been somebody banging insistently on the floor or somebody hammering to be let out. If, she thought apprehensively, they had locked somebody into one of the rooms or one of the old cupboards at the far end of the landing . . . the creaky, cold end of this old, cold house . . . Somebody. Simon.

Then there was a convincingly blood-curdling scream.

Alice jerked the door open.

"Put that light out!"

"No, it's all right"—Ronnie's voice came from the landing—"it's over."

Feet pounded downstairs again. Lights were snapped on everywhere. Everyone was shouting at everyone else. Who had been murdered? Who was it?

To Alice's relief the victim was Marion Pickering, a fluffy little blonde with eyes too knowing for her years. There was indeed quite a possibility, thought Alice uncharitably, that Marion would finish up on the front page of certain Sunday newspapers.

Boys and girls swarmed out of every cranny. The hall seemed to boil with activity, then they were all jostling into the sitting-room. There seemed to be twice as many people here as when the party began.

She could hear the shouting. Ronnie was trying to establish some kind of order.

"Who was on the stairs . . . shut up, will you . . . we've got to find who was upstairs and who was downstairs. Now sit down . . . oh, shut up a minute, will you . . ."

The inquiry was going to be a disorderly one. It needed a strong hand to control it. Instead, there was a shouting and shrieking, a carry-over from the tenseness in the dark.

It was really dark now. Alice had not realized how swiftly the evening had taken over. Twenty minutes earlier it would still have been too hazy to play murder; now there was blackness outside the windows.

Through the hubbub of voices she heard a faint but unmistakable sound. It was Tom's key in the front door.

She was halfway across the hall as he came in.

"Darling!"

He had to lean precariously forward to kiss her. He was laden with an armful of garden tools—a trowel sticking out of some torn brown paper, a pair of secateurs, and a short-handled axe.

"Going well?" He nodded towards the sitting-room door.

"I'm so glad you're back."

"Ah. That means it's getting out of hand, mm?"

"Any minute now."

It was so wonderful to see him. His lean, furrowed face was so reassuring. The smell of pipe smoke in his hair, the quiet confidence in his eyes, the sight of his competent, capable hands: everything about him strengthened her and at the same time soothed her.

Yet there was something wrong. Something nagged at her and demanded her attention.

As he turned to lay the garden tools across the umbrella stand she realized that the sound was still going on upstairs —the intermittent thumping she had heard earlier.

"I'll just dump these," Tom was saying, "and then plunge into the fray."

She was jolted into awareness of what he had done with the tools.

"Don't leave them there! For goodness' sake! With all these little monsters in and out . . ."

"All right, all right. I'll take them out to the shed right away."

"It's filthy out there. You'll get mud all over your shoes if . . ." She broke off and laughed, and Tom laughed. "I do sound a nagger, don't I?" she said.

He tucked the implements under his arm and headed for the stairs. "I'll leave them in our room," he said firmly.

Ronnie emerged abruptly and ecstatically from the sitting-room. "Dad!" He threw himself at his father and butted him, tried to get one arm round him, smiled up at him. "Come on in here—come and see—I've got lots more things. But nothing like you gave me."

"In a minute or two, son. I've just got to go upstairs with some things. I'll be right down."

Alice looked past them into the sitting-room. She moved closer to the door. Then she said:

"Ronnie, where's Simon?"

"Mm?"

"Simon. Where is he?"

Ronnie shrugged and pummelled his father again. "Dunno. Probably gone up to the lavatory."

"Ronnie, if you've done anything . . . locked him in anywhere . . ."

"Don't be long, Dad."

Ronnie twisted away and slid cunningly past his mother. She could not bring herself to pursue him into that whirlpool of arms and legs and boisterous faces.

Tom said: "Anything wrong?"

"I don't know. I just wonder if they've played some horrid joke on Simon Potter."

"Didn't think he'd been invited."

"He wasn't. But he came, poor kid. They've kept him on the edge of things. And now I think they've done something." The din from the sitting-room was so overpowering that she could not swear to hearing the spasmodic thudding from above. "If they've locked him in one of the cupboards, or one of the rooms at the far end of the landing . . ."

"I'll see," said Tom reassuringly.

She was glad to turn away towards the kitchen and leave it all to him. Now everything was going to be all right.

Two boys scuttled out of the sitting-room.

"Mrs. Jarman—where is it, please?"

"First door on the left at the top of the stairs."

They went up two stairs at a time behind Tom. Alice felt comfortable and safe when she returned to the kitchen, instead of being a frightened outcast. She began to put the cups of jelly on a large tray. In another fifteen minutes they could start eating. After that, Tom would organize them while she cleared the food away and did the washing-up.

Ronnie came in. "Mum, where's the stuff for the game? You know, the corpse stuff."

The thudding upstairs had stopped. But there was a louder thump, as though someone had fallen or banged something heavy against the floor. Perhaps it was Tom wrenching open one of the cupboard doors: they were old, stiff, and misshapen.

"Ronnie," she began, *"did* you—"

He did not wait for her to finish. He scooped up the small tray that he had so carefully prepared earlier today, covered with a sheet of thin brown paper, and was gone again.

She heard him yelling at the top of his voice.

"All right, everyone. Come on, sit down. Now, I'm going to put the lights out . . ."

"Hey, wait for us!"

Footsteps hastened down the stairs and two or three boys dashed into the sitting-room. They must have been queueing up for the lavatory. Once one wanted to go, they all wanted to go. Soon, thought Alice, the girls would begin: they would all be smitten at the same time by the idea rather than by the necessity.

"Now," Ronnie was shouting, his voice so hoarse with continuous exertion that it cracked on every third or fourth word, "there's just been a murder. We worked out who did it, but we never got round to dealing with the corpse, did we?"

"That was me," piped up Marion.

"Yes, we know, but . . . hey, shut that door!"

There was the slam of the door and the voice was muffled. After a few minutes there was a loud squeal and a burst of laughter, then another squeal. Alice arranged triangular sandwiches on a plate. She could almost follow the progress of the game by the pitch of the shrieks. "Here's the corpse's hand," Ronnie would be saying—and then he would pass a rubber glove stuffed with rags along the line in the darkness. "Here's some of its hair"—and along would go some of the coarse strands from the old sofa which was rotting away in the garden shed. "And here are its eyeballs." Two peeled grapes would pass from flinching hand to flinching hand.

Everything was ready for the party tea. She went to the door. It was time Tom came down. She could hear no sound from him.

She went to the foot of the stairs and looked up.

"Tom—are you nearly ready?"

There was no reply. Perhaps he had had to join the end of the queue for the lavatory, having more self-control than the over-excited little boys.

Alice decided to put an end to games for the time being. She went to the sitting-room door and opened it.

"Ah, Mum, close the door."

"Time for tea." She switched on the light.

There was a squeal. Then another. And all at once it

was hysteria, no longer a joke. One little girl sat staring at what was in her hand and began to scream and scream.

Alice took a step into the room, not believing.

One boy held a severed human hand from which blood dripped over his knees. The girl who could not stop screaming was holding a human eye in her right hand. The girl next to her also held a human eye, squashed and torn. On her left the pimply boy went pale and let a tuft of hair fall between his fingers to the floor.

Alice said: "No." Somehow she kept herself upright. "No. Simon—where's Simon?"

"I'm here, Mrs. Jarman."

The voice was quite calm. She turned to find him standing at one side of the room. She tried to find words. Still cool and detached, he said:

"They locked me in. Ronnie and that one over there locked me in. But I'm all right now. I was let out, and everything's all right now."

She stared at that hideous hand, chopped bloodily off at the wrist. And she recognized it and also the colour of the hair that lay on the floor.

Simon Potter stood quite still as Alice Jarman ran from the room and up the stairs.

She found her husband lying in front of the bedroom cupboard from which he had released the boy. The garden tools lay beside him, splashed with red—the axe that had first smashed in his head and then chopped off a hand, the secateurs that had snipped off a tuft of his hair, and the trowel that had clumsily gouged out his eyes.

Simon, pale but content, was now not the only boy in that room downstairs without a father.

X MARKS
THE PEDWALK

Fritz Leiber

Based on material in Ch. 7—"First Clashes of the Wheeled and Footed Sects"—of Vol. 3 of Burger's monumental *History of Traffic*, published by the Foundation for Twenty-Second Century Studies.

The raggedy little old lady with the big shopping bag was in the exact center of the crosswalk when she became aware of the big black car bearing down on her.

Behind the thick bullet-proof glass its seven occupants had a misty look, like men in a diving bell.

She saw there was no longer time to beat the car to either curb. Veering remorselessly, it would catch her in the gutter.

Useless to attempt a feint and double-back, such as any venturesome child executed a dozen times a day. Her reflexes were too slow.

Polite vacuous laughter came from the car's loud-speaker over the engine's mounting roar.

From her fellow pedestrians lining the curbs came a sigh of horror.

The little old lady dipped into her shopping bag and came up with a big blue-black automatic. She held it in both fists, riding the recoils like a rodeo cowboy on a bucking bronco.

Aiming at the base of the windshield, just as a big-game hunter aims at the vulnerable spine of a charging water buffalo over the horny armor of its lowered head, the little old lady squeezed off three shots before the car chewed her down.

From the right-hand curb a young woman in a wheelchair shrieked an obscenity at the car's occupants.

Smythe-de Winter, the driver, wasn't happy. The little old lady's last shot had taken two members of his car pool. Bursting through the laminated glass, the steel-jacketed slug had traversed the neck of Phipps-McHeath and buried itself in the skull of Horvendile-Harker.

Braking viciously, Smythe-de Winter rammed the car over the right-hand curb. Pedestrians scattered into entries and narrow arcades, among them a youth bounding high on crutches.

But Smythe-de Winter got the girl in the wheelchair.

Then he drove rapidly out of the Slum Ring into the Suburbs, a shred of rattan swinging from the flange of his right fore mudguard for a trophy. Despite the two-for-two casualty list, he felt angry and depressed. The secure, predictable world around him seemed to be crumbling.

While his companions softly keened a dirge to Horvy and Phipps and quietly mopped up their blood, he frowned and shook his head.

"They oughtn't to let old ladies carry magnums," he murmured.

Witherspoon-Hobbs nodded agreement across the front-seat corpse. "They oughtn't let 'em carry anything. God, how I hate Feet," he muttered, looking down at his shrunken legs. "Wheels forever!" he softly cheered.

The incident had immediate repercussions throughout the city. At the combined wake of the little old lady and the girl in the wheelchair, a fiery-tongued speaker inveighed against the White-Walled Fascists of Suburbia, telling to his hearers, the fabled wonders of old Los Angeles, where pedestrians were sacrosanct, even outside crosswalks. He called for a hobnail march across the nearest lawn-bowling alleys and perambulator-traversed golf courses of the motorists.

At the Sunnyside Crematorium, to which the bodies of Phipps and Horvy had been conveyed, an equally impassioned and rather more grammatical orator reminded his listeners of the legendary justice of old Chicago, where pedestrians were forbidden to carry small arms and anyone with one foot off the sidewalk was fair prey. He broadly hinted that a holocaust, primed if necessary with a few tankfuls of gasoline, was the only cure for the Slums.

Bands of skinny youths came loping at dusk out of the Slum Ring into the innermost sections of the larger doughnut of the Suburbs, slashing defenseless tires, shooting expensive watchdogs and scrawling filthy words on the pristine panels of matrons' runabouts which never ventured more than six blocks from home.

Simultaneously, squadrons of young suburban motorcyclists and scooterites roared through the outermost precincts of the Slum Ring, harrying children off sidewalks, tossing stink-bombs through second-story tenement windows and defacing hovel-fronts with paint.

Incident—a thrown brick, a cut corner, monster tracks in the portico of the Auto Club—were even reported from the center of the city, traditionally neutral territory.

The Government hurriedly acted, suspending all traffic between the Center and the Suburbs and establishing a 24-hour curfew in the Slum Ring. Government agents moved only by centipede-car and pogo-hopper to underline the point that they favored neither contending side.

The day of enforced non-movement for Feet and Wheels was spent in furtive vengeful preparations. Behind locked garage doors, machine-guns that fired through the nose ornament were mounted under hoods, illegal scythe blades were welded to oversize hubcaps and the stainless-steel edges of flange fenders were honed to razor sharpness.

While nervous National Guardsmen hopped about the deserted sidewalks of the Slum Ring, grim-faced men and women wearing black arm-bands moved through the webwork of secret tunnels and hidden doors, distributing heavy-caliber small arms and spike-studded paving blocks, piling cobblestones on strategic rooftops and sapping upward from the secret tunnels to create car-traps. Children got ready to soap intersections after dark. The Committee of Pedestrian Safety, sometimes known as Robespierre's Rats, prepared to release its two carefully hoarded anti-tank guns.

At nightfall, under the tireless urging of the Government, representatives of the Pedestrians and the Motorists met on a huge safety island at the boundary of the Slum Ring and the Suburbs.

Underlings began a noisy dispute as to whether Smythe-de Winter had failed to give a courtesy honk before charging, whether the little old lady had opened fire before the car had come within honking distance, how many wheels of Smythe-de's car had been on the sidewalk when he hit the girl in the wheelchair and so on. After a little while the High Pedestrian and the Chief Motorist exchanged cautious winks and drew aside.

The red writhing of a hundred kerosene flares and the mystic yellow pulsing of a thousand firefly lamps mounted on yellow sawhorses ranged around the safety island illumined two tragic, strained faces.

"A word before we get down to business," the Chief Motorist whispered. "What's the current S.Q. of your adults?"

"Forty-one and dropping," the High Pedestrian replied, his eyes fearfully searching from side to side for eavesdroppers. "I can hardly get aides who are halfway *compos mentis.*"

"Our own Sanity Quotient is thirty-seven," the Chief Motorist revealed. He shrugged helplessly. "The wheels inside my people's heads are slowing down. I do not think they will be speeded up in my lifetime."

"They say Government's only fifty-two," the other said with a matching shrug.

"Well, I suppose we must scrape out one more compromise," the one suggested hollowly, "though I must confess there are times when I think we're all the figments of a paranoid's dream."

Two hours of concentrated deliberations produced the new Wheel-Foot Articles of Agreement. Among other points, pedestrian handguns were limited to a slightly lower muzzle velocity and to .38 caliber and under, while motorists were required to give three honks at one-block distance before charging a pedestrian in a crosswalk. Two wheels over the curb changed a traffic kill from third-degree manslaughter to petty homicide. Blind pedestrians were permitted to carry hand grenades.

Immediately the Government went to work. The new Wheel-Foot Articles were loudspeakered and posted. Detachments of police and psychiatric social hoppers centipedaled and pogoed through the Slum Ring, seizing outsize weapons and giving tranquilizing jet-injections to the unruly. Teams of hypnotherapists and mechanics scuttled from home to home in the Suburbs and from garage to garage, in-chanting a conformist serenity and stripping illegal armament from cars. On the advice of a rogue psychiatrist, who said it would channel off aggressions, a display of bull-fighting was announced, but this had to be cancelled when a strong protest was lodged by the Decency League, which had a large mixed Wheel-Foot membership.

At dawn, curfew was lifted in the Slum Ring and traffic reopened between the Suburbs and the Center.

After a few uneasy moments it became apparent that the *status quo* had been restored.

Smythe-de Winter tooled his gleaming black machine along the Ring. A thick steel bolt with a large steel washer on either side neatly filled the hole the little old lady's slug had made in the windshield.

A brick bounced off the roof. Bullets pattered against the side windows.

Smythe-de Winter ran a handkerchief around his neck under his collar and smiled.

A block ahead children were darting into the street, cat-calling and thumbing their noses. Behind one of them limped a fat dog with a spiked collar.

Smythe-de suddenly gunned his motor. He didn't hit any of the children, but he got the dog.

A flashing light on the dash showed him the right front tire was losing pressure. Must have hit the collar as well. He thumbed the matching emergency-air button and the flashing stopped.

He turned toward Witherspoon-Hobbs and said with thoughtful satisfaction, "I like a normal orderly world, where you always have a little success, but not not champagne-heady; a little failure, but just enough to brace you."

Witherspoon-Hobbs was squinting at the next crosswalk. Its center was discolored by a brownish stain ribbon-tracked by tires.

"That's where you bagged the little old lady, Smythe-de," he remarked. "I'll say this for her now: she had spirit."

"Yes, that's where I bagged her," Smythe-de agreed flatly. He remembered wistfully the witchlike face growing rapidly larger, the jerking shoulders in black bombazine, the wild white-circled eyes. He suddenly found himself feeling that this was a very dull day.

TWO
SPINSTERS

E. Phillips Oppenheim

Erneston Grant was without doubt a very first-class detective, but as a wayfarer across Devonshire byroads with only a map and a compass to help him he was simply a washout. Even his fat little white dog, Flip, sheltered under a couple of rugs, after two hours of cold, wet, and purposeless journeying, looked at him reproachfully. With an exclamation of something like despair, Grant brought his sobbing automobile to a standstill at the top of one of the wickedest hills a Ford had ever been asked to face even on first speed, and sat looking around him.

In every direction the outlook was the same. There were rolling stretches of common divided by wooded valleys of incredible depth. There was no sign of agricultural land, no sign of the working of any human being upon the endless acres, and not a single vehicle had he passed upon the way. There were no sign-posts, no villages, no shelter of any sort. The one thing that abounded was rain—rain and mist. Gray wreaths of it hung over the commons, making them seem like falling fragments of cloud, blotted out the horizon, hung over every hopeful break in the distance—an encircling, enveloping obscurity. Then, vying with the mists in wetness, came the level rain—rain which had seemed beautiful early in the afternoon, slanting from the heavens onto the mountainside, but which had long ago lost all pretense to being anything but damnably offensive, chilling, miserably wet. Flip, whose nose only now appeared uncovered, sniffed disgustedly, and Grant, as he lit a pipe, cursed slowly but fluently under his breath. What a country! Miles of byways without a single direction post, endless stretches without a glimpse of a farmhouse or village. And the map! Grant solemnly cursed the man who had ordained it, the printer who had bound it, and the shop where he had bought it. When he had finished Flip ventured upon a gentle bark of approval.

"Somewhere or other," Grant muttered to himself, "should lie the village of Nidd. The last sign-post in this blasted region indicated six miles to Nidd. Since then we have traveled at least twelve, there has been no turning to the left or to the right, and the village of Nidd is as though it had never been."

His eyes pierced the gathering darkness ahead. Through a slight uplifting in the clouds it seemed to him that he could see for miles, and nowhere was there any sign of village or of human habitation. He thought of the road along which they had come, and the idea of retracing it made him shiver. It was at that moment, when bending forward to watch the steam from his boiling radiator, that he saw away on the left a feebly flickering light. Instantly he was out of the car. He scrambled onto the stone wall and looked eagerly in the direction from which he had seen it. There was without doubt a light; around that light must be a house. His eyes could even trace the rough track that led to it. He climbed back to his place, thrust in his clutch, drove for about forty yards, and then paused at a gate. The track on the other side was terrible, but then so was the road. He opened it and drove through, bending over his task now with every sense absorbed.

Apparently traffic here, if traffic existed at all, consisted only of an occasional farm wagon of the kind he was beginning to know all about—springless, with holes in the boarded floor and with great, slowly turning wheels. Nevertheless he made progress, skirted the edge of a tremendous combe, passed, to his joy, a semi-cultivated field, through another gate, up it seemed suddenly into the clouds, and down a fantastic corkscrew way until at last the light faced him directly ahead. He passed a deserted garden and pulled up before a broken-down iron gate which he had to get out of the car to open. He punctiliously closed it after him, traversed a few yards of grass-grown, soggy avenue, and finally reached the door of what might once have been a very tolerable farmhouse, but which appeared now, notwithstanding the flickering light burning upstairs, to be one of the most melancholy edifices the mind of man could conceive.

With scant anticipations in the way of a welcome, but with immense relief at the thought of a roof, Grant descended and knocked upon the oak door. Inside he could hear almost at once the sound of a match being struck; the light of a candle shone through the blindless windows of a room on his left. There were footsteps in the hall, and the door was opened. Grant found himself confronted by a woman who held the candle so high that it half illumined, half shadowed her features. There was a certain stateliness, however, about her figure which he realized even in those first few seconds at the door.

"What do you want?" she asked.

Grant, as he removed his hat, fancied that the answer was sufficiently obvious. Rain streamed from every angle of his be-mackintoshed body. His face was pinched with the cold.

"I am a traveler who has lost his way," he explained. "For hours I have been trying to find a village and inn. Yours is the first human habitation I have seen. Can you give me a night's shelter?"

"Is there any one with you?" the woman inquired.

"I am alone," he replied. "Except for my little dog," he added, as he heard Flip's hopeful yap.

The woman considered.

"You had better drive your car into the shed on the left-hand side of the house," she said. "Afterwards you can come in. We will do what we can for you. It is not much."

"I am very grateful, madam," Grant declared in all sincerity.

He found the shed, which was occupied only by two farm carts in an incredible state of decay. Afterwards he released Flip and returned to the front door which had been left open. Guided by the sound of crackling logs, he found his way to a huge stone kitchen. In a high-backed chair in front of the fire, seated with her hands upon her knees but gazing eagerly towards the door as though watching for his coming, was another woman, also tall, approaching middle age, perhaps, but still of striking presence and fine features. The woman who had admitted him was bending over the fire. He looked from one to the other in amazement. They were fearfully and wonderfully alike.

"It is very kind of you, ladies, to give us shelter," he began. "Flip! Behave yourself, Flip!"

A huge sheep dog had occupied the space in front of the fire. Flip without a moment's hesitation had run towards him, yapping fiercely. The dog, with an air of mild surprise, rose to his feet, and looked inquiringly downwards. Flip insinuated herself into the vacant place, stretched herself out with an air of content, and closed her eyes.

"I must apologize for my little dog," Grant continued. "She is very cold."

The sheep dog retreated a few yards and sat on his haunches considering the matter. Meanwhile the woman who had opened the door produced a cup and saucer from a cupboard, a loaf of bread, and a small side of bacon, from which she cut some slices.

"Draw your chair to the fire," she invited. "We have very little to offer you, but I will prepare something to eat."

"You are good Samaritans indeed," Grant declared fervently.

He seated himself opposite the woman who as yet had scarcely spoken or removed her eyes from his. The likeness between the two was an amazing thing, as was also their silence. They wore similar clothes—heavy, voluminous clothes they seemed to him—and their hair, brown and slightly besprinkled with gray, was arranged in precisely the same fashion. Their clothes belonged to another world, as did also their speech and manners, yet there was a curious but unmistakable distinction about them both.

"As a matter of curiosity," Grant asked, "how far am I from the village of Nidd?"

"Not far," the woman who was sitting motionless opposite to him answered. "To any one knowing the way, near enough. Strangers are foolish to trust themselves to these roads. Many people are lost who try."

"Yours is a lonely homestead," he ventured.

"We were born here," the woman answered. "Neither my sister nor I have felt the desire for travel."

The bacon began to sizzle. Flip opened one eye, licked

her mouth and sat up. In a few minutes the meal was prepared. A high-backed oak chair was placed at the end of the table. There was tea, a dish of bacon and eggs, a great loaf of bread and a small pat of butter. Grant took his place.

"You have had your supper?" he asked.

"Long ago," the woman who had prepared his meal replied. "Please to serve yourself."

She sank into the other oak chair exactly opposite her sister. Grant, with Flip by his side, commenced his meal. Neither had tasted food for many hours and for a time both were happily oblivious to anything save the immediate surroundings. Presently, however, as he poured out his second cup of tea, Grant glanced towards his hostesses. They had moved their chairs slightly away from the fire and were both watching him—watching him without curiosity, yet with a certain puzzling intentness. It occurred to him then for the first time that although both had in turn addressed him, neither had addressed the other.

"I can't tell you how good this tastes," Grant said presently. "I am afraid I must seem awfully greedy."

"You have been for some time without food, perhaps," one of them said.

"Since half past twelve."

"Are you traveling for pleasure?"

"I thought so before to-day," he answered, with a smile to which there was no response.

The woman who had admitted him moved her chair an inch or two nearer to his. He noticed with some curiosity that immediately she had done so her sister did the same thing.

"What is your name?"

"Erneston Grant," he replied. "May I know whom I have to thank for this hospitality?"

"My name is Mathilda Craske," the first one announced.

"And mine is Annabelle Craske," the other echoed.

"You live here alone?" he ventured.

"We live here entirely alone," Mathilda acquiesced. "It is our pleasure."

Grant was more than ever puzzled. Their speech was subject to the usual Devonshire intonation and soft slurring of the vowels, but otherwise it was almost curiously correct. The idea of their living alone in such a desolate part, however, seemed incredible.

"You farm here, perhaps?" he persisted. "You have laborers' cottages, or some one close at hand?"

Mathilda shook her head.

"The nearest hovel," she confided, "is three miles distant. We have ceased to occupy ourselves with the land. We have five cows—they give us no trouble—and some fowls."

"It is a lonely life," he murmured.

"We do not find it so," Annabelle said stiffly.

He turned his chair towards them. Flip, with a little gurgle of satisfaction, sprang onto his knees.

"Where do you do your marketing?" he asked.

"A carrier from Exford," Mathilda told him, "calls every Saturday. Our wants are simple."

The large room, singularly empty of furniture as he noticed looking round, was full of shadowy places, unilluminated by the single oil lamp. The two women themselves were only dimly visible. Yet every now and then in the flickering firelight he caught a clearer glimpse of them. They were so uncannily alike that they might well be twins. He found himself speculating as to their history. They must once have been very beautiful.

"I wonder whether it will be possible," he asked, after a somewhat prolonged pause, "to encroach further upon your hospitality and beg for a sofa or a bed for the night? Any place will do," he added hastily.

Mathilda rose at once to her feet. She took another candle from the mantelpiece and lit it.

"I will show you," she said, "where you may sleep."

For a moment Grant was startled. He had happened to glance towards Annabelle and was amazed at a sudden curious expression—an expression almost of malice in her face. He stooped to bring her into the little halo of lamplight more completely, and stared at her incredulously. The expression, if ever it had been there, had vanished. She was simply looking at him patiently with something in her face which he failed utterly to understand.

"If you will follow me," Mathilda invited.

Grant rose to his feet. Flip turned round with a final challenging bark to the huge sheep dog who had accepted a position remote from the fire, and failing to elicit any satisfactory response trotted after her master. They passed into a well-shaped but almost empty hall, up a broad flight of oak stairs to the first landing. Outside the room from which Grant had seen the candlelight she paused for a moment and listened.

"You have another guest?" he inquired.

"Annabelle has a guest," she replied. "You are mine. Follow me, please."

She led the way to a bedchamber in which was a huge four-poster and little else. She set the candle upon a table and turned down a sort of crazy quilt which covered the bed-clothes. She felt the sheets and nodded approvingly. Grant found himself unconsciously following her example. To his surprise they were warm. She pointed to a great brass bed-warmer with a long handle at the further end of the room, from which a little smoke was still curling upwards.

"You were expecting someone to-night?" he asked curiously.

"We are always prepared," she answered.

She left the room, apparently forgetting to wish him good-night. He called out pleasantly after her, but she made no response. He heard her level footsteps as she descended the stairs. Then again there was silence—silence down below, silence in the part of the house where he was. Flip, who was sniffing round the room, at times showed signs of excitement, at times growled. Grant, opening the window, ventured upon a cigaret.

"Don't know that I blame you, old girl," he said. "It's a queer place."

Outside there was nothing to be seen and little to be heard save the roaring of a water torrent close at hand and the patter of rain. He suddenly remembered his bag, and, leaving the door of his room open, descended the stairs. In the great stone kitchen the two women were seated exactly as they had been before his coming, and during his meal. They both looked at him but neither spoke.

"If you don't mind," he explained, "I want to fetch my bag from the car."

Mathilda, the woman who had admitted him, nodded acquiescence. He passed out into the darkness, stumbled his way to the shed, and unstrapped his bag. Just as he was turning away he thrust his hand into the tool chest and drew out an electric torch which he slipped into his pocket. When he reëntered the house the two women were still seated in their chairs and still silent.

"A terrible night," he remarked. "I can't tell you how thankful I am to you for so hospitably giving me shelter."

They both looked at him but neither made any reply. This time when he reached his room he closed the door firmly, and noticed with a frown of disappointment that except for the latch there was no means of fastening it. Then he laughed to himself softly. He, the famous captor of Ned Bullivant, the victor in a score of scraps with desperate men, suddenly nervous in this lonely farmhouse inhabited by a couple of strange women.

"Time I took a holiday," he muttered to himself. "We don't understand nerves, do we, Flip?" he added.

Flip opened one eye and growled. Grant was puzzled.

"Something about she doesn't like," he ruminated. "I wonder who's in the room with the lighted candles?"

He opened his own door once more softly and listened. The silence was almost unbroken. From downstairs in the great kitchen he could hear the ticking of a clock, and he could see the thin streak of yellow light underneath the door. He crossed the landing and listened for a moment outside the room with the candles. The silence within was absolute and complete—not even the sound of the ordinary breathing of a sleeping person. He retraced his steps, closed his own door, and began to undress. At the bottom of his bag was a small automatic. His fingers played with it for a moment. Then he threw it back. The electric torch, however, he placed by the side of his bed. Before he turned in he leaned once more out of the window. The roar of the falling water seemed more insistent than ever. Otherwise there was no sound. The rain had ceased but the sky was black and starless. With a little shiver he turned away and climbed into bed.

He had no idea of the time but the blackness outside was just as intense when he was suddenly awakened by Flip's low growling. She had shaken herself free from the coverlet at the foot of the bed and he could see her eyes, wicked little spots of light, gleaming through the darkness. He lay quite still for a moment, listening. From the first he knew that there was someone in the room. His own quick intuition had told him that, although he was still unable to detect a sound. Slowly his hand traveled out to the side of the bed. He took up the electric torch and turned it on. Then with an involuntary cry he shrank back. Standing within a few feet of him was Mathilda, still fully dressed, and in her hand, stretched out towards him, was the cruelest-looking knife he had ever seen. He slipped out of bed, and, honestly and self-confessedly afraid, kept the light fixed upon her.

"What do you want?" he demanded, amazed at the unsteadiness of his own voice. "What the mischief are you doing with that knife?"

"I want you, William," she answered, a note of disappointment in her tone. "Why do you keep so far away?"

He lit the candle. The finger which on the trigger of his automatic had kept Bullivant with his hands up for a life-long two minutes, was trembling. With the light in the room now established, however, he felt more himself.

"Throw that knife on the bed," he ordered, "and tell me what you were going to do with it?"

She obeyed at once and leaned a little towards him.

"I was going to kill you, William," she confessed.

"And why?" he demanded.

She shook her head sorrowfully.

"Because it is the only way," she replied.

"My name isn't William, for one thing," he objected, "and what do you mean by saying it is the only way?"

She smiled, sadly and disbelievingly.

"You should not deny your name," she said. "You are William Foulsham. I knew you at once, though you had been away so long. When *he* came," she added, pointing towards the other room, "Annabelle believed that he was William. I let her keep him. I knew. I knew if I waited you would come."

"Waiving the question of my identity," he struggled on, "why do you want to kill me? What do you mean by saying it is the only way?"

"It is the only way to keep a man," she answered. "Annabelle and I found that out when you left us. You knew each of us loved you, William; you promised each of us never to leave—do you remember? So we sat here and waited for you to come back. We said nothing, but we both knew."

"You mean that you were going to kill me to keep me here?" he persisted.

She looked towards the knife lovingly.

"That isn't killing," she said. "Don't you see—you could never go away. You would be here always."

He began to understand, and a horrible idea stole into his brain.

"What about the man she thought was William?" he asked.

"You shall see him if you like," she answered eagerly. "You shall see how peaceful and happy he is. Perhaps you will be sorry then that you woke up. Come with me."

He possessed himself of the knife and followed her out of the room and across the landing. Underneath the door he could see the little chink of light—the light which had been his beacon from the road. She opened the door softly and held the candle over her head. Stretched upon another huge four-poster bed was the figure of a man with a ragged, untidy beard. His face was as pale as the sheet and Grant knew from the first glance that he was dead. By his side, seated stiffly in a high-backed chair, was Annabelle. She raised her finger and frowned as they entered. She looked across at Grant.

"Step quietly," she whispered. "William is asleep."

Just as the first gleam of dawn was forcing a finger of light through the sullen bank of clouds, a distraught and disheveled-looking man, followed by a small, fat, white dog stumbled into the village of Nidd, gasped with relief at the sight of the brass plate upon a door, and pulled the bell for all he was worth. Presently a window was opened and a man's shaggy head thrust out.

"Steady there!" he expostulated. "What's the trouble with you, anyway?"

Grant looked up.

"I've spent a part of the night in a farmhouse a few

miles from here," he shouted. "There's a dead man there and two mad women and my car's broken down."

"A dead man?" the doctor repeated.

"I've seen him. My car's broken down in the road or I should have been here before."

"I'll be with you in five minutes," the doctor promised.

Presently the two men were seated in the doctor's car on their way back to the farm. It was light now, with signs of clearing, and in a short time they drew up in front of the farmhouse. There was no answer to their knock. The doctor turned the handle of the door and opened it. They entered the kitchen. The fire was out, but each in her high-backed chair, Mathilda and Annabelle were seated, facing one another, speechless, yet with wide-open eyes. They both turned their heads as the two men entered. Annabelle nodded with satisfaction.

"It is the doctor," she said. "Doctor, I am glad that you have come. You know, of course, that William is back. He came for me. He is lying upstairs but I cannot wake him. I sit with him and hold his hand and I speak to him, but he says nothing. He sleeps so soundly. Will you wake him for me, please. I will show you where he lies."

She led the way from the room, and the doctor followed her. Mathilda listened to their footsteps. Then she turned to Grant with that strange smile once more upon her lips.

"Annabelle and I do not speak," she explained. "We quarreled just after you went away. We have not spoken for so many years that I forget how long it is. I should like someone to tell her, though, that the man who lies upstairs is not William. I should like someone to make her realize that you are William, and that you have come back for *me*. Sit down, William. Presently, when the doctor has gone, I will build the fire and make you some tea."

Grant sat down and again he felt his hands trembling. The woman looked at him kindly.

"You have been gone a long time," she continued. "I should have known you anywhere, though. It is strange that Annabelle does not recognize you. Sometimes I think we have lived together so long here that she may have lost her memory. I am glad you fetched the doctor, William. Now Annabelle will know her mistake."

There was the sound of footsteps descending the stairs.

The doctor entered. He took Grant by the arm and led him to one side.

"You were quite right," he said gravely. "The man upstairs is a poor traveling tinker who has been missing for over a week. I should think that he has been dead at least four days. One of us must stay here while the other goes to the police station."

Grant caught feverishly at his hat.

"I will go for the police," he said.

THE CAGE

Ray Russell

"They say," said the Countess, absently fondling the brooch at her young throat, "that he's the devil."

Her husband snorted, "Who says that? Fools and gossips. That boy is a good overseer. He manages my lands well. He may be a little—ruthless? cold?—but I doubt very much that he is the Enemy Incarnate."

"Ruthless, yes," said the Countess, gazing at the departing black-cowled, black-hosed, black-gloved figure. "But cold? He seems to be a favorite with the women. His conquests, they say, are legion."

" 'They' say. Gossips again. But there you are—would the angel Lucifer bed women?" The Count snorted again, pleased at his logical triumph.

"He might," replied his wife. "To walk the earth, he must take the shape of a man. Might not the appetites of a man go with it?"

"I am sure I do not know. These are delicate points of theology. I suggest you discuss them with a Holy Father."

The Countess smiled. "What did he want?"

"Nothing. Business. Shall we go in to dinner?"

"Yes." The Count proffered his arm and they walked slowly through the tapestried halls of the castle. "He seemed most insistent about something," the Countess said after a moment.

"Who did?"

"Your efficient overseer."

"He was urging more stringent measures with the serfs. He said his authority had no teeth if he could not back it up with the threat of severe punishment. In my father's day, he said, the thought of the castle's torture chamber kept them in line."

"Your father's day? But does he know of your father?"

"My father's harshness, my dear, has ever been a blight on our family's escutcheon. It has created enemies on many sides. That is why I am especially careful to be lenient. History shall not call us tyrants if I can help it."

"I still believe he is the devil."

"You are a goose," said the Count, chuckling. "A beautiful goose."

"That makes you a gander, my lord."

"An old gander."

They sat at table. "My lord—" said the Countess.

"Yes?"

"That old torture chamber. How strange I've never seen it."

"In a mere three months," said the Count, "you could not possibly have seen the entire castle. Besides, it can be reached only by descending a hidden stairwell with a disguised door. We'll go down after dinner, if you like, although there's really nothing there to interest a sweet young goose."

"Three months . . ." said the Countess, almost inaudibly, fingering the brooch again.

"Does it seem longer since our marriage?" asked the Count.

"Longer?" She smiled, too brightly. "My lord, it seems like yesterday."

*   *   *

"They say," said the Countess, brushing her hair, "that you're the devil."

"Do you mind?"

"Should I mind? Will you drag me down to the Pit?"

"In one way or another."

"You speak in metaphor?"

"Perhaps."

"You are equivocal."

"Like the devil."

"And, like him, very naughty."

"Why? Because I am here in your boudoir and you are dressed in hardly anything at all?"

"Because of that, yes; and because you counsel my dear husband to be a tyrant, like his father."

"Did he tell you that?"

"Yes. And he showed me the torture chamber you advised him to reopen. How wicked of you! It is a terrible place. So dark and damp, and so deep underground—why, a poor wretch could split his lungs screaming and never be heard in the castle proper."

"Your eyes are shining. I assume you found it fascinating."

"Fascinating! Of course not! It was disgusting. That horrible rack . . . ugh! to think of the limbs stretching, the tendons tearing! . . ."

"You shudder deliciously. It becomes you."

"And that dreadful wheel, and the iron boot . . . I have a pretty foot, don't you think?"

"Perfect."

"Such a high arch; and the toes so short and even. I hate long toes. You don't have long toes, do you?"

"You forget—I have no toes at all. Only hooves."

"Careful. I may believe you. And where are your horns?"

"They are invisible. Like those your husband will be wearing very soon."

"Indeed. You think highly of your charms."

"As do you. Of yours."

"Do you know what struck me as the most horrible?"

"Eh? Horrible about what?"

"The torture chamber, of course."

"Oh, of course. What struck you as most horrible?"

"There was a cage. A little cage. It looked like something you might keep a monkey in. It was too small for anything larger. And do you know what my husband said they kept in it?"

"What?"

"People!"

"No!"

"They kept people in it," she said. "They could not stand up straight, or lie down; they could not even sit, for there were only spikes to sit on. And they kept them crouching there for days. Sometimes weeks. Until they screamed to be let out. Until they went mad. I would rather be torn apart on the rack . . ."

"Or have this pretty foot crushed in the boot?"

"Don't. That tickles . . ."

"It was meant to."

"You must leave. The Count might walk in at any moment."

"Until tomorrow then, my lady . . ."

Alone, smiling to herself, the Countess abstractedly rubbed the tops of her toes where he had kissed them. She had heard of burning kisses, they were a commonplace of bad troubadours, but until this evening she had thought the term a poetic extravagance. He wanted her—oh, how he wanted her! And he would have her. But not right away. Let him wait. Let him smoulder. Let him gaze at her in her diaphanous nightdress; let him, as she lifted her arms to brush her hair, admire the high beauty of her breasts. Allow him a kiss now and then. Oh, not on the mouth, not yet—on the feet, the fingertips, the forehead. Those burning kisses of his. Let him plead and groan. Let him suffer. She sighed happily as she turned down her bed. It was fine to be a woman and to be beautiful, to dole out little favors like little crumbs and to watch men lick them up and pant and beg for more and then to laugh in their faces and let them starve. This one was already panting. Soon he would beg. And he would starve for a long, long time. Then, some night when she thought he had suffered long enough, she would allow him to feast. What a glutton he would make of himself! He would try to make up for lost time, for all the weeks of starvation, and he would feast too rapidly and it would all be over too soon and she would have to make him hungry again very quickly so she could gorge himself again. It would all be very amusing . . .

*   *   *

"If I *am* the devil, as you say they say, then why do I not overwhelm you with my infernal magic? Why do I grovel here at your feet, sick and stiff with love?"

"Perhaps it entertains you, my Dark Prince. Here: Kiss."

"No. I want your lips."

"Oh? You grow presumptuous. Perhaps you would rather leave."

"No . . . no . . ."

"That's better. I may yet grant you a promotion."

"Ah! my love! Then—"

"Oh, sit down. Not what you call my 'favor.' Just a *little* promotion. Though I don't know if you deserve even that. You want everything but you give nothing."

"Anything. Anything."

"What a large word! But perhaps *you* could indeed give me anything . . ."

"Anything."

"But they say you demand fearful things in return. I would suffer torment without end, through eternity . . . Ah, I see you do not deny this. I do believe you *are* the devil."

"I'll give you anything you desire. You have but to ask."

"I am young. Men tell me—and so does my mirror— that I am beautiful, a delight from head to toe. Do you want all this?"

"Yes! Yes!"

"Then make this beauty never fade. Make it withstand the onslaught of time and violence. Make me—no matter what may befall—live forever."

"Forever . . ."

"Haha! I've got you, haven't I? If I never die, then what of that eternal torment? Do you grant me this boon, Evil One?"

"I cannot."

"Wonderful! Oh, what an actor you are! I begin to admire you! Other men, impersonating the Adversary, would have said Yes. But you . . . how clever you are."

"I cannot grant that."

"Stop—I'm weak with laughing! This game amuses me *so* much! It lends such spice to this dalliance! I would play it to the end. Satan, look here: you really cannot grant my wish, even if I give you in return—all this?"

"To mentress!"

"All this, my demon? In return for that one thing I desire? All this?"

"The Powers of Night will swirl and seethe, but—yes, yes, anything!"

"Ah! You disarming rogue, come take these lips, come take it all!"

* * *

"You said he was the devil and now I am inclined to believe you. The treacherous whelp! To bed my own wife in my own castle!"

"My lord, how can you think that *I*—"

"Silence! Stupid goose, do you still dissemble? He left without a word, under cover of night. Why? And your brooch—the brooch of my mother!—was found in his empty room; in your bedchamber, one of his black gloves. Wretched woman!"

"Indeed, indeed I am wretched . . ."

"Tears will avail you nothing. You must be humbled and you will be humbled. Give thanks that I am not my father. *He* would have left you crammed naked in this little cage until your mind rotted and your body after it. But I am no tyrant. All night long, without your supper, you will shiver and squirm down here in repentance, but in the morning I will release you. I hope with sincerity you will have learned your lesson by then. Now I am going. In a few hours, you will probably start screaming to be let out. Save your breath. I will not be able to hear you. Think of your sins! Repent!"

* * *

"They said he was the devil, but I place no stock in such talk. All I know is that he came to me directly from the old Count's castle where he had been overseer or something, and gave me complete plans for the storming of the battlements: information about the placement of the cannon, the least securely barricaded doors, the weakest walls, measurements, location of rooms, the exact strength of the castle guard and a schedule of its watch . . . everything I needed. My forces had been on a one-hour alert for months. I attacked that very night. Thanks to my informant, the battle was over before dawn."

"You are to be congratulated, Duke. And where is he now?"

"Gone. Vanished. I paid him handsomely, and just between the two of us, Baron, I was beginning to make plans for his disposal. A dangerous man to have near one. But the rascal was smart. He disappeared soon after my victory."

"And that head on the pike up there, with the gray beard fluttering in the wind—it belonged to the late Count?"

"Yes. To this end may *all* enemies of my family come."

"I'll drink to that. And what disposition was made of the old fool's wife?"

"The Countess? Ah. That is the only sourness in my triumph. I'd have enjoyed invading that pretty body before severing it from its pretty head. But she must have been warned. We searched and searched the castle that night. She was nowhere to be seen. She had escaped. Well . . . wherever she may be, I hope she gets wind of what I'm doing to her husband's castle."

"Razing it, aren't you?"

"Down to its foundation blocks—leaving only enough to identify it—and building on that foundation an edifice of solid stone that will be a monument to its downfall and to my victory. Forever."

"Where do you suppose the Countess is now?"

"The devil only knows. May the wench scream in torment for eternity."

CURIOUS
ADVENTURE
OF MR. BOND

Nugent Barker

Mr. Bond climbed from the wooded slopes of the valley into broad daylight. His Inverness cape, throwing his portly figure into still greater prominence against the floor of tree-tops at his back, was torn and soiled by twigs and thorns and leaves, and he stooped with prim concern to brush off the bits and pieces. After this, he eased his knapsack on his shoulder; and now he blinked his eyes upon the country stretching out before him.

Far away, across the tufted surface of the tableland, there stood a house, with its column of smoke, lighted and still, on the verge of a forest.

A house—an *inn*—he felt it in his very bones! His hunger returned, and became a source of gratification to him. Toiling on, and pulling the brim of his hat over his eyes, he watched the ruby gleam grow bigger and brighter, and when at last he stood beneath the sign, he cried aloud, scarcely able to believe in his good fortune.

"The Rest of the Traveller," he read; and there, too, ran the name of the landlord: "Crispin Sasserach."

The stillness of the night discouraged him, and he was afraid to tap at the curtained window. And now, for the first time, the full weight of his weariness fell upon the traveller. Staring into the black mouth of the porch, he imagined himself to be at rest, in bed, sprawled out, abundantly sleeping, drugged into forgetfulness by a full stomach. He shut his eyes, and drooped a little under his Inverness cape; but when he looked again into the entrance, there stood Crispin Sasserach, holding a lamp between their faces. Mr. Bond's was plump and heavy-jawed, with sagging cheeks, and eyes that scarcely reflected the lamplight; the other face was smooth and large and oval, with small lips pressed into a smile.

"Come in, come in," the landlord whispered, "*do* come in. She is cooking a *lovely* broth to-night!"

He turned and chuckled, holding the lamp above his head.

Through the doorway of this lost, upland inn, Mr. Bond followed the monstrous back of his host. The passage widened and became a hall; and here, amongst the shadows that were gliding from their lurking-places as the lamp advanced, the landlord stopped, and tilted the flat of his hand in the air, as though enjoining his guest to listen. Then Mr. Bond disturbed the silence of the house with a sniff and a sigh. Not only could he smell the "lovely broth" —already, in this outer hall, he tasted it . . . a complex and subtle flavour, pungent, heavy as honey, light as a web in the air, nipping him in the stomach, bringing tears into his eyes.

Mr. Bond stared at Crispin Sasserach, at the shadows beyond, and back again to Crispin Sasserach. The man was standing there, with his huge, oval, hairless face upturned in the light of the lamp he carried; then, impulsively, as though reluctant to cut short such sweet anticipation, he plucked the traveller by the cape and led him to the cheerful living-room, and introduced him, with a flourish of the hand, to Myrtle Sasserach, the landlord's young and small and busy wife, who at that very moment was standing at a round table of great size, beneath the massive centre-beam of the ceiling, her black hair gleaming in the light of many candles, her plump hand dipping a ladle soundlessly into a bowl of steam.

On seeing the woman, whose long lashes were once more directed towards the bowl, Mr. Bond drew his chin primly into his neckcloth, and glanced from her to Crispin Sasserach, and finally he fixed his eyes on the revolutions of the ladle. In a moment, purpose fell upon the living-room, and with swift and nervous gestures the landlord seated his guest at the table, seized the ladle from his wife, plunged it into the bowl, and thrust the brimming plate into the hands of Myrtle, who began at once to walk towards the traveller, the steam of the broth rising into her grave eyes.

After a muttered grace, Mr. Bond pushed out his lips as though he were whispering "spoon."

"Oh, what a lovely broth!" he murmured, catching a drip in his handkerchief.

Crispin Sasserach grinned with delight. "I always say it's the best in the world." Whereupon, with a rush, he broke into peals of falsetto laughter, and blew a kiss towards his wife. A moment later, the two Sasserachs were leaving their guest to himself, bending over their own platefuls of broth, and discussing domestic affairs, as though they had no other person sitting at their table. For some time their voices were scarcely louder than the sound of the broth-eating; but when the traveller's plate was empty, then, in a flash, Crispin Sasserach became again a loud and attentive host. "Now then, sir—another helping?" he suggested, picking up the ladle, and beaming down into the bowl, while Myrtle left her chair and walked a second time towards the guest.

Mr. Bond said that he would, and pulled his chair a little closer to the table. Into his blood and bones, life had returned with twice its accustomed vigour; his very feet were as light as though he had soaked them in a bath of pine needles.

"There you are, sir! Myrtle's coming! Lord a'mighty, how I wish I was tasting it for the first time!" Then, spreading his elbows, the landlord crouched over his own steaming plateful, and chuckled again. "This broth is a wine in itself! It's a wine in itself, b'God! It staggers a man!" Flushed with excitement, his oval face looked larger than ever, and his auburn hair, whirled into bellicose corkscrews, seemed to burn brighter, as though someone had brought the bellows to it.

Stirred by the broth, Mr. Bond began to describe minutely his journey out of the valley. His voice grew as prosy, his words as involved, as though he were talking at home amongst his own people. "Now, let me see—where was I?" he buzzed again and again. And later: "I was very glad to see your light, I can tell you!" he chuckled. Then Crispin jumped up from the table, his small mouth pouting with laughter.

The evening shifted to the fireside. Fresh logs cracked like pistol shots as Crispin Sasserach dropped them into the flames. The traveller could wish for nothing better than to sit here by the hearth, talking plangently to Crispin, and slyly watching Myrtle as she cleared away the supper things; though, indeed, among his own people, Mr. Bond was thought to hold women in low esteem. He found her downcast eyes modest and even pretty. One by one she blew the candles out; with each extinguishment she grew more ethereal, while reaping a fuller share of the pagan firelight. "Come and sit beside us now, and talk," thought Mr. Bond, and presently she came.

They made him very comfortable. He found a log fire burning in his bedroom, and a bowl of broth on the bedside table. "Oh, but they're overdoing it!" he cried aloud, petulantly; "they're crude, crude! They're nothing but school-children!"—and seizing the bowl, he emptied it onto the shaggy patch of garden beneath his window. The black wall of the forest seemed to stand within a few feet of his eyes. The room was filled with the mingled light of moon, fire, and candle.

Mr. Bond, eager at last for the dreamless rest, the abandoned sleep, of the traveller, turned and surveyed the room in which he was to spend the night. He saw with pleasure the four-poster bed, itself as large as a tiny room; the heavy oaken chairs and cupboards; the tall, twisting candlesticks, their candles burnt half-way, no doubt, by a previous guest; the ceiling, that he could touch with the flat of his hand. He touched it.

In the misty morning he could see no hint of the forest, and down the shallow staircase he found the hall thick with the odour of broth. The Sasserachs were seated already at the breakfast-table, like two children, eager to begin the day with their favourite food. Crispin Sasserach was lifting his spoon and pouting his lips, while Myrtle was stirring her ladle round the tureen, her eyes downcast; and Mr. Bond sighed inaudibly as he saw again the woman's dark and lustrous hair. He noticed also the flawless condition of the Sasserach skin. There was not a blemish to be seen on their two faces, on their four hands. He attributed this perfection to the beneficial qualities of the broth, no less than to the upland air; and he began to discuss, in his plangent voice, the subject of health in general. In the middle of this discourse Crispin Sasserach remarked, excitedly, that he had a brother who kept an inn a day's journey along the edge of the forest.

"Oh," said Mr. Bond, pricking up his ears, "so you have a brother, have you?"

"Certainly," whispered the innkeeper. "It is most convenient."

"Most convenient for what?"

"Why, for the inns. His name's Martin. We share our guests. We help each other. The proper brotherly spirit, b'God!"

Mr. Bond stared angrily into his broth. "They share their guests. . . . But what," he thought, "has that to do with me?" He said aloud: "Perhaps I'll meet him one day, Mr. Sasserach."

"To-day!" cried Crispin, whacking his spoon onto the table. "I'm taking you there to-day! But don't you worry," he added, seeing the look on the other's face, and flattering himself that he had read it aright; "you'll be coming back to us. Don't you worry! Day after to-morrow—day after that—one of these days! Ain't that right, Myr? Ain't that right?" he repeated, bouncing up and down in his chair like a big child.

"Quite right," answered Myrtle Sasserach to Mr. Bond, whose eyes were fixed upon her with heavy attention.

A moment later the innkeeper was out of his chair, making for the hall, calling back to Myrtle to have his boots ready. In the midst of this bustle, Mr. Bond bowed stiffly to Myrtle Sasserach, and found his way with dignity to the back garden, that now appeared wilder than he had supposed—a fenced-in plot of grass reaching above his knees and scattered with burdock, whose prickly heads clung to his clothes as he made for the gate in the fence at the foot of this wilderness. He blinked his eyes, and walked on the rough turf that lay between him and the forest. By this time the sun was shining in an unclouded sky; a fine day was at hand; and Mr. Bond was sweeping his eye along the endless wall of the forest when he heard the innkeeper's voice calling to him in the stillness. "Mr. Bond! Mr. Bond!" Turning reluctantly, and stepping carefully through the garden in order to avoid the burrs of the burdock, the traveller found Crispin Sasserach on the point of departure, in a great bustle, with a strong horse harnessed to a two-wheeled cart, and his wife putting up her face to be kissed.

"Yes, I'll go with you," cried Mr. Bond, but the Sasserachs did not appear to hear him. He lingered for a moment in the porch, scowling at Myrtle's back, scowling at the large young horse that seemed to toss its head at him with almost human insolence, then he sighed, and, slinging his knapsack over his shoulder, sat himself beside the driver; the horse was uncommonly large, restless between the shafts, and in perfect fettle, and without a word from Crispin the animal began to plunge forward rapidly over the worn track.

For some time the two men drove in silence, on the second stage of Mr. Bond's adventure above the valley. The traveller sat up stiffly, inflating his lungs methodically, glaring through his small eyes, and forcing back his shoulders. Presently he began to talk about the mountain air, and received no answer. On his right hand the wall of the forest extended as far as his eyes could see, while on his left hand ran the brink of the valley, a mile away, broken here and there by rowan trees.

The monotony of the landscape, and the continued silence of the innkeeper, soon began to pall on Mr. Bond, who liked talking and was seldom at ease unless his eyes were busy picking out new things. Even the horse behaved with the soundless regularity of a machine; so that, besides the traveller, only the sky showed a struggle to make progress.

Clouds came from nowhere, shaped and broke, and at midday the sun in full swing was riding between white puffs of cloud, glistening by fits and starts on the moist coat of the horse. The forest beneath, and the stretch of coarse grass running to the valley, were constantly shining and darkening, yet Crispin Sasserach never opened his mouth, even to whisper, though sometimes, between his teeth, he spat soundlessly over the edge of the cart. The landlord had brought with him a casserole of the broth; and during one of these sunny breaks he pulled up the horse, without a word, and poured the liquor into two pannikins, which he proceeded to heat patiently over a spirit stove.

In the failing light of the afternoon, when the horse was still making his top speed, when Crispin Sasserach was buzzing fitfully between his teeth, and sleep was flirting with the traveller, a shape appeared obscurely on the track ahead, and with it came the growing jingle of bells. Mr. Bond sat up and stared. He had not expected to meet, in such a God-forsaken spot, another cart, or carriage. He saw at length, approaching him, a four-wheeled buggy, drawn by two sprightly horses in tandem. A thin-faced man in breeches and a bowler hat was driving it. The two drivers greeted each other solemnly, raised their whips, but never slackened speed.

"Well—who was that?" asked Mr. Bond, after a pause.

"My brother Martin's manservant."

"Where is he going?" asked Mr. Bond.

"To 'The Rest of the Traveller.' With news."

"Indeed? What news?" persisted Mr. Bond.

The landlord turned his head.

"News for my Myrtle," he whispered, winking at the traveller.

Mr. Bond shrugged his shoulders. "What is the use of talking to such a boor?" he thought, and fell once more into his doze; the harvest-moon climbed up again, whitening the earth; while now and then the landlord spat towards the forest, and never spoke another word until he came to Martin Sasserach's.

Then Crispin leapt to life.

"Out with you!" he cried. "Pst! Mr. Bond! Wake up! Get out at once! We've reached 'The Headless Man,' sir!"

Mr. Bond, staggered by so much energy, flopped to the ground. His head felt as large as the moon. He heard the horse panting softly, and saw the breath from its nostrils flickering upwards in the cold air; while the white-faced Crispin Sasserach was leaping about under the moon, whistling between his teeth, and calling out enthusiastically: "Mar-tin! Mar-tin! Here he is!"

The sheer wall of forest echoed back the name. Indeed, the whole of the moonlight seemed to be filled with the name "Martin"; and Mr. Bond had a fierce desire to see this Martin Sasserach whose sign was hanging high above the traveller's head. After repeated calls from Crispin, the landlord of "The Headless Man" appeared, and Mr. Bond, expecting a very giant in physical stature, was shocked to see the small and bespectacled figure that had emerged from the house. Crispin Sasserach grew quick and calm in a moment. "Meet again," he whispered to Mr. Bond, shutting his eyes, and stretching his small mouth as though in ecstasy; then he gave the traveller a push towards the approaching Martin, and a moment later he was in his cart, and the horse was springing its way back to "The Rest of the Traveller."

Mr. Bond stood where he was, listening to the dying sound of the horse, and watching the landlord of "The Headless Man"; and presently he was staring at two grey flickering eyes behind the landlord's glasses.

"Anyone arriving at my inn from my brother's is trebly welcome. He is welcome not only for Crispin's own sake and mine, but also for the sake of our brother Stephen." The voice was as quiet and as clear as the moonlight, and the speaker began to return to his inn with scarcely a pause between speech and movement. Mr. Bond examined curiously the strongly-lighted hall that in shape and size was the very double of Crispin's. Oil-lamps, gracefully columned, gleamed almost as brightly from their fluted silver surfaces as from their opal-lighted heads; and there was Martin stooping up the very stairs, it seemed, that Mr. Bond had walked at Crispin Sasserach's—a scanty man, this brother, throwing out monstrous shadows, turning once to peer back at his guest, and standing at last in a bright and airy bedroom, where, the courteous words from which his eyes, lost in thought and gently flickering, seemed to be far distant, he invited his guest to wash before dining.

Martin Sasserach fed Mr. Bond delicately on that evening of his arrival, presenting him with small, cold dishes of various kinds and always exquisitely cooked and garnished; and these, together with the almost crystalline cleanliness of the room and of the table, seemed appropriate to the chemist-like appearance of the host. A bottle of wine was opened for Mr. Bond, who, amongst his own people, was known to drink nothing headier than bottled cider. During dinner, the wine warmed up a brief moment of attention in Martin Sasserach. He peered with sudden interest at his guest. " 'The Headless Man?' There is, in fact, a story connected with that name. If you can call it a story." He smiled briefly, tapping his finger, and a moment later was examining an ivory piece, elaborately carved, that held the bill of fare. "Lovely! Lovely! Isn't it? . . . In fact, there are many stories," he ended, as though the number of stories excused him from wasting his thought over the recital of merely one. Soon after dinner he retired, alluding distantly to work from which he never liked to be away long.

Mr. Bond went to bed early that night, suffering from dyspepsia, and glowering at the absence of home comforts in his bright and efficient bedroom.

The birds awakened him to a brisk, autumnal morning. Breathing heavily, he told himself that he was always very fond of birds and trees and flowers; and soon he was walking sleepily in Martin Sasserach's garden. The trimness of the beds began to please him. He followed the right-angled paths with dignified obesity, his very bones were proud to be alive.

A green gate at the garden-foot attracted Mr. Bond's attention; but, knowing that it would lead him on to the wild grass beyond, and thence to the forest, whose motionless crest could be seen all this while over the privet hedge, he chose to linger where he was, sniffing the clear scent of the flowers, and losing, with every breath and step, another whiff of Crispin's broth, to his intense delight.

Hunger drew him back into the house at last, and he began to pace the twilit rooms. Martin Sasserach, he saw, was very fond of ivory. He stooped and peered at the delicate things. Ivory objects of every description, perfectly carved: paper-knives, chess-men, salad-spoons; tiny busts and faces, often of grotesque appearance; and even delicate boxes, fretted from ivory.

The echo of his feet on the polished floors intensified the silence of "The Headless Man"; yet even this indoor hush was full of sound, when compared with the stillness of the scene beyond the uncurtained windows. The tufted grass was not yet lighted by the direct rays of the sun. The traveller stared towards the rowan trees that stood on the brink of the valley. Beyond them stretched a carpet of mist, raising the rest of the world to the height of the plateau; and Mr. Bond, recalling the house and town that he had left behind him, began to wonder whether he was glad or sorry that his adventures had brought him to this lost region. "Cold enough for my cape," he shivered, fetching it from the hall, and hurrying out of the inn; the desire had seized him to walk on the tufted grass, to foot it as far as the trees; and he had indeed gone some distance on his journey, wrapped in his thoughts and antique Inverness cape, when the note of a gong came up behind him, like a thread waving on the air.

"Hark at that," he whispered, staring hard at the ragged line of rowan trees on which his heart was set; then he shrugged his shoulders, and turned back to "The Headless Man," where his host was standing lost in thought at the breakfast-table that still held the crumbs of the night before.

"Ah, yes. Yes. It's you . . . You slept well?"

"Tolerably well," said Mr. Bond.

"We breakfast rather early here. It makes a longer day. Stennet will be back later. He's gone to my brother Crispin's."

"With news?" said Mr. Bond.

Martin Sasserach bowed courteously, though a trifle stiffly. He motioned his guest towards a chair at the table. Breakfast was cold and short and silent. Words were delicate things to rear in this crystalline atmosphere. Martin's skin sagged and was the colour of old ivory. Now and then he looked up at his guest, his grey eyes focused beyond mere externals; and it seemed as though they lodged themselves in Mr. Bond's very bones. On one of these occasions the traveller made great play with his appetite. "It's all this upland air," he asserted, thumping his chest.

The sun began to rise above the plateau. Again the landlord vanished, murmuring his excuses; silence flooded "The Headless Man," the garden purred in full blaze of the sun that now stood higher than the forest, and the gravelled paths crunched slowly beneath Mr. Bond's feet. "News for Myrtle," he pondered, letting his thoughts stray back over his journey; and frequently he drifted through the house where all was still and spacious: dusty, museum-like rooms brimming with sunlight, while everywhere those ivory carvings caught his eye, possessing his sight as completely as the taste of Crispin's broth had lodged in his very lungs.

Lunch was yet another meal of cold food and silence, broken only by coffee that the landlord heated on a spirit stove at the end of the table, and by a question from the traveller, to which this thin-haired Martin, delicately flicking certain greyish dust off the front of his coat and sleeve, replied that he had been a collector of carvings for years past, and was continually adding to his collection. His voice drew out in length and seemed, in fact, to trail him from the sunlit dining-room, back to his ever-lasting work . . . and now the afternoon itself began to drag and presently to settle down in the sun as though the whole of time were dozing.

"Here's my indigestion back again," sighed Mr. Bond, mooning about. At home he would have rested in his bedroom, with its pink curtains and flowered wallpaper.

He crept into the garden and eyed the back of the house. Which of those windows in the trimly-creepered stone lit up the landlord and his work? He listened for the whirring of a lathe, the scraping of a knife . . . and wondered, startled, why he had expected to hear such things. He felt the forest behind his back, and turned, and saw it looming above the privet hedge. Impulsively, he started to cross the sun-swept grass beyond the gate; but within a few yards of the forest his courage failed him again: he could not face the wall of trees: and with a cry he fled into the house, and seized his Inverness.

His eyes looked far beyond the rowans on the skyline as he plodded over the tufted grass. Already he could see himself down there below, counties and counties away, on the valley level, in the house of his neighbours the Allcards, drinking their coffee or tea and telling them of his adventures and especially of *this* adventure. It was not often that a man of his age and secure position in the world went off alone, in search of joy or trouble. He scanned the distant line of rowan trees, and nodded, harking back: "As far as it has gone. I'll tell them this adventure, as far as it ever went." And he would say to them: "The things I might have seen, if I had stayed! Yes, Allcard, I was very glad to climb down into the valley that day, I can tell you! I don't mind admitting I was a bit frightened!"

The tippet of his cape caressed his shoulders, like the hand of a friend.

Mr. Bond was not yet half-way to the rowan trees when, looking back, he saw, against the darkness of the forest wall, a carriage rapidly approaching "The Headless Man." At once there flashed into his memory the eyes of the manservant Stennet who went between the Sasserach inns.

He knew that Stennet's eyes were on him now. The sound of the horses' feet was coming up to him like a soft ball bouncing over the grass. Mr. Bond shrugged his shoulders, and stroked his pendulous cheeks. Already he was on his way back to "The Headless Man," conscious that two flying horses could have overtaken him long before he had reached the rowans. "But why," he thought, holding himself with dignity, "should I imagine that these people are expecting me to run away? And why that sudden panic in the garden? It's all that deathly quietness of the morning getting on my nerves."

The carriage had disappeared some time before he reached the inn, over whose tiled and weather-stained roof the redness of the evening was beginning to settle. And now the traveller was conscious of a welcome that seemed to run out and meet him at the very door. He found a log fire crackling in the dining-room, and Mr. Bond, holding his hands to the blaze, felt suddenly at ease, and weary. He had intended to assert himself—to shout for Martin Sasserach—to demand that he be escorted down at once from the plateau . . . but now he wished for nothing better than to stand in front of the fire, waiting for Stennet to bring him tea.

A man began to sing in the heart of the house. Stennet? The fellow's eyes and hawk-like nose were suddenly visible in the fire. The singing voice grew louder . . . died at length discreetly into silence and the tread of footsteps in the hall . . . and again the traveller was listening to the flames as they roared in the chimney.

"Let me take your coat, sir," Stennet said.

Then Mr. Bond whipped round, his cheeks shaking with anger.

Why did they want to force this hospitality upon him, making him feel like a prisoner? He glared at the large-checked riding-breeches, at the muscular shoulders, at the face that seemed to have grown the sharper through swift driving. He almost shouted: "Where's that bowler hat?"

Fear? . . . Perhaps . . . But if fear had clutched him for a moment, it had left him now. He knew that the voice had pleased him, a voice of deference breaking into the cold and irreverent silence of "The Headless Man." The cape was already off his shoulders, hanging on Stennet's bent and respectful arm. And—God be praised!—the voice was announcing that tea would be ready soon. Mr. Bond's spirits leapt with the word. He and Stennet stood there, confidentially plotting. "China? Yes, sir. We have China," Stennet said.

"And buttered toast," said Mr. Bond, softly rubbing his chin. Some time after tea he was awakened from his doze by the hand of the manservant, who told him that a can of boiling water was waiting in his room.

Mr. Bond felt that dinner would be a rich meal that night, and it was. He blushed as the dishes were put before him. Hare soup! How did they know his favourite soup? Through entrée, remove, and roast, his hands, soft and pink from washing, were busier than they had been for days. The chicken was braised to a turn. Oh, what mushrooms *au gratin!* The partridge brought tears to his eyes. The Saxony pudding caused him to turn again to Martin, in Stennet's praise.

The landlord bowed with distant courtesy. "A game of chess?" he suggested, when dinner was over. "My last opponent was a man like yourself, a traveller making a tour of the inns. We started a game. He is gone from us now. Perhaps you will take his place?" smiled Martin Sasserach, his precise voice dropping and seeming to transmit its flow of action to the thin hand poised above the board. "My move," he whispered, playing at once; he had thought it out for a week. But although Mr. Bond tried to sink his thoughts into the problem so suddenly placed before him, he could not take them off his after-dinner dyspepsia, and with apologies and groans he scraped back his chair. "I'm sorry for that," smiled Martin, and his eyes flickered over the board. "I'm very sorry. Another night

. . . undoubtedly . . . with your kind help . . . another night . . ."

The prospect of another day at "The Headless Man" was at once disturbing and pleasant to Mr. Bond as he went wheezing up to bed.

"Ah, Stennet! Do *you* ever suffer from dyspepsia?" he asked mournfully, seeing the man at the head of the staircase. Stennet snapped his fingers, and was off downstairs in a moment; and a minute later he was standing at the traveller's door, with a bowl of Crispin's famous broth. "Oh, that!" cried Mr. Bond, staring down at the bowl. Then he remembered its fine effect on his indigestion at Crispin's; and when at last he pulled the sheets over his head, he fell asleep in comfort and did not wake until the morning.

At breakfast Martin Sasserach looked up from his plate.

"This afternoon," he murmured, "Stennet will be driving you to my brother Stephen's."

Mr. Bond opened his eyes. "Another inn? Another of you Sasserachs?"

"Crispin—Martin—Stephen. Just the three of us. A perfect number . . . if you come to think of it."

The traveller strode into the garden. Asters glowed in the lustreless light of the morning. By ten o'clock the sun was shining again, and by midday a summer heat lay on the plateau, penetrating even into Mr. Bond's room. The silence of the forest pulled him to the window, made him lift up his head and shut his eyes upon that monstrous mass of trees. Fear was trying to overpower him. He did not want to go to Stephen Sasserach's; but the hours were running past him quickly now, the stillness was gone from the inn.

At lunch, to which his host contributed a flow of gentle talk, the traveller felt rising within him an impatience to be off on the third stage of his journey, if such a stage must be. He jumped up from his chair without apology, and strode into the garden. The asters were now shining dimly in the strong sunlight. He opened the gate in the privet hedge, and walked onto the tufted grass that lay between it and the forest. As he did so, he heard the flap of a wing behind him and saw a pigeon flying from a window in the roof. The bird flew over his head and over the forest and out of sight; and for the first time he remembered seeing a pigeon taking a similar course when he was standing in the garden at Crispin's inn.

His thoughts were still following the pigeon over the boundless floor of tree-tops when he heard a voice calling to him in the silence. "Mr. Bond! Mr. Bond!" He walked at once to the gate and down the garden and into the house, put on his Inverness, and hitched his knapsack onto his shoulder; and in a short while he was perched beside Stennet in the flying buggy, staring at the ears of the two horses, and remembering that Martin, at the last moment, instead of bidding his guest good-bye, had gone back to his work.

Though he never lost his fear of Stennet, Mr. Bond found Martin's man a good companion on a journey, always ready to speak when spoken to, and even able to arouse the traveller's curiosity, at times, in the monotonous landscape.

"See those rowans over there?" said Stennet, nodding to the left. "Those rowans belong to Mr. Martin. He owns them half-way to Mr. Crispin's place, and half-way on to Mr. Stephen's. And so it is with Mr. Crispin and Mr. Stephen in their turn."

"And what about the forest?"

"Same again," said Stennet, waving his hand towards the right. "It's round, you know. And they each own a third, like a huge slice of cake."

He clicked his tongue, and the horses pricked up their ears, though on either side of the dashboard the performance was no more than a formality, so swiftly was the buggy moving. "Very much quicker than Crispin's cart!" gasped the passenger, feeling the wind against his face; yet, when the evening of the autumn day was closing in, he looked about him with surprise.

He saw the moon rise up above the valley.

Later still, he asked for information regarding the names of the three inns, and Stennet laughed.

"The gentlemen are mighty proud of them, I can tell you! Romantic and a bit fearsome, that's what I call them. Poetical, too. They don't say 'The Traveller's Rest,' but

'The Rest of the Traveller,' mind you. That's poetical. I don't think it was Mr. Crispin's idea. I think it was Mr. Martin's—or Mrs. Crispin's. They're the clever ones. 'The Headless Man' is merely grim—a grim turn of mind Mr. Martin has—and it means, of course, no more than it says—a man without a head. And then again," continued Stennet, whistling to his horses, whose backs were gleaming in the moonlight, "the inn you're going to now—'The Traveller's Head'—well, inns are called 'The King's Head' sometimes, aren't they, in the King's honour? Mr. Stephen goes one better than that. He dedicates his inn to the traveller himself." By this time a spark of light had become visible in the distance, and Mr. Bond fixed his eyes upon it. Once, for a moment, the spark went out, and he imagined that Stephen's head had passed in front of the living-room lamp. At this picture, anger seized him, and he wondered, amazed, why he was submitting so tamely to the commands—he could call them no less—of these oddly hospitable brothers. Fanned by his rage, the spark grew steadily bigger and brighter, until at last it had achieved the shape and size of a glowing window through which a man's face was grinning into the moonshine.

"Look here, what's all this?" cried Mr. Bond, sliding to his feet.

" 'The Traveller's Head,' sir," answered Stennet, pointing aloft.

They both stared up at the sign above their heads, then Mr. Bond scanned the sprawling mass of the inn, and scowled at its surroundings. The night was still and vibrant, without sound; the endless forest stood like a wall of blue-white dust; and the traveller was about to raise his voice in wrath against the brothers Sasserach, when a commotion burst from the porch of the inn, and onto the moon-drenched grass there strode a tall and ungainly figure, swinging its arms, with a pack of creatures flopping and stumbling at its heels. "Here *is* Mr. Stephen," Stennet whispered, watching the approach; the landlord of "The Traveller's Head" was smiling pleasantly, baring his intensely white teeth, and when he had reached the traveller he touched his forehead with a gesture that was at once respectful and overbearing.

"Mr. Bond, sir?" Mr. Bond muttered and bowed, and

stared down at the landlord's children—large-headed, large-bellied, primitive creatures flopping round their father and pulling the skirts of the Inverness cape.

Father and children gathered round the traveller, who, lost within this little crowd, soon found himself at the entrance of "The Traveller's Head," through which his new host urged him by the arm while two of the children pushed between them and ran ahead clumsily into the depths of the hall. The place was ill-lighted and ill-ventilated; and although Mr. Bond knew from experience exactly where the living-room would be situated, yet, after he had passed through its doorway, he found no further resemblance to those rooms in which he had spent two stages of a curious adventure. The oil-lamp, standing in the middle of the round centre table, was without a shade; a moth was plunging audibly at the blackened chimney, hurling swift shadows everywhere over the ceiling and figured wall-paper; while, with the return of the children, a harmonium had started fitfully to grunt and blow.

"Let me take your cloak, your cape, Mr. Bond, sir," the landlord said, and spread it with surprising care on one of the vast sofas that looked the larger because of their broken springs and the stuffing that protruded through their soiled covers: but at once the children seized upon the cape and would have torn it to pieces had not Mr. Bond snatched it from them—at this, they cowered away from the stranger, fixing him with their eyes.

Amidst this congestion of people and furniture, Stephen Sasserach smiled and moved continuously, a stooping giant whom none but Mr. Bond obeyed. Here was the type of man whose appearance the traveller likened to that of the old-time executioner, the axe-man of the Middle Ages— harsh, loyal, simple, excessively domesticated, with a bulging forehead and untidy eyebrows and arms muscled and ready for deeds. Stephen kept no order in his house. Noise was everywhere, yet little seemed to be done. The children called their father Steve, and put out their tongues at him. They themselves were unlovely things, and their inner natures seemed to ooze through their skins and form a surface from which the traveller recoiled. Three of their names were familiar to Mr. Bond. Here were Crispin and Martin and Stephen over again, while Dorcas and Lydia were sisters whose only virtue was their mutual devotion.

The food at "The Traveller's Head" was homely and palatable, and Stephen the father cooked it and served it liberally on chipped plates. He sat in his soiled blue shirt, his knotted arms looking richly sunburnt against the blue. He was never inarticulate, and this surprised Mr. Bond. On the contrary, he spoke rapidly and almost as if to himself, in a low rugged voice that was always a pleasure to hear. At moments he dropped into silence, his eyes shut, his eyebrows lowered, and his bulging forehead grew still more shiny with thought; on such occasions, Dorcas and Lydia would steal to the harmonium, while, backed by a wail from the instrument, Crispin the Younger and Martin the Younger would jump from the sofas onto the floor.

Rousing himself at last, Stephen the Elder thumped his fist on the table, and turned in his chair to shout at the children: "Get along with you, devils! Get out your board, and *practise,* you little devils!" Whereupon the children erected a huge board, punctured with holes; and each child began to hurl wooden balls through the holes and into the pockets behind them with astonishing accuracy, except for Dorcas and Lydia. And presently their father reminded them: "The moon is shining!" At once the children scuttled out of the room, and Mr. Bond never saw them again.

The noise and the figured wall-paper, and the fat moth beating itself against the only source of light, had caused the traveller's head to grow heavy with sleep; and now it grew heavier still as he sat by the fire with Stephen after supper was over, listening to the talk of that strangely attractive man in the soiled blue shirt. "You fond of children, Mr. Bond, sir?" Mr. Bond nodded.

"Children and animals . . ." he murmured drowsily.

"One has to let them have their way," sighed Stephen Sasserach. The rugged voice came clearly and soothingly into Mr. Bond's ears, until at last it shot up, vigorously, and ordered the guest to bed. Mr. Bond pulled himself out of his chair, and smiled, and said good night, and the moth flew into his face. Where were the children, he wondered. Their voices could not be heard. Perhaps they had fallen asleep, suddenly, like animals. But Mr. Bond found it difficult to imagine those eyes in bed, asleep.

Lying, some minutes later, in his own massive bed in this third of the Sasserach inns, with an extinguished candle on his bedside table, and gazing towards the open window from which he had drawn apart one of the heavy embroidered curtains, Mr. Bond fancied that he could hear faint cries of triumph, and sounds of knocking coming from the direction of the forest. Starting up into complete wakefulness, he went to the window, and stared at the forest beyond the tufted grass. The sounds, he fancied, putting his hand to his ear, were as those given forth by the children during their game—but louder, as though the game were bigger. Perhaps strange animals were uttering them. Whatever their origin, they were coming from that depth of trees whose stillness was deepened by the light of the moon.

"Oh, God!" thought Mr. Bond, "I'm sick to death of the moonlight!"—and with a sweep of the arm he closed the curtains, yet could not shut out the sounds of the forest, nor the sight of the frosted grass beneath the moon. Together, sound and sight filled him with forboding, and his cheeks shook as he groped for the unlighted candle. He must fetch his Inverness from below, fetch it at once, and get away while there was time. He found his host still sitting by the lamp in the living-room. Stephen's fist, lying on the table, was closed; he opened it, and out flew the moth.

"He thinks he has got away," cried Stephen, looking up, and baring his teeth in a smile: "but he hasn't! He never will!"

"I've come for my Inverness," said Mr. Bond.

It was lying on one of the massive sofas. The fire was out, and the air chilly, and the depth of the room lay in darkness. An idea crossed the mind of Mr. Bond. He said, lifting up the cape: "I thought I'd like it on my bed." And he shivered to show how cold he was. From one of the folds the moth flew out, and whirled round the room like a mad thing.

"That's all right, Mr. Bond, sir. That's all right." The man had fallen into a mood of abstraction; his forehead shone in the rays of the lamp; and the traveller left the room, holding himself with dignity in his gay dressing-gown, the Inverness hanging on his arm.

He was about to climb the staircase when a voice spoke softly in his ear, and wished him good night.

Stennet! What was the man doing here? Mr. Bond lifted his candle and gazed in astonishment at the back of Martin's manservant. The figure passed into the shadows, and the soft and deliberate ticking of the grandfather clock in the hall deepened the silence and fear of the moments that followed.

Mr. Bond ran to his room, locked himself in, and began to dress. His dyspepsia had seized him again. If only he were back at Crispin's! He parted the curtains, and peeped at the night. The shadow of the inn lay on the yard and the tufted grass beyond, and one of the chimneys, immensely distorted, extended as far as the forest. The forest-wall itself was solid with moonlight; from behind it there came no longer the sounds of the knocking, and the silence set Mr. Bond trembling again.

"I shall escape at dawn," he whispered, "when the moon's gone down."

Feeling no longer sleepy, he took from his knapsack a volume of *Mungo Park,* and, fully dressed, settled himself in an easy chair, with the curtains drawn again across the window, and the candle burning close beside him. At intervals he looked up from his book, frowning, running his eye over the group of three pagodas, in pale red, endlessly repeated on the wallpaper. The restful picture made him drowsy, and presently he slept and snored and the candle burned on.

At midnight he was awakened by crashing blows on his door; the very candle seemed to be jumping with fear, and Mr. Bond sprang up in alarm.

"Yes? Who's that?" he called out feebly.

"What in the name of God is *that?*" he whispered, as the blows grew louder.

"What are they up to now?" he asked aloud, with rising terror.

A splinter flew into the room, and he knew in a flash that the end of his journey had come. Was it Stephen or Stennet, Stephen or Stennet behind the door? The candle flickered as he blundered to and fro. He had no time to think, no time to act. He stood and watched the corner of the axe-blade working in the crack in the panel. "Save me, save me," he whispered, wringing his hands. They fluttered towards his Inverness, and struggled to push themselves into the obstinate sleeves. "Oh, come on, come on," he whimpered, jerking his arms about, anger rising with terror. The whole room shuddered beneath the axe. He plunged at the candle and blew it out. In the darkness a ray of light shot through a crack in the door, and fell on the window curtain.

Mr. Bond remembered the creeper clinging beneath his window and as soon as possible he was floundering, scrambling, slipping down to the house-shadowed garden below. Puffing out his cheeks, he hurried onward, while the thuds of the axe grew fainter in his ears. Brickbats lay in his path, a zinc tub wrenched at his cape and ripped it loudly, an iron hoop caught in his foot and he tottered forward with outstretched hands. And now, still running in the far-flung shadow of the house, he was on the tufted grass, whimpering a little, struggling against desire to look back over his shoulder, making for the forest that lay in the full beams of the moonlight. He tried to think, and could think of nothing but the size and safety of the shadow on which he was running. He reached the roof of the inn at last: plunged aside from his course of flight: and now he was running up the monstrous shadow of the chimney, thinking of nothing at all because the forest stood so near. Blindingly, a moon-filled avenue stretched before him: the chimney entered the chasm, and stopped: and it was as though Mr. Bond were a puff of smoke blowing into the forest depths. His shadow, swinging its monstrously distorted garments, led him to an open space at the end of the avenue. The thick-set trees encircled it with silence deeper than any Mr. Bond had known. Here, in this glade, hung silence within a silence. Yet, halting abruptly, and pressing the flat of his hands to his ribs in the pain of his sudden burst of breathing, Mr. Bond had no ears for the silence, nor eyes for anything beyond the scene that faced him in the centre of the forest glade: a group of upright posts, or stakes, set in a concave semicircle, throwing long shadows, and bearing on each summit a human skull. " 'The Traveller's Head,' 'The Headless Man,' " he whispered, stricken with terror, whipping his back on the skulls; and there was

Stephen Sasserach in silhouette, leaping up the avenue, brandishing his axe as though he were a demented wood-cutter coming to cut down trees.

The traveller's mind continued to run swiftly through the names of the three inns. " 'The Traveller's Head,' " he thought, 'The Headless Man,' 'The Rest of the Traveller.' " He remembered the carrier pigeons that had flown ahead of him from inn to inn; he remembered the dust on the front of Martin's coat. . . .

He was staring at the figure in the soiled blue shirt. It had halted now, as still as a tree, on the verge of the moon-filled glade: but the whirling thoughts of Mr. Bond were on the verge of light more blinding than this; they stopped, appalled: and the traveller fled beyond the skulls, fruitlessly searching for cover in the farthest wall of trees.

Then Stephen sprang in his wake, flinging up a cry that went knocking against the tree-trunks.

The echoes were echoed by Mr. Bond, who, whipping round to face his enemy, was wriggling and jerking in his Inverness cape, slipping it off at last, and swinging it in his hand, for his blood was up. And now he was deep in mortal combat, wielding his Inverness as the gladiators used to wield their nets in the old arenas. Time and again the axe and the cape engaged each other; the one warding and hindering; the other catching and ripping, clumsily enough, as though in sport. Around the skulls the two men fought and panted, now in darkness, now in the full light pouring down the avenue. Their moon-cast shadows fought another fight together, wilder still than theirs. Then Stephen cried: "Enough of this!" and bared his teeth for the first time since the strife had started.

"B-but you're my friend!" bleated Mr. Bond; and he stared at the shining thread of the axe.

"The best you ever had, sir, Mr. Bond, sir!" answered Stephen Sasserach; and, stepping back, the landlord of "The Traveller's Head" cut off the traveller's head.

The thump of the head on the sticks and leaves and grass of the forest glade was the first sound in the new and peaceful life of Mr. Bond, and he did not hear it; but to the brothers Sasserach it was a promise of life itself, a signal that all was ready now for them to apply their respective talents busily and happily in the immediate future.

Stephen took the head of Mr. Bond, and with gentle though rather clumsy fingers pared it to a skull, grinning back at it with simple satisfaction when the deed was over, and after that he set it up as a fine mark for his brood of primitives, the game's endeavour being to see who could throw the ball into the eyesockets; and to his brother Martin, landlord of "The Headless Man," he sent the headless man, under the care of Stennet: and Martin, on a soft, autumnal day, reduced the headless body to a skeleton, with all its troubles gone, and through the days and nights he sat at work, with swift precision in his fingers, carving and turning, powdering his coat with dust, creating his figures and trinkets, his paper-knives and salad-spoons and fretted boxes and rare chess-men; and to his brother Crispin, landlord of "The Rest of the Traveller," Martin sent the rest of the traveller, the soft and yielding parts, the scraps, the odds and ends, the miscellaneous pieces, all the internal lumber that had gone to fill the skin of the man from the Midlands and to help to render him in middle years a prey to dyspepsia. Crispin received the parcel with a pursing of his small mouth, and a call to Myrtle in his clear falsetto: "Stennet's here!"

She answered from the kitchen. "Thank you, Cris!" Her hands were soft and swollen as she scoured the tureen. The back of the inn was full of reflected sunlight, and her dark hair shone.

"It's too late in the season now," she said, when tea-time came. "I don't suppose we'll have another one before the spring."

Yet she was wrong. That very evening, when the moon had risen from beyond the valley, Myrtle murmured: "There he comes," and continued to stir her ladle in the bowl.

Her husband strolled into the hall and wound the clock.

He took the lamp from its bracket on the wall.

He went to the door, and flung it open to the moonlight; holding the lamp above his head.

"Come in, come in," he said, to the stranger standing there. "She is cooking a *lovely* broth to-night!"

OUT OF
THE DEEPS

John Wyndham

PHASE **1**

I'm a reliable witness, you're a reliable witness, practically all God's children are reliable witnesses in their own estimation—which makes it funny how such different ideas of the same affair get about. Almost the only people I know who agree word for word on what they saw on the night of July fifteenth are Phyllis and I. And as Phyllis happens to be my wife, people said, in their kindly way behind our backs, that I "overpersuaded" her, a thought that could proceed only from someone who did not know Phyllis.

The time was 11:15 P.M.; the place, latitude thirty-five, some twenty-four degrees west of Greenwich; the ship, the *Guinevere;* the occasion, our honeymoon. About these facts there is no dispute. The cruise had taken us to Madeira, the Canaries, Cape Verde Islands, and had then turned north to show us the Azores on our way home. We, Phyllis and I, were leaning on the rail, taking a breather. From the saloon came the sound of the dance continuing, and the crooner yearning for somebody. The sea stretched in front of us like a silken plain in the moonlight. The ship sailed as smoothly as if she were on a river. We gazed out silently at the infinity of sea and sky. Behind us the crooner went on baying.

"I'm so glad I don't feel like him; it must be devastating," Phyllis said. "Why, do you suppose, do people keep on mass-producing these dreary moanings?"

I had no answer ready for that one, but I was saved the trouble of trying to find one when her attention was suddenly caught elsewhere.

"Mars is looking pretty angry tonight, isn't he? I hope it isn't an omen," she said.

I looked where she pointed at a red spot among myriads of white ones, and with some surprise. Mars does look red, of course, though I had never seen him look quite as red as that—but then, neither were the stars, as seen at home, quite as bright as they were here. Being practically in the tropics might account for it.

"Certainly a little inflamed," I agreed.

We regarded the red point for some moments. Then Phyllis said: "That's funny. It seems to be getting bigger."

I explained that that was obviously an hallucination formed by staring at it. We went on staring, and it became quite indisputably bigger. Moreover: "There's another one. There can't be two Marses," said Phyllis.

And sure enough there was. A smaller red point, a little up from, and to the right of, the first. She added: "*And* another. To the left. See?"

She was right about that, too, and by this time the first one was glowing as the most noticeable thing in the sky.

"It must be a flight of jets of some kind, and that's a cloud of luminous exhaust we're seeing," I suggested.

We watched all three of them slowly getting brighter and also sinking lower in the sky until they were little above the horizon line, and reflecting in a pinkish pathway across the water toward us.

"Five now," said Phyllis.

We've both of us been asked many times since to describe them, but perhaps we are not gifted with such a precise eye for detail as some others. What we said at the time, and what we still say, is that on this occasion there was no real shape visible. The center was solidly red, and a kind of fuzz round it was less so. The best suggestion I can make is that you imagine a brilliantly red light as seen in a fairly thick fog so that there is a strong halation, and you will have something of the effect.

Others besides ourselves were leaning over the rail, and in fairness I should perhaps mention that between them they appear to have seen cigar-shapes, cylinders, discs, ovoids, and, inevitably, saucers. We did not. What is more, we did not see eight, nine, or a dozen. We saw five.

The halation may or may not have been due to some kind of jet drive, but it did not indicate any great speed. The things grew in size quite slowly as they approached.

There was time for people to go back into the saloon and fetch their friends out to see, so that presently a line of us leaned all along the rail, looking at them and guessing.

With no idea of scale we could have no judgment of their size or distance; all we could be sure of was that they were descending in a long glide which looked as if it would take them across our wake.

When the first one hit the water a great burst of steam shot up in a pink plume. Then, swiftly, there was a lower, wider spread of steam which had lost the pink tinge, and was simply a white cloud in the moonlight. It was beginning to thin out when the sound of it reached us in a searing hiss. The water round the spot bubbled and seethed and frothed. When the steam drew off, there was nothing to be seen there but a patch of turbulence, gradually subsiding.

Then the second of them came in, in just the same way, on almost the same spot. One after another all five of them touched down on the water with great whooshes and hissings of steam. Then the vapor cleared, showing only a few contiguous patches of troubled water.

Aboard the *Guinevere,* bells clanged, the beat of the engines changed, we started to change course, crews turned out to man the boats, men stood by to throw lifebelts.

Four times we steamed slowly back and forth across the area, searching. There was no trace whatever to be found. But for our own wake, the sea lay all about us in the moonlight, placid, empty, unperturbed . . .

The next morning I sent my card in to the captain. In those days I had a staff job with the E.B.C., and I explained to him that they would be pretty sure to take a piece from me on the previous night's affair. He gave the usual response: "You mean *B.B.C.?*"

The E.B.C. was comparatively young then. People long accustomed to the B.B.C.'s monopoly of the British air were still finding it difficult to become used to the idea of a competitive radio service. Life would have been a great deal simpler, too, if somebody had not had the idea in the early days of sailing as near the wind as possible by calling us the English Broadcasting Company. It was one of those pieces of foolishness that becomes more difficult to undo as time goes on, and led continually to one's explaining as I did now: "Not the *B*.B.C.; the *E*.B.C. Ours is the largest all-British commercial radio network . . ." etc. And when I was through with that I added:

"Our news-service is a stickler for accuracy, and as every passenger has his own version of this business, I hoped you would let me check mine against your official one."

He nodded approval of that.

"Go ahead and tell me yours," he invited me.

When I had finished, he showed me his own entry in the log. Substantially we were agreed; certainly in the view that there had been five, and on the impossibility of attributing a definite shape to them. His estimates of speed, size, and position were, of course, technical matters. I noticed that they had registered on the radar screens, and were tentatively assumed to have been aircraft of an unknown type.

"What's your own private opinion?" I asked him. "Did you ever see anything at all like them before?"

"No, I never did," he said, but he seemed to hesitate.

"But what—?" I asked.

"Well, but not for the record," he said, "I've heard of two instances, almost exactly similar, in the last year. One time it was three of the things by night; the other, it was half a dozen of them by daylight—even so, they seem to have looked much the same; just a kind of red fuzz. They were in the Pacific, though, not over this side."

"Why 'not for the record'?" I asked.

"In both cases there were only two or three witnesses —and it doesn't do a seaman any good to get a reputation for seeing things, you know. The stories just get around professionally, so to speak—among ourselves we aren't quite as skeptical as landsmen: some funny things can still happen at sea, now and then."

"You can't suggest an explanation I can quote?"

"On professional grounds I'd prefer not. I'll just stick to my official entry. But reporting it is a different matter this time. We've a couple of hundred witnesses and more."

"Do you think it'd be worth a search? You've got the spot pinpointed."

He shook his head. "It's deep there—over three thousand fathoms. That's a long way down."

"There wasn't any trace of wreckage in those other cases, either?"

"No. That would have been evidence to warrant an inquiry. But they had no evidence."

We talked a little longer, but I could not get him to put forward any theory. Presently I went away, and wrote up my account. Later, I got through to London, and dictated it to an E.B.C. recorder. It went out on the air the same evening as a filler, just an oddity which was not expected to do more than raise a few eyebrows.

So it was by chance that I was a witness of that early stage—almost the beginning, for I have not been able to find any references to identical phenomena earlier than those two spoken of by the captain. Even now, years later, though I am certain enough in my own mind that this was the beginning, I can still offer no *proof* that it was not an unrelated phenomenon. What the end that will eventually follow this beginning may be, I prefer not to think too closely. I would also prefer not to dream about it, either, if dreams were within my control.

It began so unrecognizably. Had it been more obvious —and yet it is difficult to see what could have been done effectively even if we had recognized the danger. Recognition and prevention don't necessarily go hand in hand. We recognized the potential dangers of atomic fission quickly enough—yet we could do little about them.

If we had attacked immediately—well, perhaps. But until the danger was well established we had no means of knowing that we *should* attack—and then it was too late.

However, it does no good to cry over our shortcomings. My purpose is to give as good a brief account as I can of how the present situation arose—and, to begin with, it arose very scrappily . . .

In due course the *Guinevere* docked at Southampton without being treated to any more curious phenomena. We did not expect any more, but the event had been memorable; almost as good, in fact, as having been in a position to say, upon some remote future occasion: "When your grandmother and I were on our honeymoon we saw a sea serpent," though not quite. Still, it was a wonderful honeymoon, I never expect to have a better; and Phyllis said something to much the same effect as we leaned on the rail, watching the bustle below.

"Except," she added, "that I don't see why we shouldn't have one nearly as good, now and then."

So we disembarked, sought our brand-new home in Chelsea, and I turned up at the E.B.C. offices the following Monday morning to discover that *in absentia* I had been rechristened Fireball Watson. This was on account of the correspondence. They handed it to me in a large sheaf, and said that since I had caused it, I had better do something about it. One letter, referring to a recent experience off the Philippines, I identified with fair certainty as being a confirmation of what the captain of the *Guinevere* had told me. One or two others seemed worth following up, too—particularly a rather cagey approach which invited me to meet the writer at La Plume D'Or, where lunch is always worth having.

I kept that appointment a week later. My host turned out to be a man two or three years older than myself who ordered four glasses of Tio Pepe, and then opened up by admitting that the name under which he had written was not his own, and that he was a Flight Lieutenant, R.A.F.

"It's a bit tricky, you see," he said. "At the moment I am considered to have suffered some kind of hallucination, but if enough evidence turns up to show that it was *not* a hallucination, then they're almost certain to make it an official secret. Awkward, you see."

I agreed that it must be.

"Still," he went on, "the thing worries me, and if you're collecting evidence, I'd like you to have it—though maybe not to make direct use of it. I mean, I don't want to find myself on the carpet."

I nodded understandingly. He went on:

"It was about three months ago. I was flying one of the regular patrols, a couple of hundred miles or so east of Formosa—"

"I didn't know we—" I began.

"There are a number of things that don't get publicity, though they're not particularly secret," he said. "Anyway, there I was. The radar picked these things up when they were still out of sight behind me, but coming up fast from the west."

He had decided to investigate, and climbed to intercept. The radar continued to show the craft on a straight course behind and above him. He tried to communicate, but couldn't raise them. By the time he was getting the ceiling of them they were in sight, as three red spots, quite bright, even by daylight, and coming up fast though he was doing close to five hundred himself. He tried again to radio them, but without success. They just kept on coming, steadily overtaking him.

"Well," he said, "I was there to patrol. I told base that they were a completely unknown type of craft—if they were craft at all—and as they wouldn't talk I proposed to have a pip at them. It was either that, or just let 'em go—in which case I might as well not have been patrolling at all. Base agreed, kind of cautiously.

"I tried them once more, but they didn't take a damn bit of notice of either me or my signals. And as they got closer I was doubtful whether they were craft at all. They were just as you said on the radio—a pink fuzz, with a deeper red center: might have been miniature red suns for all I could tell. Anyway, the more I saw of them the less I liked 'em, so I set the guns to radar-control, and let 'em get on ahead.

"I reckoned they must be doing seven hundred or more as they passed me. A second or two later the radar picked up the foremost one, and the guns fired.

"There wasn't any lag. The thing seemed to blow up almost as the guns went off. And, boy, did it blow! It suddenly swelled immensely, turning from red to pink to white, but still with a few red spots here and there—and then my aircraft hit the concussion, and maybe some of the debris too. I lost quite a lot of seconds, and probably had a lot of luck, because when I got sorted out I found that I was coming down fast. Something had carried away three-quarters of my starboard wing, and messed up the tip of the other. So I reckoned it was time to try the ejector, and rather to my surprise it worked."

He paused reflectively. Then he added: "I don't know that it gives you a lot besides confirmation, but there are one or two points. One is that they are capable of traveling a lot faster than those you saw. Another is that, whatever they are, they are highly vulnerable."

And that, as we talked it over in detail, was about all the additional information he did provide—that, and the fact that when they hit they did not disintegrate into sections, but exploded completely, which should, perhaps, have conveyed more than it seemed to at the time.

During the next few weeks several more letters trickled in without adding much, but then it began to look as if the whole affair were going the way of the Loch Ness Monster. What there was came to me because it was generally conceded at E.B.C. that fireball stuff was my pigeon. Several observatories confessed themselves puzzled by detecting small red bodies traveling at high speeds, but were extremely guarded in their statements. None of the newspapers really played it because, in editorial opinion, the whole thing was suspect in being too similar to the flying saucer business, and their readers would prefer more novelty in their sensations. Nevertheless, bits and pieces did slowly accumulate—though it took nearly two years before they acquired serious publicity and attention.

This time it was a flight of thirteen. A radar station in the north of Finland picked them up first, estimating their speed as fifteen hundred miles per hour, and their direction as approximately southwest. In passing the information on they described them simply as "unidentified aircraft." The Swedes picked them up as they crossed their territory, and managed to spot them visually, describing them as small red dots. Norway confirmed, but estimated the speed at under thirteen hundred miles per hour. A Scottish station logged them as traveling at a thousand miles per hour, and just visible to the naked eye. Two stations in Ireland reported them as passing directly overhead, on a line slightly west of southwest. The more southerly station gave their speed as eight hundred and claimed that they were "clearly visible." A weather ship at about 65 degrees North, gave a description which tallied exactly with that of the earlier fireballs, and calculated a speed close to 500 m.p.h. They were not sighted again.

There was a sudden spate of fireball observation after that. Reports came in from so far and wide that it was impossible to do more than sort out the more wildly imaginative and put the rest aside to be considered at more leisure, but I noticed that among them were several accounts of fireballs descending into the sea that tallied well with my own observation—so well, indeed, that I could not be absolutely sure that they did not derive from my own broadcast. All in all, it appeared to be such a muddle of guesswork, tall stories, thirdhand impressions, and thoroughgoing invention that it taught me little. One negative point, however, did strike me—not a single observer claimed to have seen a fireball descend on land. Ancillary to that, not a single one of those descending on water had been observed from the shore: all had been noticed from ships, or from aircraft well out to sea.

For a couple of weeks reports of sightings in groups large or small continued to pour in. The skeptics were weakening; only the most obstinate still maintained that they were hallucinations. Nevertheless, we learned nothing more about them than we had known before. No pictures. So often it seemed to be a case of the things you see when you don't have a gun. But then a flock of them came up against a fellow who did have a gun—literally.

The fellow in this case happened to be the U.S.S. *Tuskegee*, a carrier. The message from Curaçao that a flight of eight fireballs was headed directly toward her reached her when she was lying off San Juan, Puerto Rico. The captain breathed a short hope that they would commit a violation of the territory, and made his preparations. The fireballs, true to type, kept on in a dead straight line which would bring them across the island, and almost over the ship herself. The captain watched their approach on his radar with great satisfaction. He waited until the technical violation was indisputable. Then he gave the word to release six guided missiles at three-second intervals, and went on deck to watch, against the darkling sky.

Through his glasses he watched six of the red dots change as they burst, one after another, into big white puffs.

"Well, that's settled them," he observed, complacently. "Now it's going to be mighty interesting to see who beefs," he added, as he watched the two remaining red dots dwindle away to the northward.

But the days passed, and nobody beefed. Nor was there any decrease in the number of fireball reports.

For most people such a policy of masterly silence pointed only one way, and they began to consider the responsibility as good as proved.

In the course of the following week, two more fireballs that had been incautious enough to pass within range of the experimental station at Woomera paid for that temerity, and three others were exploded by a ship off Kodiak after flying across Alaska.

Washington, in a note of protest to Moscow regarding repeated territorial violations, ended by observing that in several cases where drastic action had been taken it regretted the distress that must have been caused to the relatives of the crews aboard the craft, but that responsibility lay at the door not of those who dealt with the craft, but with those who sent them out under orders which transgressed international agreements.

The Kremlin, after a few days of gestation, produced a rejection of the protest. It proclaimed itself unimpressed by the tactics of attributing one's own crime to another, and went on to state that its own weapons, recently developed by Russian scientists for the defense of peace, had now destroyed more than twenty of these craft over Soviet territory, and would, without hesitation, give the same treatment to any others detected in their work of espionage . . .

The situation thus remained unresolved. The non-Russian world was, by and large, divided sharply into two classes—those who believed every Russian pronouncement, and those who believed none. For the first class no question arose; their faith was firm. For the second, interpretation was less easy. Was one to deduce, for instance, that the whole thing was a lie? Or merely that when the Russians claimed to have accounted for twenty fireballs, they had only, in fact, exploded five or so?

An uneasy situation, constantly punctuated by an exchange of notes, drew out over months. Fireballs were undoubtedly more numerous than they had been, but just how much more numerous, or more active, or more frequently reported was difficult to assess. Every now and then a few more were destroyed in various parts of the world, and from time to time, too, it would be announced that numbers of capitalistic fireballs had been effectively shown the penalties that awaited those who conducted espionage upon the territory of the only true People's Democracy.

Public interest must feed to keep alive; and as novelty waned, an era of explaining-away set in.

Nevertheless, in Admiralty and Air Force Headquarters all over the world these notes and reports came together. Courses were plotted on charts. Gradually a pattern of a kind began to emerge.

At E.B.C. I was still regarded as the natural sifting place for anything to do with fireballs, and although the subject was dead mutton for the moment, I kept up my files in case it should revive. Meanwhile, I contributed in a small way to the building up of the bigger picture by passing along to the authorities such snippets of information as I thought might interest them.

In due course I found myself invited to the Admiralty to be shown some of the results.

It was a Captain Winters who welcomed me there, explaining that while what I should be shown was not exactly an official secret, it was preferred that I should not make public use of it yet. When I had agreed to that, he started to bring out maps and charts.

The first one was a map of the world hatched over with fine lines, each numbered and dated in minute figures. At first glance it looked as if a spider's· web had been applied to it; and, here and there, there were clusters of little red dots, looking much like the monkey spiders who had spun it.

Captain Winters picked up a magnifying glass and held it over the the area southeast of the Azores.

"There's your first contribution," he told me.

Looking through it, I presently distinguished one red dot with a figure 5 against it, and the date and time when Phyllis and I had leaned over the *Guinevere*'s rail watching the fireballs vanish in steam. There were quite a number of other red dots in the area, each labeled, and more of them were strung out to the northeast.

"Each of these dots represents the descent of a fireball?" I asked.

"One or more," he told me. "The lines, of course, are only for those on which we have had good enough information to plot the course. What do you think of it?"

"Well," I told him, "my first reaction is to realize that there must have been a devil of a lot more of them than I ever imagined. The second is to wonder why in thunder they should group in spots, like that."

"Ah!" he said. "Now stand back from the map a bit. Narrow your eyes, and get a light and shade impression."

I did, and saw what he meant.

"Areas of concentration," I said.

He nodded, "Five main ones, and a number of lesser. A dense one to the southwest of Cuba; another, six hundred miles south of the Cocos Islands; heavy concentrations off the Philippines, Japan, and the Aleutians. I'm not going to pretend that the proportions of density are right—in fact, I'm pretty sure that they are not. For instance, you can see a number of courses converging toward an area northeast of the Falklands, but only three red dots there. It very likely means simply that there are precious few people around those parts to observe them. Anything else strike you?"

I shook my head, not seeing what he was getting at. He produced a bathymetric chart, and laid it beside the first. I looked at it.

"All the concentrations are in deep water areas?" I suggested.

"Exactly. There aren't many reports of descents where the depth is less than four thousand fathoms, and none at all where it is less than two thousand."

I thought that over, without getting anywhere.

"So—just what?" I inquired.

"Exactly," he said again. "So what?"

We contemplated the proposition awhile.

"All descents," he observed. "No reports of any coming up."

He brought out maps on a large scale of the various main areas. After we had studied them a bit I asked: "Have you any idea at all what all this means—or wouldn't you tell me if you had?"

"On the first part of that, we have only a number of

theories, all unsatisfactory for one reason or another, so the second doesn't really arise."

"What about the Russians?"

"Nothing to do with them. As a matter of fact, they're a lot more worried about it than we are. Suspicion of capitalists being part of their mother's milk, they simply can't shake themselves clear of the idea that we must be at the bottom of it somehow, and they just can't figure out, either, what the game can possibly be. But what both we and they are perfectly satisfied about is that the things are not natural phenomena, nor are they random."

"And you'd know if it were any other country pulling it?"

"Bound to—not a doubt of it."

We considered the charts again in silence.

"The other obvious question is, of course, what do they seem to be doing?"

"Yes," he said.

"Meaning, no clue?"

"They come," he said. "Maybe they go. But certainly they come. That's about all."

I looked down at the maps, the crisscrossing lines, and the red-dotted areas.

"Are you doing anything about it? Or shouldn't I ask?"

"Oh, that's why you're here. I was coming round to that," he told me. "We're going to try an inspection. Just at the moment it is not considered to be a matter for a direct broadcast, nor even for publication, but there ought to be a record of it, and we shall need one ourselves. So if your people happened to feel interested enough to send you along with some gear for the job . . ."

"Where would it be?" I inquired.

He circled his finger round an area.

"Er—my wife has a passionate devotion to tropical sunshine, the West Indian kind in particular," I said.

"Well, I seem to remember that your wife has written some pretty good documentary scripts," he remarked.

"And it's the kind of thing E.B.C. might be very sorry about afterwards if they'd missed it," I reflected.

Not until we had made our last call and were well out of sight of land were we allowed to see the large object which rested in a specially constructed cradle aft. When the Lieutenant Commander in charge of technical operations ordered the shrouding tarpaulin to be removed, there was quite an unveiling ceremony. But the mystery revealed was something of an anticlimax: it was simply a sphere of metal some ten feet in diameter. In various parts of it were set circular, porthole-like windows; at the top it swelled into a protuberance which formed a massive lug. The Lieutenant Commander, after regarding it a while with the eye of a proud mother, addressed us in the manner of a lecturer.

"This instrument that you now see," he said, impressively, "is what we call the Bathyscope." He allowed an interval for appreciation.

"Didn't Beebe—?" I whispered to Phyllis.

"No," she said. "That was the bathysphere."

"Oh," I said.

"It has been constructed," he went on, "to resist a pressure approaching two tons to the square inch, giving it a theoretical floor of fifteen hundred fathoms. In practice we do not propose to use it at a greater depth than twelve hundred fathoms, thus providing for a safety factor of something over six hundred pounds to the square inch. Even at this it will considerably surpass the achievements of Dr. Beebe who descended a little over five hundred fathoms, and Barton who reached a depth of seven hundred and fifty fathoms . . ." He continued in this vein for a time, leaving me somewhat behind. When he seemed to have run down for a bit I said to Phyllis,

"I can't think in all these fathoms. What is it in God's feet?"

She consulted her notes.

"The depth they intend to go to is seven thousand, two hundred feet; the depth they *could* go to is nine thousand feet."

"Either of them sounds an awful lot of feet," I said.

Phyllis is, in some ways, more precise and practical.

"Seven thousand, two hundred feet is just over a mile and a third," she informed me. "The pressure will be a little more than a ton and a third."

"That's my continuity-girl," I said. "I don't know where

I'd be without you." I looked at the bathyscope. "All the same—" I added doubtfully.

"What?" she asked.

"Well, that chap at the Admiralty, Winters; he was talking in terms of four or five tons pressure—meaning, presumably, four or five miles down." I turned to the Lieutenant Commander. "How deep is it where we're bound for?" I asked him.

"It's an area called the Cayman Trench, between Jamaica and Cuba," he said. "In parts it reaches nearly four thousand."

"But—" I began, frowning.

"Fathoms, dear," said Phyllis. "Getting on for twenty-four thousand feet."

"Oh," I said. "That'll be—er—something like four and a half miles?"

"Yes," she said.

"Oh," I said, again.

He returned to his public address manner.

"That," he told the assembled crowd of us, "is the present limit of our ability to make direct visual observations. However—" He paused to make a gesture somewhat in the manner of a conjuror towards a party of sailors, and watched while they pulled the tarpaulin from another, similar, but smaller sphere. "—here," he continued, "we have a new instrument with which we hope to be able to make observations at something like twice the depth attainable by the bathyscope, perhaps even more. It is entirely automatic. In addition to registering pressures, temperature, currents, and so on, and transmitting the readings to the surface, it is equipped with five small television cameras, four of them giving all round horizontal coverage, and one transmitting the view vertically beneath the sphere."

"This instrument," continued another voice in good imitation of his own, "we call the telebath."

Facetiousness could not put a man like the Commander off his stroke. He continued his lecture. But the instrument had been christened, and the telebath it remained.

The three days after we reached our position were occupied with tests and adjustments of both the instruments. In one test Phyllis and I were allowed to make a dive of three hundred feet or so, cramped up in the bathyscope, "just to get the feel of it." It gave us no envy of anyone making a deeper dive. Then, with all the gear fully checked, the real descent was announced for the morning of the fourth day.

Soon after sunrise we were clustering round the bathyscope where it rested in its cradle. The two naval technicians, Wiseman and Trant, who were to make the descent, wriggled themselves in through the narrow hole that was the entrance. The warm clothing they would need in the depths was handed in after them, for they could never have squeezed in wearing it. Then followed the packets of food and the vacuum flasks of hot drinks. They made their final checks, gave their okays. The circular entrance-plug was swung over by the hoist, screwed gradually down into its seating, and bolted fast. The bathyscope was hoisted outboard, and hung there, swinging slightly. One of the men inside switched on his hand television camera, and we ourselves, as seen from within the instrument, appeared on the screen.

"Okay," said a voice from the loudspeaker, "lower away now."

The winch began to turn. The bathyscope descended, and the water lapped at it. Presently it had disappeared from sight beneath the surface.

The descent was a long business which I do not propose to describe in detail. Frankly, as seen on the screen in the ship, it was a pretty boring affair to the noninitiate. Life in the sea appears to exist in fairly well-defined levels. In the better-inhabited strata the water is full of plankton which behaves like a continuous dust storm and obscures everything but creatures that approach very closely. At other levels where there is no plankton for food, there are consequently few fish. In addition to the tediousness of very limited views or dark emptiness, continuous attention to a screen that is linked with a slightly swinging and twisting camera has a dizzying effect. Both Phyllis and I spent much of the time during the descent with our eyes shut, relying on the loud-speaking telephone to draw our attention to anything interesting. Occasionally we slipped on deck for a cigarette.

There could scarcely have been a better day for the job. The sun beat fiercely down on decks that were occasionally sluiced with water to cool them off. The ensign hung limp, barely stirring. The sea stretched out flat to meet the dome of the sky which showed only one low bank of cloud, to the north, over Cuba, perhaps. There was scarcely a sound, either, except for the muffled voice of the loudspeaker in the mess, the quiet drone of the winch, and from time to time the voice of a deck hand calling the tally of fathoms.

The group sitting in the mess scarcely spoke; they left that to the men now far below.

At intervals, the Commander would ask: "All in order, below there?"

And, simultaneously two voices would reply: "Aye, aye, sir!"

Once a voice inquired: "Did Beebe have an electrically heated suit?"

Nobody seemed to know.

"I take my hat off to him if he didn't," said the voice.

The Commander was keeping a sharp eye on the dials as well as watching the screen.

"Half-mile coming up. Check," he said.

The voice from below counted:

"Four thirty-eight . . . Four thirty-nine . . . *Now!* Half mile, sir."

The winch went on turning. There wasn't much to see. Occasional glimpses of schools of fish hurrying off into the murk. A voice complained: "Sure as I get the camera to one window a damn great fish comes and looks in at another."

"Five hundred fathoms. You're passing Beebe now," said the Commander.

"Bye-bye, Beebe," said the voice. "But it goes on looking much the same."

Presently the same voice said: "More life around just here. Plenty of squid, large and small. You can probably see 'em. There's something out this way, keeping on the edge of the light. A big thing. I can't quite—might be a giant squid—no! my God! It *can't* be a whale! Not down here!"

"Improbably, but not impossible," said the Commander.

"Well, in that case—oh, it's sheered off now, anyway. Gosh! We mammals do get around a bit, don't we?"

In due course the moment arrived when the Commander announced: "Passing Barton now," and then added with an unexpected change of manner, "From now on it's all yours, boys. Sure you're quite happy there? If you're not perfectly satisfied you've only to say."

"That's all right, sir. Everything functioning okay. We'll go on."

Up on deck the winch droned steadily.

"One mile coming up," announced the Commander. When that had been checked he asked, "How are you feeling now?"

"What's the weather like up there?" asked a voice.

"Holding well. Flat calm. No swell."

The two down below conferred.

"We'll go on, sir. Could wait weeks for conditions like this again."

"All right—if you're both sure."

"We are, sir."

"Very good. About three hundred fathoms more to go then."

There was an interval. Then: "Dead," remarked the voice from below. "All black and dead now. Not a thing to be seen. Funny thing the way these levels are quite separate. Ah, now we can begin to see something below . . . Squids again . . . luminous fish . . . Small shoal there, see? . . . There's . . . Gosh! Gosh—"

He broke off, and simultaneously a nightmare fishy horror gaped at us from the screen.

"One of nature's careless moments," he remarked.

He went on talking, and the camera continued to give us glimpses of unbelievable monstrosities, large and small.

Presently the Commander announced: "Stopping you now. Twelve hundred fathoms." He picked up the telephone and spoke to the deck. The winch slowed and then ceased to turn.

"That's all, boys," he said.

"Huh," said the voice from below, after a pause. "Well, whatever it was we came here to find, we've not found it."

The Commander's face was expressionless. Whether he

had expected tangible results or not I couldn't tell. I imagined not. In fact, I wondered if any of us there really had. After all, these centers of activity were all Deeps. And from that it would seem to follow that the reason must lie at the bottom. The echogram gave the bottom hereabouts as still three miles or so below where the two men now dangled . . .

"Hullo, there, bathyscope," said the Commander. "We're going to start you up now. Ready?"

"Aye, aye, sir! All set," said the two voices.

The Commander picked up his telephone.

"Haul away there!"

We could hear the winch start, and slowly gather speed.

"On your way now. All okay?"

"All correct, sir."

There was an interval without talk for ten minutes or more. Then a voice said: "There's something out there. Something big—can't see it properly. Keeps just on the fringe of the light. Can't be that whale again—not at this depth. Try to show you."

The picture on the screen switched and then steadied. We could see the light-rays streaming out through the water, and the brilliant speckles of small organisms caught in the beam. At the very limits there was a suspicion of a faintly lighter patch. It was hard to be sure of it.

"Seems to be circling us. We're spinning a bit, too, I think. I'll try—ah, got a bit better glimpse of it then. It's not the whale, anyway. There, see it now?"

This time we could undoubtedly make out a lighter patch. It was roughly oval, but indistinct, but there was nothing to give it scale.

"H'm," said the voice from below. "That's certainly a new one. Could be a fish—or maybe something else kind of turtle-shaped. Monstrous-sized brute, anyway. Circling a bit closer now, but I still can't make out any details. Keeping pace with us."

Again the camera showed us a glimpse of the thing as it passed one of the bathyscope's ports, but we were little wiser; the definition was too poor for us to be sure of anything about it.

"It's going up now. Rising faster than we are. Getting

beyond our angle of view. Ought to be a window in the top of this thing . . . Lost it now. Gone somewhere up above us. Maybe it'll—"

The voice cut off dead. Simultaneously, there was a brief, vivid flash on the screen, and it, too, went dead. The sound of the winch outside altered as it speeded up.

We sat looking at one another without speaking. Phyllis's hand sought mine, and tightened on it.

The Commander started to stretch his hand towards the telephone, changed his mind, and went out without a word. Presently the winch speeded up still more.

It takes quite a time to reel in more than a mile of heavy cable. The party in the mess dispersed awkwardly. Phyllis and I went up into the bows and sat there without talking much.

After what seemed a very long wait the winch slowed down. By common consent we got up, and moved aft together.

At last, the end came up. We all, I suppose, expected to see the end of the wire rope unraveled, with the strands splayed out, brushlike.

They were not. They were melted together. Both the main and the communication cables ended in a blob of fused metal.

We all stared at them, dumbfounded.

In the evening the Captain read the service, and three volleys were fired over the spot.

The weather held, and the glass was steady. At noon the next day the Commander assembled us in the mess. He looked ill, and very tired. He said, briefly, and unemotionally: "My orders are to proceed with the investigation, using our automatic instrument. If our arrangements and tests can be completed in time, and providing the weather remains favorable, we shall conduct the operation tomorrow morning, commencing as soon after dawn as possible. I am instructed to lower the instrument to the point of destruction, so there will be no other opportunity for observation."

The arrangement in the mess the following morning was different from that on the former occasion. We sat facing a bank of five television screens, four for the quadrants about the instrument, and one viewing vertically beneath it. There was also a movie camera photographing all five screens simultaneously for the record.

Again we watched the descent through the ocean layers, but this time instead of a commentary we had an astonishing assortment of chirrupings, raspings, and gruntings picked up by externally-mounted microphones. The deep sea is, in its lower inhabited strata, it seems, a place of hideous cacophony. It was something of a relief when at about three-quarters of a mile down silence fell, and somebody muttered: "Huh! Said those mikes'd never take the pressure."

The display went on. Squids sliding upwards past the cameras, shoals of fish darting nervously away, other fish attracted by curiosity—monstrosities, grotesque, huge monsters dimly seen. On and on. A mile down, a mile and a half, two miles, two and a half . . . And then, at about that point, something came into view which quickened all attention on the screens. A large, uncertain, oval shape at the extreme of visibility that moved from screen to screen as it circled round the descending instrument. For three or four minutes it continued to show on one screen or another, but always tantalizingly ill-defined, and never quite well enough illuminated for one to be certain even of its shape. Then, gradually, it drifted towards the upper edges of the screen, and presently it was left behind.

Half a minute later all the screens went blank . . .

Why not praise one's wife? Phyllis can write a thundering good feature script—and this was one of her best. It was too bad that it was not received with the immediate enthusiasm it deserved.

When it was finished, we sent it round to the Admiralty for checking. A week later we were asked to call. It was Captain Winters who received us. He congratulated Phyllis on the script, as well he might, even if he had not been so taken with her as he so obviously was. Once we were settled in our chairs, however, he shook his head regretfully.

"Nevertheless," he said, "I'm afraid I'm going to have to ask you to hold it up for a while."

Phyllis looked understandably disappointed; she had worked hard on that script. Not just for cash, either. She had tried to make it a tribute to the two men, Wiseman and Trant, who had vanished with the bathyscope. She looked down at her toes.

"I'm sorry," said the Captain, "but I did warn your husband that it wouldn't be for immediate release."

Phyllis looked up at him. "Why?" she asked.

That was something I was equally anxious to know about. My own recordings of the preparations, of the brief descent we had both made in the bathyscope, and of various aspects that were not on the official tape record of the dive, had been put into cold storage, too.

"I'll explain what I can. We certainly owe you that," agreed Captain Winters. He sat down and leaned forward, elbows on knees, fingers interlaced between them, and looked at us both in turn.

"The crux of the thing—and of course you will both of you have realized that long ago—is those fused cables," he said. "Imagination staggers a bit at the thought of a creature capable of snapping through steel hawsers—all the same, it might just conceivably admit the possibility. When, however, it comes up against the suggestion that there is a creature capable of cutting through them like an oxyacetylene flame, it recoils. It recoils, and definitely rejects.

"Both of you saw what had happened to those cables, and I think you must agree that their condition opens a whole new aspect. A thing like that is not just a hazard of deep-sea diving—and we want to know more about just what kind of hazard it is before we give a release on it."

We talked it over for a little time. The Captain was apologetic and understanding, but he had his orders.

"Honestly, Captain Winters—and off the record, if you like—have you any idea what can have done it?"

He shook his head. "On or off the record, Mrs. Watson, I can think of no explanation that approaches being possible—and, though this is not for publication, I doubt whether anyone else in the Service has an idea, either."

And so, with the affair left in that unsatisfactory state, we parted.

The prohibition, however, lasted a shorter time than

we expected. A week later, just as we were sitting down to dinner, he telephoned. Phyllis took the call.

"Oh, hullo, Mrs. Watson. I'm glad it's you. I have some good news for you," Captain Winters' voice said. "I've just been talking to your E.B.C. people, and giving them the okay, so far as we are concerned, to go ahead with that feature of yours, and the whole story."

Phyllis thanked him for the news. "But what's happened?" she added.

"The story's broken, anyway. You'll hear it on the nine o'clock news tonight, and see it in tomorrow's papers. In the circumstances it seemed to me that you ought to be free to take your chance as soon as possible. Their Lordships saw the point—in fact, they would like your feature to go out as soon as possible. So there it is. And the best of luck to you."

Phyllis thanked him again, and hung up. "Now what do you suppose can have happened?" she inquired.

We had to wait until nine o'clock to find that out. The notice on the news was scanty, but sufficient from our point of view. It reported simply that an American naval unit conducting research into deep-sea conditions somewhere off the Philippines had suffered the loss of a depth chamber, with its crew of two men.

Almost immediately afterwards E.B.C. came through on the telephone with a lot of talk about priorities, and altered program schedules, and available cast.

Audio-assessment told us later that the feature had rated an excellent reception figure. Coming so soon after the American announcement, we hit the peak of popular interest. Their Lordships were pleased too. It gave them the opportunity of showing that they did not always have to follow the American lead—though I still think there was no need to make the U.S. a present of the first publicity. Anyway, in view of what has followed, I don't suppose it greatly matters.

Phyllis rewrote a part of the script, making greater play with the fusing of the cables than before. A flood of correspondence came in, but when all the tentative explanations and suggestions had been winnowed none of us was any wiser than before.

Perhaps it was scarcely to be expected that we should be. Our listeners had not even seen the maps, and at this stage it had not occurred to the general public that there could be any link between the diving catastrophes and the somewhat *démodé* topic of fireballs.

But if, as it seemed, the Royal Navy was disposed simply to sit still for a time and ponder the problem theoretically, the U.S. Navy was not. Deviously we heard that they were preparing to send a second expedition to the same spot where their loss had occurred. We promptly applied to be included, and were refused. How many other people applied, I don't know, but enough for them to allocate a second small craft. We couldn't get a place on that either. All space was reserved for their own correspondents and commentators who would cover for Europe, too.

Well, it was their own show. They were paying for it. All the same, I'm sorry we missed it because, though we did think it likely they would lose their apparatus again, it never crossed our minds that they might lose their ship as well . . .

About a week after it happened one of the N.B.C. men who had been covering it came over. We more or less shanghaied him for lunch and the personal dope.

"Never saw anything like it," he said, "but if ever lightning were to strike upwards from the sea, I guess that'd be about the way it'd look. The sparks ran around all over the ship for a few seconds. Then she blew up."

"I never heard of anything like that," Phyllis said.

"It certainly isn't on the record," he agreed. "But there has to be a first time."

"Not very satisfactory," Phyllis commented.

He looked us over. "Seeing that you two were on that British fishing party, do I take it you know why we were there?"

"I'd not be surprised," I told him.

He nodded. "Well, look," he said, "I'm told it isn't possible to persuade a high charge, say a few million volts to run up an uninsulated hawser in sea water, so I must accept that; it's not my department. All I say is that *if* it were possible, then I guess the effect might be quite a bit like what we saw."

"There'd be insulated cables, too—to the cameras, microphones, thermometers and things," Phyllis said.

"Sure. And there was an insulated cable relaying the TV to our ship; but it couldn't carry that charge, and burned out—which was a darned good thing for us. That would make it look to me like it followed the main hawser—if it didn't so happen that the physics boys won't have it."

"They've no alternative suggestions?" I asked.

"Oh, sure. Several. Some of them could sound quite convincing—to a fellow who hadn't seen it happen."

"If you are right, this is very queer indeed," Phyllis said, reflectively.

The N.B.C. man looked at her. "A nice British understatement—but it's queer enough, even without me," he said, modestly. "However they explain this away, the physics boys are still stumped on those fused cables, because, whatever this may be, those cable severances *couldn't* have been accidental."

"On the other hand, all that way down, all that pressure . . . ?" Phyllis said.

He shook his head. "I'm making no guesses. I'd want more data than we've got, even for that. Could be we'll get it before long."

We looked questioning.

He lowered his voice. "Seeing you're in this too, but strictly under your hats, they've got a couple more probes lined up right now. But no publicity this time—the last lot had a nasty taste."

"Where?" we asked, simultaneously.

"One off the Aleutians, some place. The other in a deep spot in the Guatemala Basin. What're your folks doing?"

"We don't know," we said honestly.

He shook his head. "Always kinda close, your people," he said, sympathetically.

And close they remained. During the next few weeks we kept our ears uselessly wide open for news of either of the two new investigations, but it was not until the N.B.C. man was passing through London again a month later that we learned anything. We asked him what had happened.

He frowned. "Off Guatemala they drew a blank," he said. "The ship south of the Aleutians was transmitting by radio while the dive was in progress. It cut out suddenly. She's reported as lost with all hands."

Official cognizance of these matters remained underground—if that can be considered an acceptable term for their deep-sea investigations. Every now and then we would catch a rumor which showed that the interest had not been dropped, and from time to time a few apparently isolated items could, when put in conjunction, be made to give hints. Our naval contacts preserved an amiable evasiveness, and we found that our opposite numbers across the Atlantic were doing little better with their naval sources. The consoling aspect was that had they been making any progress we should most likely have heard of it, so we took silence to mean that they were stalled.

Public interest in fireballs was down to zero, and few people troubled to send in reports of them any more. I still kept my files going though they were not so unrepresentative that I could not tell how far the apparently low incidence was real.

As far as I knew, the two phenomena had never so far been publicly connected, and presently both were allowed to lapse unexplained, like any silly-season sensation.

In the course of the next three years we ourselves lost interest almost to vanishing point. Other matters occupied us. There was the birth of our son, William—and his death, eighteen months later. To help Phyllis to get over that I wangled myself a traveling-correspondent series, sold the house, and for a time we roved.

In theory, the appointment was simply mine; in practice, most of the gloss and finish on the scripts which pleased the E.B.C., were Phyllis's, and most of the time when she wasn't dolling up my stuff she was working on scripts of her own. When we came back home, it was with enhanced prestige, a lot of material to work up, and a feeling of being set on a smooth, steady course.

Almost immediately, the Americans lost a cruiser off the Marianas.

The report was scanty, an Agency message, slightly blown up locally; but there was a something about it—just a kind of feeling. When Phyllis read it in the newspaper, it struck her, too. She pulled out the atlas, and considered the Marianas.

"It's pretty deep round three sides of them," she said.

"That report's not handled quite the regular way. I can't exactly put my finger on it. But the approach is a bit off the line, somehow," I agreed.

"We'd better try the grapevine," Phyllis decided.

We did, without result. It wasn't that our sources were holding out on us; there seemed to be a blackout somewhere. We got no further than the official handout: this cruiser, the *Keweenaw,* had, in fair weather, simply gone down. Twenty survivors had been picked up. There would be an official inquiry.

Possibly there was: I never heard the outcome. The incident was somehow overlayed by the inexplicable sinking of a Russian ship, engaged on some task never specified, to eastward of the Kurils, that string of islands to the south of Kamchatka. Since it was axiomatic that any Soviet misadventure must be attributable in some way to capitalist jackals or reactionary fascist hyenas, this affair assumed an importance which quite eclipsed the American loss, and the acrimonious innuendoes went on echoing for some time. In the noise of vituperation the mysterious disappearance of the survey vessel *Utskarpen,* in the Southern Ocean, went almost unnoticed outside her native Norway.

Several others followed, but I no longer have my records to give me the details. It is my impression that quite half a dozen vessels, all seemingly engaged in ocean research in one way or another had vanished before the Americans suffered again, off the Philippines. This time they lost a destroyer, and with it, their patience.

The ingenuous announcement that since the water about Bikini was too shallow for a contemplated series of deep-water atomic-bomb tests the locale of these experiments would be shifted westwards by a little matter of a thousand miles or so, may possibly have deceived a portion of the general public, but in radio and newspaper circles it touched off a scramble for assignments.

Phyllis and I had better standing now, and we were lucky, too. We flew out there, and a few days later we formed part of the complement of a number of ships lying at a strategic distance from the point where the *Keweenaw* had gone down off the Marianas.

I can't tell you what that specially designed depth bomb looked like, for we never saw it. All we were allowed to see was a raft supporting a kind of semispherical, metal hut which contained the bomb itself, and all we were told was that it was much like one of the more regular types of atomic bomb, but with a massive casing that would resist the pressure at five miles deep, if necessary.

At first light on the day of the test a tug took the raft in tow, and chugged away over the horizon with it. From then on we had to observe by means of unmanned television cameras mounted on floats. In this way we saw the tug cast off the raft, and put on full speed. Then there was an interval while the tug hurried out of harm's way and the raft pursued a calculated drift towards the exact spot where the *Keweenaw* had disappeared. The hiatus lasted for some three hours, with the raft looking motionless on the screens. Then a voice through the loudspeakers told us that the release would take place in approximately thirty minutes. It continued to remind us at intervals until the time was short enough for it to start counting in reverse, slowly and calmly. There was a complete hush as we stared at the screens and listened to the voice: "—three—two—one—*NOW!*"

On the last word a rocket sprang from the raft, trailing red smoke as it climbed.

"Bomb away!" said the voice.

We waited.

For a long time, as it seemed, everything was intensely still. Around the vision screens no one spoke. Every eye was on one or another of the frames which showed the raft calmly afloat on the blue, sunlit water. There was no sign that anything had occurred there, save the plume of red smoke drifting slowly away. For the eye and the ear there was utter serenity; for the feelings, a sense that the whole world held its breath.

Then it came. The placid surface of the sea suddenly belched into a vast white cloud which spread, and boiled as it writhed upwards. A tremor passed through the ship.

We left the screens, and rushed to the ship's side. Already the cloud was above our horizon. It still writhed and convolved upon itself in a fashion that was somehow obscene as it climbed monstrously up the sky. Only then did the sound reach us, in a buffeting roar. Much later, amazingly delayed, we saw the dark line which was the first wave of turbulent water rushing toward us.

That night we shared a dinner table with Mallarby of *The Tidings* and Bennell of *The Senate*. This was Phyllis's show, and she had them more or less where she wanted them between the entree and the roast. They argued a while along familiar lines, but after a while the name Bocker began to crop up with increasing frequency and some acrimony. Apparently this Bocker had some theory about deep-sea disturbances which had not come our way, and did not seem to be held in great repute by either party.

Phyllis was on it like a hawk. One would never have guessed that she was utterly in the dark, from the judicial way she said: "Surely the Bocker line can't be altogether dismissed?" frowning a little as she spoke.

It worked. In a little time we were adequately briefed on the Bocker view, and without either of them guessing that as far as we were concerned he had come into it for the first time.

The name of Alastair Bocker was not, of course, entirely unknown to us: it was that of an eminent geographer, a name customarily followed by several groups of initials. However, the information on him that Phyllis now prompted forth was something quite new to us. When reordered and assembled it amounted to this: Almost a year earlier Bocker had presented a memorandum to the Admiralty in London. Because he was Bocker it succeeded in getting itself read at some quite important levels although the gist of its argument was as follows: The fused cables and electrification of certain ships must be regarded as indisputable evidence of intelligence at work in certain deeper parts of the oceans.

Conditions, such as pressure, temperature, perpetual darkness, etc., in those regions made it inconceivable that any intelligent form of life could have evolved there—and this statement he backed with several convincing arguments.

It was to be assumed that no nation was capable of constructing mechanisms that could operate at such depths as indicated by the evidence, nor would they have any purpose in attempting to do so.

But, if the intelligence in the depths were not indigenous, then it must have come from elsewhere. Also, it must be embodied in some form able to withstand a pressure of tons to the square inch—two tons certainly from present evidence, probably five or six tons, even seven tons if it was capable of existing in the very deepest Deeps. Now, was there anywhere else on Earth where a mobile form could find conditions of such pressure to evolve in? Clearly, there was not.

Very well, then if it could not have evolved on Earth, it must have evolved somewhere else—say, on a large planet where the pressures were normally very high. If so, how did it cross space and arrive here?

Bocker then recalled attention to the fireballs which had aroused so much speculation a few years ago, and were still occasionally to be seen. None of these had been known to descend on land; none, indeed, had been known to descend anywhere but in areas of very deep water. Moreover, such of them as had been struck by missiles had exploded with such violence as to suggest that they had been retaining a very high degree of pressure.

It was significant, also, that these fireball globes invariably sought the only regions of the Earth in which high-pressure conditions compatible with movement were available.

Therefore, Bocker deduced, we were in the process, while almost unaware of it, of undergoing a species of interplanetary immigration. If he were to be asked the source of it, he would point to Jupiter as being most likely to fulfill the conditions of pressure.

His memorandum had concluded with the observation that such an incursion need not necessarily be regarded as hostile. It seemed to him that the interests of a type of creation which existed at fifteen pounds to the square inch were unlikely to overlap seriously with those of a form which required several tons per square inch. He advocated, therefore, that the greatest efforts should be made to develop some means of making a sympathetic approach to the new dwellers in our depths, with the aim of facilitating an exchange of science, using the word in its widest sense.

The views expressed by Their Lordships upon these elucidations and suggestions are not publicly recorded. It is known, however, that no long interval passed before Bocker withdrew his memorandum from their unsympathetic desks, and shortly afterwards presented it for the personal consideration of the Editor of *The Tidings*. Undoubtedly *The Tidings*, in returning it to him, expressed itself with its usual tact. It was only for the benefit of his professional brethren that the Editor remarked: "This newspaper has managed to exist for more than one hundred years without a comic strip, and I see no reason to break that tradition now."

In due course, the memorandum appeared in front of the Editor of *The Senate,* who glanced at it, called for a synopsis, lifted his eyebrows, and dictated an urbane regret.

Subsequently it ceased to circulate, and was known only by word of mouth within a small circle.

"The best you can say of it," said Mallarby, "is that he does include more factors than anyone else has—and that anything that includes even most of the factors is bound to be fantastic. We may decry it but, for all that, until something better turns up, it's the best we have."

"That's true," said Bennell. "But whatever the top naval men may think about Bocker, it is clear enough that they too must have been assuming for some time that there *is* something intelligent down there. You don't design and make a special bomb like that all in five minutes, you know. Anyway, whether the Bocker theory is sheer hot-air or not, he's lost his main point. This bomb was not the amiable and sympathetic approach that he advocated."

Mallarby paused, and shook his head. "I've met Bocker several times. He's a civilized, liberal-minded man—with the usual trouble of liberal-minded men; that they think others are, too. He has an interested, inquiring mind. He has never grasped that the average mind when it encounters something new is scared, and says: 'Better smash it, or suppress it, quick.' Well, he's just had another demonstration of the average mind at work."

"But," Bennell objected, "if, as you say, it is officially believed that these ship losses have been caused by an intelligence, then there's something to be scared about, and you *can't* put today's affair down as nothing stronger than retaliation."

Mallarby shook his head again. "My dear Bennell, I not only can, but I do. Suppose, now, that something were to come dangling down to us on a rope out of space; and suppose that that thing was emitting rays on a wave length that acutely discomforted us, perhaps even caused us physical pain. What should we do? I suggest that the first thing we should do would be to snip the rope, and put it out of action. Then we should examine the strange object and find out what we could about it. And if more of the same followed, we should forthwith take what steps we could to discourage them. This might be done simply in the spirit of ending a nuisance, or it might be done with some animosity, and regarded as—retaliation. Now, would it be we, or the thing above, that was to blame?

"It is difficult to imagine any kind of intelligence that would not resent what we've just done. If this were the only Deep where trouble has occurred, there might well be no intelligence left to resent it—but this *isn't* the only place, as you know; not by any means. So, what form that very natural resentment will take remains for us to see."

"You think there really will be some kind of response, then?" Phyllis asked.

He shrugged. "To take up my analogy again: suppose that some violently destructive agency were to descend from space upon one of our cities. What should we do?"

"Well, what *could* we do?" asked Phyllis, reasonably enough.

"We could turn the backroom boys on to it. And if it happened a few times more, we should soon be giving the backroom boys full priorities. No," he shook his head, "no, I'm afraid Bocker's idea of fraternization never had the chance of a flea in a furnace."

That was, I think, very likely as true as Mallarby made it sound; but if there ever had been any chance at all, it was gone by the time we reached home. Somehow, and apparently overnight, the public had put several twos together at last. The halfhearted attempt to represent the depth bomb as one of a series of tests had broken down altogether. The vague fatalism with which the loss of the *Keweenaw* and the other ships had been received was succeeded by a burning sense of outrage, a satisfaction that the first step in vengeance had been taken, and a demand for more.

The atmosphere was similar to that at a declaration of war. Yesterday's phlegmatics and skeptics were, all of a sudden, fervid preachers of a crusade against the—well, against whatever it was that had had the insolent temerity to interfere with the freedom of the seas. Agreement on that cardinal point was virtually unanimous, but from that hub speculation radiated in every direction, so that not only fireballs, but every other unexplained phenomenon that had occurred for years was in some way attributed to, or at least connected with, the mystery in the Deeps.

The wave of world-wide excitement struck us when we stopped off for a day at Karachi on our way home. The place was bubbling with tales of sea serpents and visitations from space, and it was clear that whatever restrictions Bocker might have put on the circulation of his theory, a good many million people had now arrived at a similar explanation by other routes. This gave me the idea of telephoning to the E.B.C. in London to find out if Bocker himself would now unbend enough for an interview.

They told me that others had had the same idea, and that Bocker would be giving a restricted press conference on Friday. They would do their best to get us in on it. They did, and we arrived back in London with a couple of hours to spare before it took place.

Alastair Bocker was recognizable from his photographs, but they had not done him justice. The main facial architecture, with its rather full, middle-aged-infant quality, the broad eyebrows, the lock of gray hair tending to stray forward, the shapes of the nose and mouth, were all familiar; but the camera by its inability to convey the liveliness of his eyes, the mobility of the mouth and the whole face, the sparrow-like quality of his movements, had falsified him.

"One of those so unrestful small-boys-grown-up," observed Phyllis, studying him before the affair began.

For some minutes longer people continued to arrive and settle down, then Bocker stepped up to the table in front. The way he did it managed to convey that he had not come there to conciliate. When the babble had died he stood looking us over for some seconds. Then he spoke, without script or notes.

"I don't suppose for a moment that this meeting is going to be useful," he began. "However I did not call it, and I am not concerned now whether I get a good press or not.

"A couple of years ago I should have welcomed the chance of this publicity. One year ago I attempted to achieve it, though my hopes that we might be able to deflect the probable course of events were no more than slight, even then. I find it somewhat ironical, therefore, that you should honor me in this way now that they have become nonexistent.

"A version of my arguments, very likely a garbled one, may have reached you, but I will summarize them now so that at least we shall know what we are talking about."

The summary differed little from the version we had already heard. At the end of it he paused. "Now. Your questions," he said.

At this distance in time I cannot pretend to remember who asked what questions, but I recall that the few first fatuous ones were slapped down pretty sharply. Then someone asked: "Doctor Bocker, I seem to recall that originally you made some deliberate play with the word "immigration," but just now you spoke of "invasion." You have changed your mind?"

"It has been changed for me," Bocker told him. "For all I know, it may have been, in intention, just a peaceful immigration—but the evidence is that it is not so now."

"So," said somebody else, "you are telling us that this is our old blood-chiller, the interplanetary war, come at last."

"It might be put that way—by the facetious," agreed Bocker, calmly. "It is certainly an invasion, and from some place unknown." He paused. "Almost equally remarkable," he went on, "is the fact that in this sensation-seeking world it has managed to take place almost unrecognized for what it is. Only now, several years after its inception, is it starting to be taken seriously."

"It doesn't look like an interplanetary war to me now, whatever it is," a voice remarked.

"That," remarked Bocker, "I would ascribe to two main causes. First, constipation of the imagination; and, secondly, the influence of the late Mr. H. G. Wells.

"One of the troubles about writing a classic is that it sets a pattern of thinking. Everybody reads it, with the result that everybody thinks he knows exactly the form which an interplanetary invasion not only ought to, but must, take. If a mysterious cylinder were to land close to London or Washington tomorrow, we should all of us immediately recognize it as a right and proper subject for alarm. It seems to have been overlooked that Mr. Wells was simply employing one of a number of devices that he might have used for a work of fiction, so one might point out that he did not pretend to be laying down a law for the conduct of interplanetary campaigns. And the fact that his choice remains the only prototype for the occurrence in so many minds is a better compliment to his skill in writing than it is to those minds' skill in thinking.

"There could be quite a large variety of invasions against which it would be no good to call out the marines. This one is much more difficult to come to grips with than Mr. Wells' Martians were. It still remains to be seen whether the weapons we shall have to face will be more or less effective than those he imagined."

Somebody put in: "All right. Say, for purposes of discussion, that this is an invasion. Now why, would you say, have we been invaded?"

Bocker regarded him for a long moment, then he said: "I imagine that 'Why?' to have been the cry of every invaded party throughout history."

"But there must be some reason," the questioner persisted.

"Must there?—Well, I suppose, in the widest sense there must. But it does not follow from that that it is a reason we should understand, even if we knew it. I do not suppose the original Americans had much understanding of the reasons why they were being invaded by the Spaniards . . .

"But what you are, in fact, asking is that I should explain to you the motives that are animating an alien form of intelligence. In modesty I must decline to make that much of a fool of myself. The way to have found out, if not to have understood perhaps, would have been to get into communication with these things in our Deeps. But it would appear that whatever chance there may once have been of that, we have now very surely spoiled it."

The questioner was not satisfied with that. "But if we can't assign a reason," he said, "then surely the whole thing becomes very little different from a natural disaster—something like, say, an earthquake or a cyclone?"

"True enough," agreed Bocker. "And why not? I imagine that it is just so that the bird appears to the insect. Also, for the common people involved in a great war its distinction from a natural disaster is not very sharp. I know that you have all taught your readers to expect oversimplified explanations of everything, not excluding God Himself, in words of one syllable, so go ahead, and satisfy their lust for wisdom; no one can contradict you. But if you try to hang your explanations on me, I'll sue you.

"I'll go just as far as this: I can think of just two *human* motives for migration across space, if it were possible, on any scale. One would be simple expansion and aggrandizement; the other, flight from intolerable conditions on the home planet. But those things in the Deeps are certainly not human, whatever they may be; therefore, their reasons and motives may, but much more likely will not, be similar to human motives."

He paused and looked round again. "You know," he said, "this 'Why?' business is a waste of breath. If we were to go to another planet, and the people we found there promptly threw bombs at us, the 'Why?' of our going there wouldn't make the least difference; we should simply assume that if we did not take steps to stop it, we should be exterminated. And there, possibly, we do have some common ground with these things in the Deeps—the life-force, in whatever shape it is embodied, must have, collectively or individually, the will to survive, or it will soon cease to be."

"Then it is definitely your opinion that this is a *hostile* invasion?" someone asked.

Bocker regarded him with interest. "You know, you'd better stay after class. What I say is that it *is* an invasion, that it *is* hostile now, but it *may* not have been hostile in intention.

"And now," he concluded, "all I ask is that you convince your readers that this is no stunt, but a very serious matter—those of you whom editorial and proprietorial policies permit, of course."

What happened, in point of fact, was that almost all reports presented Bocker as a crackpot, with the kind of implied comment: "This is the sort of thing you might believe if you were a crackpot, too—but of course you are not, you are a sensible man."

There were signs that the playing-down was not accidental. The public was in a mood in which it would have taken anything, but there was pointed neglect of the opportunity to exploit the situation. Nor, just then, did anything sensational occur to interrupt the soothing process.

Then, by degrees, a feeling got about that this was not at all the way anyone had expected an interplanetary war to be; so very likely it was not an interplanetary war after all. From there, of course, it was only a step to deciding that it must be the Russians.

The Russians had all along encouraged, within their dictatorate, suspicion of capitalistic warmongers. When whispers of the interplanetary notion did in some way penetrate their curtain, they were countered by the statements that, (a) it was all a lie, a verbal smoke screen to cover the preparations of warmongers, (b) that it was true; and the capitalists, true to type, had immediately attacked the unsuspecting strangers with atom bombs, and, (c) whether it was true or not, the U.S.S.R. would fight unswervingly for Peace with all the weapons it possessed, except germs.

The swing continued. People were heard to say: "Huh —that interplanetary stuff? Don't mind telling you that I very nearly fell for it all the time. But, of course, when you start to actually *think* about it—! Wonder what the Russian game really is? Must've been something pretty big to make 'em use A-bombs on it." Thus, in quite a short time, the *status quo ante bellum hypotheticum* was restored, and we were back on the familiar comprehensible basis of international suspicion. The only lasting result was that marine insurance stayed up one per cent.

A couple of weeks later we had a little dinner party—with Captain Winters sitting at Phyllis's right hand. They looked to be getting on very well. Afterward, in our domestic privacy, I inquired: "If you aren't too sleepy, how did it go? What did the Captain have to say?"

"Oh, lots of nice things. Irish blood there, I think."

"But, passing from the really important to matters of mere worldwide interest—?" I suggested, patiently.

"He wouldn't let go of much, but what he did say wasn't encouraging. Some of it was rather horrid."

"Tell me."

"Well, the main situation doesn't seem to have altered a lot on the surface, but they're getting increasingly worried about what's happening below. He didn't actually *say* that investigation has made no progress, either, but what he did say implied it.

"He says for instance that atomic bombs are out, for the moment at any rate. You can only use them in isolated places, and even then the radioactivity spreads widely. The fisheries experts on both sides of the Atlantic have been raising hell, and saying that it's because of the bombings that some shoals have been failing to turn up in the proper places at the proper times. They've been blaming the bombs for upsetting the ecology, whatever that is, and affecting the migratory habits. But a few of them are saying that the data isn't sufficient to be absolutely sure that it is the bombs that have done it, but something certainly has, and it may have serious effects on food supplies. And so, as nobody seems to be quite clear what the bombs were expected to do, and all they do do is to kill and bewilder lots of fish at great expense, they've become unpopular just now.

"And here's something else. Two of those bombs they've sent down haven't gone off."

"Oh," I said, "and what do we infer from that?"

"I don't know. But it has them worried, very worried. You see, the way they are set to operate is by the pressure at a given depth; simple and pretty accurate."

"Meaning that they never reached the right pressure zone? Must have got hung up somewhere on the way down?"

Phyllis nodded. "It's made them extremely anxious."

"Understandably, too. I'd not feel too happy myself if I'd mislaid a couple of live atom bombs," I admitted. "What else?"

"Three cable-repair ships have unaccountably disappeared. One of them was cut off in the middle of a radio message. She was known to be grappling for a defective cable at the time."

"When was this?"

"One about six months ago, one about three weeks ago, and one last week."

"They might not have anything to do with it."

"They *might* not—but everyone's pretty sure they have."

"No survivors to tell what happened?"

"None."

Presently I asked: "Anything more?"

"Let me see. Oh, yes. They are developing some kind of guided depth missile which will be high-explosive, not atomic. But it hasn't been tested yet."

I turned to look at her admiringly. "That's the stuff, darling. The real Mata Hari touch."

Phyllis ignored that one. "The most important thing is that he is going to give me an introduction to Dr. Matet, the oceanographer."

I sat up. "But, darling, the Oceanographical Society has more or less threatened to excommunicate anybody who deals with us after that last script—it's part of their anti-Bocker line."

"Well, Dr. Matet happens to be a friend of the Captain's. He's seen his fireball-incidence maps, and he's a half-convert. Anyway, we're not convinced Bockerites, are we?"

"What we think we are isn't necessarily what other people think we are. Still, if he's willing—when can we see him?"

"*I* hope to see him in a few days' time, darling."

"Don't you think I should—"

"No. But it's sweet of you not to trust me still."

"But—"

"No. And now it's time we went to sleep," she said, firmly.

The beginning of Phyllis's interview was, she reported, almost standard: "*E.B.C.*?" said Dr. Matet, raising eyebrows like miniature door mats. "I thought Captain Winters said *B.B.C.*"

He was a man with a large frame sparingly covered, which gave his head the appearance of properly belonging to a still larger frame. His tanned forehead was high, and well polished back to the crown. He gave one, Phyllis said, a feeling of being overhung.

She sighed inwardly, and started on the routine justification of the English Broadcasting Company's existence, and worked him round gradually until he had reached the position of considering us nice-enough people striving manfully to overcome the disadvantages of being considered a slightly second-class oracle. Then, after making it quite clear that any material he might supply was strictly anonymous in origin, he opened up a bit.

The trouble from Phyllis's point of view was that he did it on a pretty academic level, full of strange words and instances which she had to interpret as best she could. The gist of what he had to tell her, however, seemed to be this: A year ago there had begun to be reports of discolorations in certain ocean currents. The first observation of the kind had been made in the Kuroshio current in the North Pacific—an unusual muddiness flowing northeast, becoming less discernible as it gradually widened out along the West Wind Drift until it was no longer perceptible to the naked eye.

"Samples were taken and sent for examination, of course, and what do you think the discoloration turned out to be?" said Dr. Matet.

Phyllis looked properly expectant. He told her: "Mainly radiolarian ooze, but with an appreciable percentage of diatomaceous ooze."

"How very remarkable!" Phyllis said, safely. "Now what on earth could produce a result like that?"

"Ah," said Dr. Matet, "that is the question. A disturbance on a quite remarkable scale—even in samples taken on the other side of the ocean, off the coast of California, there was still quite a heavy impregnation of both these oozes."

He went on and on, until Phyllis finally managed to interrupt him. "Something, then," she said, "not only was, but still is, going on down there?"

"Something is," he agreed, looking at her. Then, with a sudden descent to the vernacular, he added: "But, to be honest with you, Lord knows what it is."

"Too much geography," said Phyllis, "and too much oceanography, and too much bathyography: too much of all the ographies, and lucky to escape ichthyology."

"Tell me," I said.

She did, with notes. "And," she concluded, "I'd like to see anyone scribe a script out of that lot."

"H'm," I said.

"There's no 'H'm' about it. Some kind of ographer might give a talk on it to high brows and low listening-figures, but even if he were intelligible, where'd it get anybody?"

"That," I remarked, "is the key question each time. But little by little the bits do accumulate. This is another bit. You didn't really expect to come back with the stuff for a whole script, anyway. He didn't suggest how this might link up with the rest of it?"

"No. I said it was sort of funny how everything seemed to be happening down in the most inaccessible parts of the ocean lately, and a few things like that, but he didn't rise. Very cautious. I think he was rather wishing he had not agreed to see me, so he stuck to verifiable facts. Eminently nonwheedlable—at first meeting, anyhow. He admitted that might send his reputation the way Bocker's has gone."

"Look," I said. "Bocker must have got to know about this as soon as anyone did. He ought to have some views on it, and it might be worth trying to find out what they are. The select press conference of his that we went to was almost an introduction."

"He went very coy after that," she said doubtfully. "Not surprising, really. Still, we weren't among the ones who panned him publicly—in fact, we were very objective."

"Toss you which of us rings him up," I offered.

"I'll do it," she said.

So I leaned back comfortably in my chair, and listened to her going through the opening ceremony of making it clear that she was the *E.B.C.*

I will say for Bocker that having proposed his mouthful of a theory and then sold it to himself, he had not backed out of the deal when he found it unpopular. At the same time he had no great desire to be involved in a further round of controversy when he would be pelted with cheap cracks and drowned in the noise from empty vessels. He made that quite clear when we met. He looked at us earnestly, his head a little to one side, the lock of gray hair hanging slightly forward, his hands clasped together. He nodded thoughtfully, and then said: "You want a theory from me because nothing you can think of will explain this phenomenon. Very well, you shall have one. I don't suppose you'll accept it, but I do ask you if you use it at all to use it anonymously. When people come round to my view again, I shall be ready, but I prefer not to be thought of as keeping my name before the public by letting out sensational driblets—is that quite clear?"

We nodded. We are becoming used to this general desire for anonymity.

"What we are trying to do," Phyllis explained, "is to fit a lot of bits and pieces into a puzzle. If you can show us where one of them should go, we'll be very grateful. If you would rather not have the credit for it, well, that is your own affair."

"Exactly. Well, you already know my theory of the origin of the deepwater intelligences, so we'll not go into that now. We'll deal with their present state, and I deduce that to be this: having settled into the environment best suited to them, these creatures' next thought would be to develop that environment in accordance with their ideas of what constitutes a convenient, orderly, and, eventually, civilized condition. They are, you see, in the position of—well, no, they are *actually* pioneers, colonists. Once they have safely arrived they set about improving and exploiting their new territory. What we have been seeing are the results of their having started work on the job."

"By doing what?" I asked.

He shrugged his shoulders. "How can we possibly tell? But judging by the way we have received them, one would imagine that their primary concern would be to provide themselves with some form of defense against us. For this they would presumably require metals. I suggest to you, therefore, that somewhere down in the Mindanao Trench, and also somewhere in the Deep in the southeast of the Cocos-Keeling Basin, you would, if you could go there, find mining operations now in progress."

I glimpsed the reason of his demand for anonymity. "Er—but the working of metals in such conditions—?" I said.

"How can we guess what technology they may have developed? We ourselves have plenty of techniques for doing things which would at first thought appear impossible in an atmospheric pressure of fifteen pounds per square inch; there are also a number of unlikely things we can do under water."

"But, with a pressure of tons, and in continual darkness, and—" I began, but Phyllis cut across me with that decisiveness which warns me to shut up and not argue.

"Dr. Bocker," she said, "you named two particular Deeps then, why was that?"

He turned from me to her. "Because that seems to me the only reasonable explanation where those two are concerned. It may be, as Mr. Holmes once remarked to your husband's illustrious namesake, 'a capital mistake to theorize before one has data,' but it is mental suicide to funk the data one has. I know of nothing, and can imagine nothing, that could produce the effect Dr. Matet spoke of except some exceedingly powerful machine for continuous ejection."

"But," I said, a little firmly, for I get rather tired of being dogged by the ghost of Mr. Holmes, "if it is mining as you suggest, then why is the discoloration due to ooze, and not grit?"

"Well, firstly there would be a great deal of ooze to be shifted before one could get at the rock, immense deposits, most likely, and secondly the density of the ooze is little more than that of water, whereas the grit, being heavy, would begin to settle long before it got anywhere near the surface, however fine it might be."

Before I could pursue that, Phyllis cut me off again: "What about the other places, Doctor. Why mention just those two?"

"I don't say that the others don't also signify mining, but I suspect, from their locations, that they may have another purpose."

"Which is—?" prompted Phyllis, looking at him, all girlish expectation.

"Communications, I think. You see, for instance, close to, though far below, the area where discoloration begins to occur in the equatorial Atlantic lies the Romanche Trench. It is a gorge through the submerged mountains of the Atlantic Ridge. Now, when one considers the fact that it forms the only deep link between the eastern and western Atlantic Basins, it seems more than just a coincidence that signs of activity should show up there. In fact, it strongly suggests to me that something down below is not satisfied with the natural state of that Trench. It is quite likely that it is blocked here and there by falls of rock. It may be that in some parts it is narrow and awkward; almost certainly, if there were a prospect of using it, it would be an advantage to clear it of ooze deposits down to a solid bottom. I don't *know*, of course, but the fact that something is undoubtedly taking place in that strategic Trench leaves me with little doubt that whatever is down there is concerned to improve its methods of getting about in the depths—just as we have improved our ways of getting about on the surface."

There was a silence while we took in that one, and its implications. Phyllis rallied first. "Er—and the other two main places—the Caribbean one, and the one west of Guatemala?" she asked.

Dr. Bocker offered us cigarettes, and lit one himself.

"Well, now," he remarked, leaning back in his chair, "doesn't it strike you as probable that, for a creature of the depths, a tunnel connecting the Deeps on either side of the isthmus would offer advantages almost identical with those that we ourselves obtain from the existence of the Panama Canal?"

People may say what they like about Bocker, but they can never truthfully claim that the scope of his ideas is mean or niggling. What is more, nobody has ever actually *proved* him wrong. His chief trouble was that he usually provided such large, indigestible slabs that they stuck in all gullets—even mine, and I would class myself as a fairly wide-gulleted type. That, however, was a subsequent reflection. At the climax of the interview I was chiefly occupied with trying to convince myself that he really meant what he had said, and finding nothing but my own resistance to suggest that he did not.

Before we left, he gave us one more thing to think about, too. He said: "Since you are following this along, you've probably heard of two atomic bombs that failed to go off?"

We told him we had.

"And have you heard that there was an unsponsored atomic explosion yesterday?"

"No. Was it one of them?" Phyllis asked.

"I should very much hope so—because I should hate to think it could be any other," he replied. "But the odd thing is that though one was lost off the Aleutians, and the other in the process of trying to give the Mindanao Trench another shake up, the explosion took place not so far off Guam—a good twelve hundred miles from Mindanao."

PHASE 2

We made an early start the next morning. The car, ready loaded, had stood out all night, and we were away a few minutes after five, with the intention of putting as much of southern England behind us as we could before the roads got busy. It was two hundred and sixty-eight point eight (when it wasn't point seven or point nine) miles to the door of the cottage that Phyllis had bought with a small legacy from her Aunt Helen.

I had rather favored the idea of a cottage a mere fifty

miles or so away from London, but it was Phyllis's aunt who was to be commemorated with what was now Phyllis's money, so we became the proprietors of Rose Cottage, Penllyn, Nr. Constantine, Cornwall, Telephone Number: Navasgan 333. It was a gray stone, five-roomed cottage set on a southeasterly sloping, heathery hillside, with its almost eaveless roof clamped down tight on it in true Cornish manner. Straight before us we looked across the Helford River, and on toward the Lizard where, by night, we could see the flashing of the lighthouse. To the left was a view of the coast stretching raggedly away on the other side of Falmouth Bay, and if we walked a hundred yards ahead, and so out of the lee of the hillside which protected us from the southwesterly gales, we could look across Mount's Bay, towards the Scilly Isles, and the open Atlantic beyond. Falmouth, seven miles; Helston, nine; elevation 332 feet above sea level; several, though not all, mod. con.

We used it in a migratory fashion. When we had enough commissions and ideas on hand to keep us going for a time we would withdraw there to drive our pens and bash our typewriters in pleasant, undistracting seclusion for a few weeks. Then we would return to London for a while, market our wares, cement relations, and angle for commissions until we felt the call to go down there again with another accumulated batch of work—or we might, perhaps, simply declare a holiday.

That morning, I made pretty good time. It was still only half-past eight when I removed Phyllis's head from my shoulder and woke her up to announce: "Breakfast, darling." I left her trying to pull herself together to order breakfast intelligibly while I went to get some newspapers. By the time I returned she was functioning better, and had already started on the cereal. I handed over her paper, and looked at mine. The main headline in both was given to a shipping disaster. That this should be so when the ship concerned was Japanese suggested that there was little news from elsewhere.

I glanced at the story below the picture of the ship. From a welter of human interest I unearthed the fact that the Japanese liner, *Yatsushiro*, bound from Nagasaki to Amboina, in the Moluccas, had sunk. Out of some seven hundred people on board, only five survivors had been found.

Before I could settle down to the story, however, Phyllis interrupted with an exclamation. I looked across. Her paper carried no picture of the vessel; instead, it printed a small sketch-map of the area, and she was intently studying the spot marked "X."

"What is it?" I asked.

She put her finger on the map. "Speaking from memory, and always supposing that the cross was made by somebody with a conscience," she said, "doesn't that put the scene of this sinking pretty near our old friend the Mindanao Trench?"

I looked at the map, trying to recall the configuration of the ocean floor around there.

"It can't be far off," I agreed.

I turned back to my own paper, and read the account there more carefully. "Women," apparently, "screamed when—" "Women in night attire ran from their cabins," "Women, wide-eyed with terror, clutched their children—," "Women" this and "Women" that when "death struck silently at the sleeping liner." When one had swept all this woman jargon, and the London Office's repertoire of phrases suitable for trouble at sea, aside, the skeleton of a very bare Agency message was revealed—so bare that for a moment I wondered why two large newspapers had decided to splash it instead of giving it just a couple of inches. Then I perceived the real mystery angle which lay submerged among all the phoney dramatics. It was that the *Yatsushiro* had, without warning, and for no known reason, suddenly gone down like a stone.

I got hold of a copy of this Agency message later, and I found its starkness a great deal more alarming and dramatic than this business of dashing about in "night attire." Nor had there been much time for that kind of thing, for, after giving particulars of the time, place, etc., the message concluded laconically: "Fair weather, no (no) collision, no (no) explosion, cause unknown. Foundered less one (one) minute alarm. Owners state quote impossible unquote."

So there can have been very few shrieks that night. Those unfortunate Japanese women—and men—had time to wake, and then, perhaps, a little time to wonder, bemused with sleep, and then the water came to choke them: there were no shrieks, just a few bubbles as they sank down, down, down in their nineteen-thousand-ton steel coffin.

When I read what there was I looked up. Phyllis was regarding me, chin on hands, across the breakfast table. Neither of us spoke for a moment. Then she said: "It says here: '—in one of the deepest parts of the Pacific Ocean.' Do you think this can be *it*, Mike—so soon?"

I hesitated. "It's difficult to tell. So much of this stuff's obviously synthetic—If it actually was only one minute— No, I suspend judgment, Phyl. We'll see *The Times* tomorrow and find what really happened—if anyone knows."

We drove on, making poorer time on the busier roads, stopped to lunch at the usual little hotel on Dartmoor, and finally arrived in the late afternoon—two hundred and sixty-eight point seven, this time. We were sleepy and hungry again, and though I did remember when I telephoned to London to ask for cuttings on the sinking to be sent, the fate of the *Yatsushiro* on the other side of the world seemed as remote from the concerns of a small gray Cornish cottage as the loss of the *Titanic*.

The Times noticed the affair the next day in a cautious manner which gave an impression of the staff pursing their lips and staying their hands rather than mislead their readers in any way. Not so, however, the reports in the first batch of cuttings which arrived on the afternoon of the following day. We put the stack between us, and drew from it. Facts were evidently still meager, and comments curiously similar.

"All got a strong dose of not-before-the-children this time," I said, as we finished. "And not altogether surprising, seeing the hell the advertisers would raise."

Phyllis said coldly: "Mike, this isn't a game, you know. After all, a big ship *has* gone down, and seven hundred poor people have been drowned. That is a terrible thing. I dreamed last night that I was shut up in one of those little cabins when the water came bursting in."

"Yesterday——" I began, and then stopped. I had been about to say that Phyllis had poured a kettle of boiling water down a crack in order to kill a lot more than seven hundred ants, but thought better of it. "Yesterday," I amended, "a lot of people were killed in road accidents, a lot will be today."

"I don't see what that has to do with it," she said.

She was right. It was not a very good amendment—but neither had it been the right moment to postulate the existence of a menace that might think no more of us than we, of ants.

"As a race," I said, "we have allowed ourselves to become accustomed to the idea that the proper way to die is in bed, at a ripe age. It is a delusion. The normal end for all creatures comes suddenly. The——"

But that wasn't the right thing to say at that time, either. She withdrew, using those short, brisk, hard-on-the-heel steps.

I was sorry. I was worried, too, but it takes me differently.

Later, I found her staring out of the living room window. From where she stood, at the side of it, she had a view of the blue water stretching to the horizon.

"Mike," she said, "I'm sorry about this morning. The thing—this ship going down like that—suddenly got me. Until now this has been a sort of guessing game, a puzzle. Losing the bathyscope with poor Wiseman and Trant was bad, and so was losing the naval ships. But this—well, it suddenly seemed to put it into a different category—a big liner full of ordinary, harmless men, women, and children peacefully asleep, to be wiped out in a few seconds in the middle of the night! It's somehow a different *class* of thing altogether. Do you see what I mean? Naval people are always taking risks doing their jobs—but these people on a liner hadn't anything to do with it. It made me feel that those things down there had been a working hypothesis that I had hardly believed in, and now, all at once, they had become horribly real. I don't like it, Mike. I suddenly started to feel afraid. I don't quite know why."

I went over and put my arm round her. "I know what you mean," I said. "I think it is part of it—the thing is not to let it get us down."

She turned her head. "Part of what?" she asked, puzzled.

"Part of the process we are going through—the instinctive reaction. The idea of an alien intelligence here *is* intolerable to us, we *must* hate and fear it. We can't help it —even our own kind of intelligence when it goes a bit off the rails in drunks and crazies alarms us not very rationally."

"You mean I'd not be feeling quite the same way about it if I knew that it had been done by—well, the Chinese, or somebody?"

"Do you think you would?"

"I—I'm not sure."

"Well, for myself, I'd say I'd be roaring with indignation. Knowing that it was somebody hitting well below the belt, I'd at least have a glimmering of who, how, and why, to give me focus. As it is, I've only the haziest impressions of the who, no idea about the how, and a feeling about the why that makes me go cold inside, if you really want to know."

She pressed her hand on mine. "I'm glad to know that, Mike. I was feeling pretty lonely this morning."

"My protective coloration isn't intended to deceive you, my sweet. It is intended to deceive me."

She thought. "I must remember that," she said, with an air of extensive implication that I am not sure I have fully understood yet.

A pleasant month followed as we settled down to our tasks—Phyllis to the search for something which had not already been said about Beckford of Fonthill. I, to the less literary occupation of framing a series on royal love matches, to be entitled provisionally either, "The Heart of Kings" or "Cupid Wears a Crown."

The outer world intruded little. Phyllis finished the Beckford script, and two more, and picked up the threads of the novel that never seemed to get finished. I went steadily ahead with the task of straining the royal love-lives free from any political contaminations, and writing an article or two in between, to clear the air a bit. On days that we thought were too good to be wasted we went down to the coast and bathed, or hired a sailing dinghy. The newspapers forgot about the *Yatsushiro*. The deep sea and all our speculations concerning it, seemed very far away.

Then, on a Wednesday night, the nine o'clock bulletin

announced that the *Queen Anne* had been lost at sea . . .

The report was very brief. Simply the fact, followed by: "No details are available as yet, but it is feared that the list of the missing may prove to be very heavy indeed." There was silence for fifteen seconds, then the announcer's voice resumed: "The *Queen Anne,* the current holder of the Transatlantic record, was a vessel of ninety thousand tons displacement. She was built . . ."

I leaned forward, and turned it off. We sat looking at one another. Tears came into Phyllis's eyes. The tip of her tongue appeared, wetting her lips.

"The *Queen Anne!*—Oh, God!" she said.

She searched for a handkerchief. "Oh, Mike. That lovely ship!"

I crossed to sit beside her. For the moment she was seeing simply the ship as we had last seen her, putting out from Southampton. A creation that had been somewhere between a work of art and a living thing, shining and beautiful in the sunlight, moving serenely out towards the high seas, leaving a flock of little tugs bobbing behind. But I knew enough of my wife to realize that in a few minutes she would be on board, dining in the fabulous restaurant, or dancing in the ballroom, or up on one of the decks, watching it happen, feeling what they must have felt there. I put both my arms around her, and held her close.

I am thankful that such imagination as I, myself, have is more prosaic, and seated further from the heart.

Half an hour later the telephone rang. I answered it, and recognized the voice with some surprise.

"Oh, hullo, Freddy. What is it?" I asked, for nine-thirty in the evening was not a time that one expected to be called by the E.B.C.'s Director of Talks & Features.

"Good. 'Fraid you might be out. You've heard the news?"

"Yes."

"Well, we want something from you on this deep-sea menace of yours, and we want it quick. Half-hour feature."

"But, look here, the last thing I was told was to lay off any hint——"

"This has altered all that. It's a *must,* Mike. You don't want to be too sensational, but you *do* want to be convincing. Make 'em really believe there is something down there."

"Look here, Freddy, if this is some kind of legpull—"

"It isn't. It's an urgent commission."

"That's all very well, but for over a year now I've been regarded as the dumb coot who can't let go of an exploded crackpot theory. Now you suddenly ring me at about the time when a fellow might have made a fool bet at a party, and say——"

"Hell, I'm not at a party. I'm at the office, and likely to be here all night."

"You'd better explain," I told him.

"It's like this. There's a rumor running wild here that the Russians did it. Somebody launched that one off within a few minutes of the news coming through on the tape. Why the hell anybody'd think they would want to start anything that way, heaven knows, but you know how it is when people are emotionally worked up; they'll swallow anything for a bit. My own guess is that it is the let's-have-a-showdown-now school of thought seizing the opportunity, the damn fools. Anyway, it's got to be stopped. If it isn't there might be enough pressure worked up to force the Government out, or make it send an ultimatum, or something. So stopped it's damned well going to be, and the line is your deep-sea menace. Tomorrow's papers are using it, the Admiralty is willing to play, we've got several big scientific names already, the B.B.C.'s next bulletin, and ours, will have good strong hints in order to start the ball rolling, the American networks have started already, and some of their evening editions are coming on the streets with it. So if you want to put in your own pennyworth towards stopping the atom bombs falling, get cracking right away." I hung up and turned to Phyllis. "Work for us, darling."

The next morning, with one accord, we decided to go back to London. The first thing we did upon reaching the flat was to switch on the radio. We were just in time to hear of the sinking of the aircraft carrier *Meritorious,* and the liner *Carib Princess.*

The *Meritorious,* it will be recalled, went down in mid-Atlantic, eight hundred miles southwest of the Cape Verde Islands: the *Carib Princess* not more than twenty miles from Santiago de Cuba: both sank in a matter of two or three minutes, and from each very few survived. It is difficult to say whether the British were the more shocked by the loss of a brand-new naval unit, or the Americans by their loss of one of their best cruise liners with her load of wealth and beauty; both had already been somewhat stunned by the *Queen Anne,* for in the great Atlantic racers there was community of pride. Now, the language of resentment differed, but both showed the characteristics of a man who had been punched in the back in the crowd, and is looking round, both fists clenched, for someone to hit.

The American reaction appeared more extreme for, in spite of the violent nervousness of the Russians existing there, a great many found the idea of the deep-sea menace easier to accept than did the British, and a clamor for drastic, decisive action swelled up, giving a lead to a similar clamor at home. The Americans decided to make the placating gesture of depth-bombing the Cayman Trench close to the point where the *Carib Princess* had vanished —they can scarcely have expected any decisive result from the random bombing of a Deep some fifty miles wide and four hundred miles long.

The occasion was well-publicized on both sides of the Atlantic. American citizens were proud that their forces were taking the lead in reprisals: British citizens, though vocal in their dissatisfaction at being left standing at the post when the recent loss of two great ships should have given them the greater incentive to swift action, decided to applaud the occasion loudly, as a gesture of reproof to their own leaders. The flotilla of ten vessels commissioned for the task was reported as carrying a number of H. E. bombs specially designed for great depth, as well as two atomic bombs. It put out from Chesapeake Bay amid an acclamation which entirely drowned the voice of Cuba plaintively protesting at the prospect of atomic bombs on her doorstep.

None of those who heard the broadcast put out from one of the vessels as the task force neared the chosen area will ever forget the sequel. The voice of the announcer when it suddenly broke off from his description of the scene to say sharply: "Something seems to be——my God! She's blown up!" and then the boom of the explosion. The announcer gabbling incoherently, then a second boom. A clatter, a sound of confusion and voices, a clanging of bells, then the announcer's voice again: breath short, sounding unsteady, talking fast: "That explosion you heard —the first one—was the destroyer, *Cavort*. She has entirely disappeared. Second explosion was the frigate, *Redwood*. She has disappeared, too. The *Redwood* was carrying one of our two atomic bombs. It's gone down with her. It is constructed to operate by pressure at five miles depth——

"The other eight ships of the flotilla are dispersing at full speed to get away from the danger area. We shall have a few minutes to get clear. I don't know how long. Nobody here can tell me. A few minutes, we think. Every ship in sight is using every ounce of power to get away from the area before the bomb goes off. The deck is shuddering under us. We're going full speed . . . Everyone's looking back at the place where the *Redwood* went down——Hey, doesn't anybody here know how long it'll take that thing to sink five miles——? Hell, *somebody must* know——We're pulling away, pulling away for all we're worth——All the other ships, too. All getting the hell out of it, fast as we can make it——Anybody know what the area of the main spout's reckoned to be——? For crysake! Doesn't anybody know any damn thing around here? We're pulling off now, pulling off—Maybe we *will* make it——wish I knew how long——? Maybe——maybe——Faster, now faster, for heaven's sake——Pull the guts out of her, what's it matter?——Hell, slog her to bits——Cram her along——

"Five minutes now since the *Redwood* sank——How far'll she be down in five minutes——? For God's sake, somebody: *How long does that damn thing take to sink*——?

"Still going——Still keeping going——Still beating it for all we're worth——Surely to heaven we must be beyond the main spout area by now——Must have a chance now ——We're keeping it up——Still going——Still going full speed——Everybody looking astern——Everybody watching and waiting for it——And we're still going——How can a thing be sinking all this time?——But thank God it is ——Over seven minutes now——Nothing yet——Still going——And the other ships, with great white wakes behind them——Still going——Maybe it's a dud——Or maybe the bottom isn't five miles around here——Why can't somebody tell us how long it *ought* to take——? Must be getting clear of the worst now——Some of the other ships are just black dots on white spots now——still going——We're still hammering away——Must have a chance now——I guess we've really got a chance now——Everybody still staring aft——Oh, God! The whole sea's——"

And there it cut off.

But he survived, that radio announcer. His ship and five others out of the flotilla of ten came through, a bit radioactive, but otherwise unharmed. And I understand that the first thing that happened to him when he reported back to his office after treatment was a reprimand for the use of overcolloquial language which had given offense to a number of listeners by its neglect to the Third Commandment.

That was the day on which argument stopped, and propaganda became unnecessary. Two of the four ships lost in the Cayman Trench disaster had succumbed to the bomb, but the end of the other two had occurred in a glare of publicity that routed the skeptics and the cautious alike. At last it was established beyond doubt that there was something—and a highly dangerous something, too—down there in the Deeps.

Such was the wave of alarmed conviction spreading swiftly round the world that even the Russians sufficiently overcame their national reticence to admit that they had lost one large freighter and one unspecified naval vessel, both, again, off the Kurils, and one more survey craft off eastern Kamchatka. In consequence of this, they were, they said, willing to co-operate with other powers in putting down this menace to the cause of world Peace.

The following day the British Government proposed that an International Naval Conference should meet in London to make a preliminary survey of the problem. A disposition among some of those invited to quibble about the locale was quenched by the unsympathetically urgent mood of the public. The conference assembled in Westminster within three days of the announcement, and, as far as England was concerned, none too soon. In those three days cancellations of sea passages had been wholesale, overwhelmed airline companies had been forced to apply priority schedules, the Government had clamped down fast on the sales of oils of all kinds, and was rushing out a rationing system for essential services.

On the day before the conference opened Phyllis and I met for lunch.

"You ought to see Oxford Street," she said. "Talk about panic-buying! Cottons particularly. Every hopeless line is selling out at double prices, and they're scratching one another's eyes out for things they wouldn't have been seen dead in last week."

"From what they tell me of the City," I told her, "it's about as good there. Sounds as if you could get control of a shipping line for a few bob, but you couldn't buy a single share in anything to do with aircraft for a fortune. Steel's all over the place; rubbers are, too; plastics are soaring; distilleries are down; about the only thing that's holding its own seems to be breweries."

"I saw a man and a woman loading two sacks of coffee beans into a Rolls, in Piccadilly. And there were——" She broke off suddenly as though what I had been saying had just registered. "You *did* get rid of Aunt Mary's shares in those Jamaican Plantations?" she inquired, with the expression that she applies to the monthly housekeeping accounts.

"Some time ago," I reassured her. "The proceeds went, oddly enough, into airplace engines, and plastics."

She gave an approving nod, rather as if the instructions had been hers. Then another thought occurred to her. "What about the press tickets for tomorrow?" she asked.

"There aren't any for the conference proper," I told her. "There will be a statement afterwards."

She stared at me. *"Aren't any?* For heaven's sake! How do they expect us to do our job?" she exclaimed, and sat there brooding.

When Phyllis said "our job" the words did not connote

exactly what they would have implied a few days before. The job somehow changed quality under our feet. The task of persuading the public of the reality of the unseen, indescribable menace had turned suddenly into one of keeping up morale in the face of a menace which everyone now accepted to the point of panic. E.B.C. ran a feature called "News-Parade" in which we appeared to have assumed the roles of special oceanic correspondents, without being quite sure how it had occurred. In point of fact, Phyllis had never been on the E.B.C. staff, and I had technically left it when I ceased, officially, to have an office there some two years before. Nobody, however, seemed to be aware of this except the accounts department which now paid by the piece instead of by the month. All the same, there was not going to be much freshness of treatment in our assignment if we could get no nearer to the sources than official handouts. Phyllis was still brooding about it when I left her to go back to the office I officially didn't have in E.B.C.

We did our best during the next few days to play our part in putting across the idea of firm hands steady on the wheel, and of the backroom boys who had produced radar, asdic, and other marvels nodding confidently, and saying, in effect: "Sure. Just give us a few days to think, and we'll knock together something that will settle this lot!" There was a satisfactory feeling that confidence was gradually being restored.

Perhaps the main stabilizing factor, however, emerged from a difference of opinion on one of the technical committees.

General agreement had been reached that a torpedolike weapon designed to give submerged escort to a vessel could profitably be developed to counter the assumed mine form of attack. The motion was accordingly put that all should pool information likely to help in the development of such a weapon.

The Russian delegates demurred. Remote control of missiles, they pointed out was, of course, a Russian invention in any case. Moreover, Russian scientists, zealous in the fight for Peace, had already developed such control to a degree greatly in advance of that achieved by the capitalist-ridden science of the West. It could scarcely be expected of the Soviets that they should make a present of their discoveries to warmongers.

The Western spokesman replied that, while respecting the intensity of the fight for Peace and the fervor with which it was being carried on in every department of Soviet science except, of course, the biological, the West would remind the Soviets that this was a conference of peoples faced by a common danger and resolved to meet it by cooperation.

The Russian leader responded frankly that he doubted whether, if the West had happened to possess a means of controlling a submerged missile by radio, such as had been invented by Russian engineers, they would care to share such knowledge with the Soviet people.

The Western spokesman assured the Soviet representative that since the West had called the conference for the purpose of co-operation, if felt in duty bound to state that it had indeed perfected such a means of control as the Soviet delegate had mentioned.

Following a hurried consultation, the Russian delegate announced that *if* he believed such a claim to be true, he would also know that it could only have come about through theft of the work of Soviet scientists by capitalist hirelings. And, since neither a lying claim, nor the admission of successful espionage showed that disinterest in national advantage which the conference had professed, his delegation was left with no alternative but to withdraw.

This action, with its reassuring ring of normality, exerted a valuable tranquilizing influence.

Amid the widespread satisfaction and resuscitating confidence, the voice of Bocker, dissenting, rose almost alone: It was late, he proclaimed, but it still might not be too late to make some last attempt at a pacific approach to the sources of the disturbance. They had already been shown to possess a technology equal to, if not superior to, our own. In an alarming short time they had been able not only to establish themselves, but to produce the means of taking effective action for their self-defense. In the face of such a beginning one was justified in regarding their powers with respect and, for his part, with apprehension.

The very differences of environment that they required

made it seem unlikely that human interests and those of these xenobathetic intelligences need seriously overlap. Before it should be altogether too late, the very greatest efforts should be made to establish communication with them in order to promote a state of compromise which would allow both parties to live peacefully in their separate spheres.

Very likely this was a sensible suggestion—though whether the attempt would ever have produced the desired result is a different matter. Where there was no will whatever to compromise, however, the only evidence that his appeal had been noticed at all was that the word, "xenobathetic," and a derived noun, "xenobath," and its diminutive, "bathy," began to be used in print.

"More honored in the dictionary than in the observance," remarked Bocker, with some bitterness. "If it is Greek words they are interested in, there are others— Cassandra, for instance."

Hard on Bocker's words, but with a significance that was not immediately recognized, came the news first from Saphira, and then from April Island.

Saphira, a Brazilian island in the Atlantic, lies a little south of the Equator and some four hundred miles southeast of the larger island of Fernando de Noronha. In that isolated spot a population of a hundred or so lived in primitive conditions, largely on its own produce, content to get along in its own way, and little interested in the rest of the world. It is said that the original settlers were a small party who, arriving on account of a shipwreck sometime in the eighteenth century, remained perforce. By the time they were discovered they had settled to the island life and already become interestingly inbred. In due course, and without knowing or caring much about it, they had ceased to be Portuguese and become technically Brazilian citizens, and a token connection with their foster mother country was maintained by a ship which called at roughly six-month intervals to do a little barter.

Normally, the visiting ship had only to sound its siren, and the Saphirans would come hurrying out of their cottages down to the minute quay where their few fishing boats lay, to form a reception committee which included almost the entire population. On this occasion, however, the hoot of the siren echoed emptily back and forth in the little bay, and set the sea birds wheeling in flocks, but no Saphiran appeared at the cottage doors. The ship hooted again . . .

The coast of Saphira slopes steeply. The ship was able to approach to within a cable's length of the shore, but there was nobody to be seen—nor, still more ominously, was there any trace of smoke from the cottages' chimneys.

A boat was lowered and a party, with the mate in charge, rowed ashore. They made fast to a ringbolt and climbed the stone steps up to the little quay. They stood there in a bunch, listening and wondering. There was not a sound to be heard but the cries of the sea birds and the lapping of the water.

"Must've made off, the lot of 'em. Their boat's gone," said one of the sailors, uneasily.

"Huh!" said the mate. He took a deep breath, and gave a mighty hail, as though he had greater faith in his own lungs than in the ship's siren.

They listened for an answer, but none came save the sound of the mate's voice echoing faintly back across the bay.

"Huh!" said the mate again. "Better take a look."

The uneasiness which had come over the party kept them together. They followed him in a bunch as he strode towards the nearest of the small, stone-built cottages. The door was standing half-open. He pushed it back.

"Phew!" he said.

Several putrid fish decomposing on a dish accounted for the smell. Otherwise the place was tidy and, by Saphiran standards, reasonably clean. There were no signs of disorder or hasty packing-up. In the inner room the beds were made up, ready to be slept in. The occupant might have been gone only a matter of a few hours, but for the fish and the lack of warmth in the turf-fire ashes.

In the second and third cottages there was the same air of unpremeditated absence. In the fourth they found a dead baby in its cradle in the inner room. The party returned to the ship, puzzled and subdued.

The situation was reported by radio to Rio. Rio in its reply suggested a thorough search of the island. The crew started on the task with reluctance and a tendency to keep in close groups, but, as nothing fearsome revealed itself, gradually gained confidence.

On the second day of their three-day search they discovered a party of four women and six children in two caves on a hillside. All had been dead for some weeks, apparently from starvation. By the end of the third day they were satisfied that if there were any living person left, he must be deliberately hiding. It was only then, on comparing notes, that they realized also that there could not be more than a dozen sheep and two or three dozen goats left out of the island's normal flocks of some hundreds.

They buried the bodies they had found, radioed a full report to Rio, and then put to sea again, leaving Saphira, with its few surviving animals, to the sea birds.

In due course the news came through from the Agencies and won an inch or two of space here and there, but no one at the time inquired further into the matter.

The April Island affair was set in quite a different key and might have continued undiscovered for some time but for the coincidence of official interest in the place.

The interest stemmed from the existence of a group of Javanese malcontents variously described as smugglers, terrorists, communists, patriots, fanatics, gangsters, or merely rebels who, whatever their true affiliations, operated upon a troublesome scale. For many years they had dropped out of sight, but recently an informer had managed to reach the authorities with the news that they had taken over April Island. The authorities set out immediately to capture them.

In order to minimize the risk to a number of innocent people who were being held hostage by the criminals, the approach to April Island was made by night. Under starlight the gunboat stole quietly into a little-used bay which was masked from the main village by a headland. There, a well-armed party, accompanied by the informant who was to act as their guide, was put ashore with the task of taking the village by surprise. The gunboat then drew off, moved a little way along the coast, and lay in lurk behind the point of the headland until the landing party should summon her to come in and dominate the situation.

Three-quarters of an hour had been the length of time

estimated for the party's crossing of the isthmus, and then perhaps another ten or fifteen minutes for its disposal of itself about the village. It was, therefore, with concern that after only forty minutes had passed the men aboard the gunboat heard the first burst of automatic fire, succeeded presently by several more.

With the element of surprise lost, the Commander ordered full speed ahead, but even as the boat surged forward the sound of firing was drowned by a dull, reverberating boom. The crew of the gunboat looked at one another with raised eyebrows: the landing party had carried no higher forms of lethalness than automatic rifles and grenades. There was a pause, then the hammering of the automatic rifles started again. This time, it continued longer in intermittent bursts until it was ended again by a similar boom.

The gunboat rounded the headland. In the dim light it was impossible to make out anything that was going on in the village two miles away. For the moment all there was dark. Then a twinkling broke out, and another, and the sound of firing reached them again. The gunboat, continuing at full speed, switched on her searchlight. The village and the trees behind it sprang into sudden miniature existence. No figures were visible among the houses. The only sign of activity was some froth and commotion in the water, a few yards out from the edge. Some claimed afterwards to have seen a dark, humped shape showing above the water a little to the right of it.

As close inshore as she dared go the gunboat put her engines astern, and hove to in a flurry. The searchlight played back and forth over the huts and their surroundings. Everything lit by the beam had hard lines, and seemed endowed with a curious glistening quality. The man on the oerlikons followed the beam, his fingers steady on the triggers. The light made a few more slow sweeps and then stopped. It was trained on several submachine guns lying on the sand, closer to the water's edge.

A stentorian voice from the hailer called the landing party from cover. Nothing stirred. The searchlight roved again, prying between the huts, among the trees. Nothing moved there. The patch of light slid back across the beach and steadied upon the abandoned arms. The silence seemed to deepen.

The Commander refused to allow landing until daylight.
The gunboat dropped anchor. She rode there for the rest
of the night, her searchlight making the village look like a
stage-set upon which at any moment the actors might
appear, but never did.

When there was full daylight the First Officer, with a
party of five armed men rowed cautiously ashore under
cover from the ship's oerlikons. They landed close to the
abandoned arms, and picked them up to examine them. All
the weapons were covered with a thin slime. The men put
them in the boat, and then washed their hands clean of the
stuff.

The beach was scored in four places by broad furrows
leading from the water's edge towards the huts. They were
something over eight feet wide, and curved in section. The
depth in the middle was five or six inches; the sand at the
edges was banked a trifle above the level of the surrounding beach. Some such track, the First Officer thought,
might have been left if a large boiler had been dragged
across the foreshore. Examining them more closely he
decided from the lie of the sand that though one of the
tracks led towards the water, the other three undoubtedly
emerged from it. It was a discovery which caused him to
look at the village with increased wariness. As he did so, he
became aware that the scene which had glistened oddly in
the searchlight was still glistening oddly. He regarded it
curiously for some minutes. Then he shrugged. He tucked
the butt of his submachine gun comfortably under his
right arm, and slowly, with his eyes flicking right and left
for the least trace of movement, led his party up the
beach.

The village was formed of a semicircle of huts of various sizes fringing upon an open space, and as they drew
closer the reason for the glistening look became plain. The
ground, the huts themselves, and the surrounding trees,
too, all had a thin coating of the slime which had been on
the guns.

The party kept steadily, slowly on until they reached the
center of the open space. There they paused, bunched
together, facing outwards, examining each foot of cover
closely. There was no sound, no movement but a few

fronds stirring gently in the morning breeze. The men began to breathe more evenly.

The First Officer removed his gaze from the huts, and examined the ground. It was littered with a wide scatter of small metal fragments, most of them curved, all of them shiny with the slime. He turned one over curiously with the toe of his boot, but it told him nothing. He looked about them again, and decided on the largest hut. "We'll search that," he said.

The whole front of it glistened stickily. He pushed the unfastened door open with his foot, and led the way inside. There was little disturbance; only a couple of overturned stools suggested a hurried exit. No one, alive or dead, remained in the place.

They came out again. The First Officer glanced at the next hut, then he paused, and looked at it more closely. He went round to examine the side of the hut they had already entered. The wall there was quite dry and clear of slime. He considered the surroundings again. "It looks," he said, "as if everything had been sprayed with this muck by something in the middle of the clearing."

A more detailed examination supported the idea, but took them little further.

"But how?" the officer asked, meditatively. "Also what? And why?"

"Something came out of the sea," said one of his men, looking back uneasily toward the water.

"Some things—three of them," the First Officer corrected him.

They returned to the middle of the open semicircle. It was clear that the place was deserted, and there did not seem to be much more to be learned there at present.

"Collect a few of these bits of metal—they may mean something to somebody," the officer instructed.

He himself went across to one of the huts, found an empty bottle, scraped some of the slime into it, and corked it up. "This stuff's beginning to stink now the sun's getting at it," he said, on his return. "We might as well clear out. There's nothing we can do here."

Back on board, he suggested that a photographer should take pictures of the furrows on the beach, and showed the Commander his trophies, now washed clean of the slime.

"Queer stuff," he said, holding a piece of the thick, dull metal. "A shower of it around." He tapped it with a knuckle. "Sounds like lead; weighs like feathers. Cast, by the look of it. Ever seen anything like that, sir?"

The Commander shook his head. He observed that the world seemed to be full of strange alloys these days.

Presently the photographer came rowing back from the beach. The Commander decided: "We'll give 'em a few blasts on the siren. If nobody shows up we'd better make a landing some other place and find a local inhabitant who can tell us what the hell goes on."

A couple of hours later the gunboat cautiously nosed her way into a bay on the northeast coast of April Island. A similar though smaller village stood there in a clearing, close to the water's edge. The similarity was uncomfortably emphasized by an absence of life as well as by a beach displaying four broad furrows to the water's edge.

Closer investigation, however, showed some differences: of these furrows, two had been made by some objects ascending to the beach; the other two, apparently, the same objects *de*scending it. There was no trace of the slime either in or about the deserted village.

The Commander frowned over his charts. He indicated another bay. "All right. We'll try there, then," he said.

This time there were no furrows to be seen on the beach, though the village was just as thoroughly deserted. Again the gunboat's siren gave a forlorn, unheeded wail. They examined the scene through glasses, then the First Officer, scanning the neighborhood more widely, gave an exclamation. "There's a fellow up on that hill there, sir. Waving a shirt, or something."

The Commander turned his own glasses that way. "Two or three others, a bit to the left of him, too."

The gunboat gave a couple of hoots, and moved closer inshore. The boat was lowered.

"Stand off a bit till they come," the Commander directed. "Find out whether there's been an epidemic of some kind before you try to make contact."

He watched from his bridge. In due course a party of natives, eight or nine strong appeared from the trees a couple of hundred yards east of the village, and hailed the boat. It moved in their direction. Some shouting and countershouting between the two parties ensued, then the boat went in and grounded on the beach. The First Officer beckoned the natives with his arm, but they hung back in the fringe of the trees. Eventually he jumped ashore and walked across the strand to talk to them. An animated discussion took place. Clearly an invitation to some of them to visit the gunboat was being declined with vigor. Presently the First Officer descended the beach alone, and the landing party headed back.

"What's the trouble there?" the Commander inquired as the boat came alongside.

The First Officer looked up. "They won't come, sir."

"What's the matter with them?"

"They're okay themselves, sir, but they say the sea isn't safe."

"They can see it's safe enough for us. What do they mean?"

"They say several of the shore villages have been attacked, and they think theirs may be at any moment."

"Attacked! What by?"

"Er—perhaps if you'd come and talk to them yourself, sir—?"

"I sent a boat so that they could come to me—that ought to be good enough for them."

"I'm afraid they'll not come, short of force, sir."

The Commander frowned. *"That* scared are they? What's been doing this attacking?"

The First Officer moistened his lips; his eyes avoided his commander's. "They—er, they say—whales, sir."

The Commander stared at him. "They say—*what?*" he demanded.

The First Officer looked unhappy. "Er—I know, sir. But that's what they keep on *saying.* Er—whales, and er—giant jellyfish. I think that if you'd speak to them yourself, sir . . . ?"

The news about April Island did not exactly "break" in the accepted sense. Curious goings on on an atoll which could not even be found in most atlases had, on the face of it, little news value, and the odd line or two which recorded the matter was allowed to slip past. Possibly it would not have attracted attention nor been remembered until much later, if at all, but for the chance that an American journalist who happened to be in Jakarta discovered the story for himself, took a speculative trip to April Island, and wrote the affair up for a weekly magazine.

A pressman, reading it, recalled the Saphira incident, linked the two, and splashed a new peril across a Sunday newspaper. It happened that this preceded by one day the most sensational communiqué yet issued by the Standing Committee for Action, with the result that the Deeps had the big headlines once more. Moreover, the term "Deeps" was more comprehensive than formerly, for it was announced that shipping losses in the last month had been so heavy, that the areas in which they had occurred so much more extensive that, pending the development of a more efficient means of defense, all vessels were strongly advised to avoid crossing deep water and keep, as far as was practicable, to the areas of the continental shelves.

It was obvious that the Committee would not have dealt such a blow to a confidence in shipping which had been recovering, without the gravest reasons. Nevertheless, the answering outburst of indignation from the shipping interests accused it of everything from sheer alarmism to a vested interest in airlines. To follow such advice, they protested, would mean routing transatlantic liners into Iceland and Greenland waters, creeping coastwise down the Bay of Biscay and the West African coast, etc. Transpacific commerce would become impossible, and Australia and New Zealand, isolated. It showed a shocking and lamentable lack of a sense of responsibility that the Committee should be allowed to advise in this way, without full consultation of all interested parties, these panic-inspired measures which would, if heeded, bring the maritime commerce of the world virtually to a stop. Advice which could never be implemented, should never have been given.

The Committee hedged slightly under the attack. It had not ordered, it said. It had simply suggested that wherever possible vessels should attempt to avoid crossing any extensive stretch of water where the depth was greater than two thousand fathoms, and thus avoid exposing itself to danger unnecessarily.

This, retorted the shipowners, curtly, was virtually putting the same thing in different words; and their case, though not their cause, was upheld by the publication in almost every newspaper of sketch-maps showing hurried and somewhat varied impressions of the two-thousand fathom line.

Before the Committee was able to re-express itself in still different words the Italian liner, *Sabina,* and the German liner, *Vorpommern,* disappeared on the same day— the one in mid-Atlantic, the other in the South Pacific— and reply became superfluous.

The news of the latest sinkings was announced on the 8 A.M. news bulletin on a Saturday. The Sunday papers took full advantage of their opportunity. At least six of them slashed at official incompetence with almost eighteenth century gusto, and set the pitch for the dailies.

On the Wednesday I rang up Phyllis.

It used to come upon her periodically when we had had a longer spell than usual in London that she could not stand the works of civilization any longer without a break for refreshment. If it happened that I were free, I was allowed along, too; if not, she went off to commune with nature on her own. As a rule, she returned spiritually refurbished in the course of a week or so. This time, however, the communion had already been going on for almost a fortnight, and there was still no sign of the postcard which customarily preceded her return by a short head, when it did not come on the following day.

The telephone down in Rose Cottage rang forlornly for some time. I was on the point of giving up when she answered it.

"Hullo, darling!" said her voice.

"I might have been the butcher, or the income tax man," I reproved her.

"They'd have given up more quickly. Sorry if I've been long answering. I was busy outside."

"Digging the garden?" I asked hopefully.

"No, as a matter of fact. I was bricklaying."

"This line's not good. It sounded like bricklaying."

"It was, darling."

"Oh," I said. "Bricklaying."

"It's very fascinating when you get into it. Did you know there are all kinds of bonds and things; Flemish Bond, and

English Bond, and so on? And you have things called "headers" and other things called——"

"What is this, darling? A tool shed, or something?"

"No. Just a wall, like Balbus and Mr. Churchill. I read somewhere that in moments of stress Mr. Churchill used to find that it gave him tranquility, and I thought that anything that could tranquilize Mr. Churchill was probably worth following up."

"Well, I hope it has cured the stress."

"Oh, it has. It's very soothing. I love the way when you put the brick down the mortar squidges out at the sides and you——"

"Darling, the minutes are ticking up. I rang you to say that you are wanted here."

"That's sweet of you, darling. But leaving a job half——"

"It's not me—I mean—it is me, but not only. The E.B.C. want a word with us."

"What about?"

"I don't really know. They're being cagey, but insistent."

"Oh. When do they want to see us?"

"Freddy suggested dinner on Friday. Can you manage that?"

There was a pause. "Yes. I think I'll be able to finish— All right. I'll be on that train that gets into Paddington about six."

"Good. I'll meet it. There is the other reason, too, Phyl."

"It being?"

"The running sand, darling. The unturned coverlet. The tarnished thimble. The dull, unflavored drops from life's clepsydra. The——"

"Mike, you've been rehearsing."

"What else had I to do?"

We were only twenty minutes late, but Freddy Whittier might have been desiccating for some hours from the urgency with which we were swept into the bar. He disappeared into the mob round the counter with a nicely controlled violence and presently emerged with a selection of double and single sherries on a tray.

"Doubles first," he said.

Soon his mind broadened out of the single track. He looked more himself, and noticed things. He even noticed Phyllis's hands; the abraded knuckles on the right, the large piece of plaster on the left. He frowned and seemed about to speak, but thought better of it. I observed him covertly examining my face, and then my hands.

"My wife," I explained, "has been down in the country. The start of the bricklaying season, you know."

He looked relieved rather than interested. "Nothing wrong with the old team spirit?" he inquired, with a casual air.

We shook our heads.

"Good," he said, "because I've got a job for two."

He went on to expound. It seemed that one of E.B.C.'s favorite sponsors had put a proposition to them. This sponsor had apparently been feeling for some time that a description, some photographs, and definite evidence of the nature of the Deeps creatures was well overdue.

"A man of perception," I said. "For the last five or six years—"

"Shut up, Mike," said my dear wife, briefly.

"Things," Freddy went on, "have in his opinion now reached a pass where he might as well spend some of his money while it still has value, and might even bring in some valuable information. At the same time, he doesn't see why he shouldn't get some benefit out of the information if it is forthcoming. So he proposes to fit out and send out an expedition to find out what it can—and of course the whole thing will be tied up with exclusive rights and so on. By the way, this is highly confidential: we don't want the B.B.C. to get on to it first."

"Look, Freddy," I said. "For several years now everybody has been trying to get on it, let alone the B.B.C. What the—?"

"Expedition where to?" asked Phyllis, practically.

"That," said Freddy, "was naturally our first question. But he doesn't know. The whole decision on a location is in Bocker's hands."

"Bocker!" I exclaimed. "Is he becoming un-untouchable, or something?"

"His stock has recovered quite a bit," Freddy admitted.

"And, as this fellow, the sponsor, said: 'If you leave out all the outer-space nonsense, the rest of Bocker's pronouncements have had a pretty high score'—higher than anyone else's, anyway. So he went to Bocker, and said: 'Look here. These things that came up on Saphira and April Island; where do you think they are most likely to appear next—or, at any rate, soon?' Bocker wouldn't tell him, of course. But they talked; and the upshot was that the sponsor will subsidize an expedition led by Bocker to a region to be selected by Bocker. What is more, Bocker also selects the personnel. And part of the selection, with E.B.C.'s blessing and your approval, could be you two."

"He was always my favorite ographer," said Phyllis. "When do we start?"

"Wait a minute," I put in. "Once upon a time an ocean voyage used to be recommended for health. Recently, however, so far from being healthy—"

"Air," said Freddy. "Exclusively air. People have doubtless got a lot of personal information about the things the other way, but we would prefer you to be in a position to bring it back."

Phyllis wore an abstracted air at intervals during the evening.

When we got home I said: "If you'd rather not take this up—"

"Nonsense. Of course we're going," she said. "But do you think 'subsidize' means we can get suitable clothes and things on expenses?"

"I like idleness—in the sun," said Phyllis.

From where we sat at an umbrella-ed table in front of the mysteriously named Grand Hotel Britannia y la Justicia it was possible to direct idle contemplation on tranquility or activity. Tranquility was on the right. Intensely blue water glittered for miles until it was ruled off by a hard, straight horizon line. The shore, running round like a bow, ended in a palm-tufted headland which trembled mirage-wise in the heat. A backcloth which must have looked just the same when it formed a part of the Spanish Main.

To the left was a display of life as conducted in the capital, and only town of the island of Escondida.

The island's name derived, presumably, from erratic

seamanship in the past which had caused ships to arrive mistakenly at one of the Caymans, but through all the vicissitudes of those parts it had managed to retain it, and much of its Spanishness, too. The houses looked Spanish, the temperament had a Spanish quality, in the language there was more Spanish than English, and, from where we were sitting at the corner of the open space known indifferently as the Plaza, or the Square, the church at the far end with the bright market-stalls in front of it looked positively picture-book Spanish. The population, however, was somewhat less so, and ranged from sunburnt-white to coal-black. Only a bright-red British mailbox prepared one for the surprise of learning that the place was called Smithtown—and even that took on romance when one learned also that the Smith commemorated had been a pirate in a prosperous way.

Behind us, and therefore behind the hotel, one of the two mountains which made Escondida climbed steeply, emerging far above as a naked peak with a scarf of greenery about its shoulders. Between the mountain's foot and the sea stretched a tapering rocky shelf, with the town clustered on its wider end.

And there, also, had clustered for five weeks the Bocker Expedition.

Bocker had contrived a probability-system all his own. Eventually his eliminations had given him a list of ten islands as likely to be attacked, and the fact that four of them were in the Caribbean area had settled our course.

That was about as far as he cared to go simply on paper, and it landed us all at Kingston, Jamaica. There we stayed a week in company with Ted Jarvey, the cameraman; Leslie Bray, the recordist; and Muriel Flynn, one of the technical assistants while Bocker himself and his two male assistants flew about in an armed coastal-patrol aircraft put at his disposal by the authorities, and considered the rival attractions of Grand Cayman, Little Cayman, Cayman Brac, and Escondida. The reasoning which led to their final choice of Escondida was no doubt very nice, so that it seemed a pity that two days after the aircraft had finished ferrying us and our gear to Smithtown it should have been a large village on Grand Cayman which suffered the first visitation in those parts.

But if we were disappointed, we were also impressed. It was clear that Bocker really had been doing something more than a high-class eeny meeny miney mo, and had brought off a very near miss.

The plane took four of us over there as soon as he had the news. Unfortunately we learned little. There were grooves on the beach, but they had been greatly trampled by the time we arrived. Out of two hundred and fifty villagers about a score had got away by fast running. The rest had simply vanished. The whole affair had taken place in darkness, so that no one had seen much. Each survivor felt an obligation to give any inquirer his money's worth, and the whole thing was almost folklore already.

Bocker announced that we should stay where we were. Nothing would be gained by dashing hither and thither; we should be just as likely to miss the occasion as to find it. Even more likely, for Escondida in addition to its other qualities had the virtue of being a one-town island so that when an attack did come (and he was sure that sooner or later it would) Smithtown must almost certainly be the objective.

We hoped he knew what he was doing, but in the next two weeks we doubted it. The radio brought reports of a dozen raids—all, save one small affair in the Azores, were in the Pacific. We began to have a depressed feeling that we were in the wrong hemisphere.

When I say "we," I must admit I mean chiefly me. The others continued to analyze the reports and go stolidly ahead with their preparations. One point was that there was no record of an assault taking place by day; lights, therefore, would be necessary. Once the town council had been convinced that it would cost them nothing we were all impressed into the business of fixing improvised flood-lights on trees, posts and the corners of buildings all over Smithtown, though with greater proliferation toward the waterside, all of which, in the interests of Ted's cameras had to be wired back to a switchboard in his hotel room.

The inhabitants assumed that a fiesta of some kind was in preparation, the council considered it a harmless form of lunacy, but were pleased to be paid for the extra current we consumed. Most of us were slowly growing more cynical, until the affair at Gallows Island which, though Gallows was in the Bahamas, unnerved the whole Caribbean, nevertheless.

Port Anne, the chief town on Gallows, and three large coastal villages there were raided the same night. About half the population of Port Anne, and a much higher proportion from the villages disappeared entirely. Those who survived had either shut themselves in their houses or run away, but this time there were plenty of people who agreed that they had seen things like tanks—like military tanks, they said, but larger—emerge from the water and come sliding up the beaches. Owing to the darkness, the confusion, and the speed with which most of the informants had either made off or hidden themselves, there were only imaginative reports of what these tanks from the sea had then done. The only verifiable fact was that from the four points of attack more than a thousand people in all had vanished during the night.

All around there was a prompt change of heart. Every islander in every island shed his indifference and sense of security, and was immediately convinced that his own home would be the next scene of assault. Ancient, uncertain weapons were dug out of cupboards, and cleaned up. Patrols were organized, and for the first night or two of their existence went on duty with a fine swagger. Talks on an interisland flying defense system were proposed.

When, however, the next week went by without trace of further trouble anywhere in the area enthusiasm waned. Indeed, for that week there was a pause in subsea activity all over. The only report of a raid came from the Kurils, for some Slavonic reason, undated, and therefore assumed to have spent some time under microscopic examination from every security angle.

By the tenth day after the alarm Escondida's natural spirit of *mañana* had fully reasserted itself. By night and siesta it slept soundly; the rest of the time it drowsed, and we with it. It was difficult to believe that we shouldn't go on like that for years, so we were settling down to it, some of us. Muriel explored happily among the island flora; Johnny Tallton, the pilot, who was constantly standing by, did most of it in a café where a charming *señorita* was teaching him the patois; Leslie had also gone native to the extent of acquiring a guitar which we could now hear tinkling through the open window above us; Phyllis and I occasionally told one another about the scripts we might write if we had the energy; only Bocker and his two closest assistants, Bill Weyman and Alfred Haig, retained an air of purpose. If the sponsor could have seen us he might well have felt dubious about his money's worth.

I began to feel that I had had about enough of it. There was a suggestion of the Anglo-Saxon draining out, and the tropical Latin seeping in, and, while the sensation was not unpleasant, I felt it was a bit early in my life to let myself get fixed that way.

"This can't continue indefinitely," I said to Phyllis. "I suggest we give Bocker a time limit—a week from now to produce his phenomenon."

"Well—" she began reluctantly. "Yes, I suppose you're right."

"I'm damned sure I am," I told her. "In fact, I'm not at all sure that even another week may not prove fatal."

Which was, in an unintended way, truer than I knew.

"Darling, stop worrying that moon now, and come to bed."

"No soul—that's the trouble. I often wonder why I married you."

So I got up and joined her at the window.

"See?" she said. " 'A ship, an isle, a sickle moon . . .' So fragile, so eternal—isn't it lovely?"

We gazed out, across the empty Plaza, past the sleeping houses, over the silvered sea.

"I want it. It's one of the things I'm putting away to remember," she said.

Faintly from behind the opposite houses, down by the waterfront, came the tinkling of a guitar.

"*El amor tonto—y dulce,*" she sighed.

And then, suddenly, the distant player dropped his guitar, with a clang.

Down by the waterfront a voice called out, unintelligible but alarming. Then other voices. A woman screamed. We turned to look at the houses that hid the little harbor.

"Listen!" said Phyllis. "Mike, do you think—?" She broke off at the sound of a couple of shots. "It must be! Mike, they must be coming!"

There was an increasing hubbub in the distance. In the Square itself windows were opening, people calling questions from one to another. A man ran out of a door, round the corner, and disappeared down the short street that led to the water. There was more shouting now, more screaming, too. Among it the crack of three or four more shots. I turned from the window and thumped on the wall which separated us from the next room.

"Hey, Ted!" I shouted. "Turn up your lights! Down by the waterfront, man. Lights!"

I heard his faint okay. He must have been out of bed already, for almost as I turned back to the window the lights began to go on in batches.

There was nothing unusual to be seen except a dozen or more men pelting across the Square towards the harbor. Quite abruptly the noise which had been rising in crescendo was cut off. Ted's door slammed. His boots thudded along the corridor past our room. Beyond the houses the yelling and screaming broke out again, louder than before, as if it had gained force from being briefly dammed.

"I must—" I began, and then stopped when I found that Phyllis was no longer beside me.

I looked across the room, and saw her in the act of locking the door. I went over. "I must go down there. I must see what's—"

"No!" she said.

She turned and planted her back firmly against the door. She looked rather like a severe angel barring a road, except that angels are assumed to wear respectable cotton night dresses, not nylon.

"But, Phyl—it's the job. It's what we're here for."

"I don't care. We wait a bit."

She stood without moving, severe angel expression now modified by that of mutinous small girl. I held out my hand. "Phyl. Please give me that key."

"No!" she said, and flung it across the room, through the window. It clattered on the cobbles outside. I gazed after it in astonishment. That was not at all the kind of thing one associated with Phyllis. All over the now floodlit Square people were now hurriedly converging towards the street on the opposite side. I turned back.

"Phyl. Please get away from that door."

She shook her head. "Don't be a fool, Mike. You've got a job to do."

"That's just what I—"

"No, it isn't. Don't you see? The only reports we've had at all were from the people who *didn't* rush to find out what was happening. The ones who either hid, or ran away."

I was angry with her, but not too angry for the sense of that to reach me and make me pause. She followed up: "It's what Freddy said—the point of our coming at all is that we should be able to go back and tell them about it."

"That's all very well, but—"

"No! Look there." She nodded towards the window.

People were still converging upon the streets that led to the waterside; but they were no longer going into it. A solid crowd was piling up at the entrance. Then, while I still looked, the previous scene started to go into reverse. The crowd backed, and began to break up at its edges. More men and women came out of the street, thrusting it back until it was dispersing all over the Square.

I went closer to the window to watch. Phyllis left the door and came and stood beside me. Presently we spotted Ted, turret-lensed movie camera in hand, hurrying back.

"What is it?" I called down.

"God knows. Can't get through. There's a panic up the street there. They all say it's coming this way, whatever it is. If it does, I'll get a shot from my window. Can't work this thing in that mob." He glanced back, and then disappeared into the hotel doorway below us.

People were still pouring into the Square, and breaking into a run when they reached a point where there was room to run. There had been no further sound of shooting, but from time to time there would be another outbreak of shouts and screams somewhere at the hidden far end of the short street.

Among those headed back to the hotel came Dr. Bocker himself, and the pilot, Johnny Tallton. Bocker stopped below, and shouted up. Heads popped out of various windows. He looked them over. "Where's Alfred?" he asked.

No one seemed to know.

"If anyone sees him, call him inside," Bocker instructed. "The rest of you stay where you are. Observe what you can, but don't expose yourselves till we know more about it. Ted, keep all your lights on. Leslie—"

"Just on my way with the portable recorder, Doc," said Leslie's voice.

"No, you're not. Sling the mike outside the window if you like, but keep under cover yourself. And that goes for everyone, for the present."

"But, Doc, what is it? What's—"

"We don't know. So we keep inside until we find out why it makes people scream. Where the hell's Miss Flynn? Oh, you're there. Right. Keep watching, Miss Flynn."

He turned to Johnny, and exchanged a few inaudible words with him. Johnny nodded, and made off round the back of the hotel. Bocker himself looked across the Square again, and then came in, shutting the door behind him.

Running, or at least hurrying, figures were still scattering over the Square in all directions, but no more were emerging from the street. Those who had reached the far side turned back to look, hovering close to doorways or alleys into which they could jump swiftly if necessary. Half a dozen men with guns or rifles laid themselves down on the cobbles, their weapons all aimed at the mouth of the street. Everything was much quieter now. Except for a few sounds of sobbing, a tense, expectant silence held the whole scene. And then, in the background, one became aware of a grinding, scraping noise; not loud, but continuous.

The door of a small house close to the church opened. The priest, in a long back robe, stepped out. A number of people nearby ran towards him, and then knelt around him. He stretched out both arms as though to encompass and guard them all.

The noise from the narrow street sounded like the heavy dragging of metal upon stone.

Three or four rifles fired suddenly, almost together. Our angle of view still stopped us from seeing what they fired at, but they let go a number of rounds each. Then the men jumped to their feet and ran further back, almost to the further side of the Square. There they turned round, and reloaded.

From the street came a noise of crackling timbers and falling bricks and glass.

Then we had our first sight of a "sea-tank." A curve of dull, gray metal sliding into the Square, carrying away the lower corner of a housefront as it came.

Shots cracked at it from half a dozen different directions. The bullets splattered or thudded against it without effect. Slowly, heavily, with an air of inexorability, it came on, grinding and scraping across the cobbles. It was inclining slightly to its right, away from us and toward the church, carrying away more of the corner house, unaffected by the plaster, bricks and beams that fell on it and slithered down its sides.

More shots smacked against it or ricocheted away whining, but it kept steadily on, thrusting itself into the Square at something under three miles an hour, massively indeflectable. Soon we were able to see the whole of it.

Imagine an elongated egg which has been halved down its length and set flat side to the ground, with the pointed end foremost. Consider this egg to be between thirty and thirty-five feet long, of a drab, lusterless leaden color, and you will have a fair picture of the "sea-tank" as we saw it pushing into the Square.

There was no way of seeing how it was propelled; there may have been rollers beneath, but it seemed, and sounded, simply to grate forward on its metal belly with plenty of noise, but none of machinery. It did not jerk to turn, as a tank does, but neither did it steer like a car. It simply moved to the right on a diagonal, still pointing forwards. Close behind it followed another, exactly similar contrivance which slanted its way to the left, in our direction, wrecking the housefront on the nearest corner of the street as it came. A third kept straight ahead into the middle of the Square, and then stopped.

At the far end the crowd that had knelt about the priest scrambled to its feet, and fled. The priest himself stood his ground. He barred the thing's way. His right hand held a cross extended against it, his left was raised, fingers spread and palm outward, to halt it. The thing moved on, neither faster nor slower, as if he had not been there. Its curved flank pushed him aside a little as it came. Then it, too, stopped.

A few seconds later the one at our end of the Square

reached what was apparently its appointed position and also stopped.

"Troops will establish themselves at first objective in extended order," I said to Phyllis as we regarded the three evenly spaced out in the Square. "This isn't haphazard. Now what?"

For almost half a minute it did not appear to be now anything. There was a little more sporadic shooting, some of it from windows which, all round the Square, were full of people hanging out to see what went on. None of it had any effect on the targets, and there was some danger from ricochets.

"Look!" said Phyllis suddenly. "This one's bulging."

She was pointing at the nearest. The previously smooth fore-and-aft sweep of its top was now disfigured at the highest point by a small, domelike excrescence. It was lighter colored than the metal beneath; a kind of off-white, semiopaque substance which glittered viscously under the floods. It grew as one watched it.

"They're all doing it," she added.

There was a single shot. The excrescence quivered, but went on swelling. It was growing faster now. It was no longer dome-shaped, but spherical, attached to the metal by a neck, inflating like a balloon, and swaying slightly as it distended.

"It's going to pop. I'm sure it is," Phyllis said, apprehensively.

"There's another coming up further down its back," I said. "Two more, look."

The first excrescence did not pop. It was already some two foot six in diameter and still swelling fast.

"It *must* pop soon," she muttered.

But still it did not. It kept on expanding until it must have been all of five feet in diameter. Then it stopped growing. It looked like a huge, repulsive bladder. A tremor and a shake passed through it. It shuddered jellywise, became detached, and wobbled into the air with the uncertainty of an overblown bubble.

In a lurching, amoebic way it ascended for ten feet or so. There it vacillated, steadying into a more stable sphere. Then, suddenly, something happened to it. It did not explode. Nor was there any sound. Rather, it seemed to slit open, as if it had been burst into instantaneous bloom by a vast number of white cilia which rayed out in all directions.

The instinctive reaction was to jump back from the window away from it. We did.

For or five of the cilia, like long white whiplashes, flicked in through the window, and dropped to the floor. Almost as they touched it they began to contract and withdraw. Phyllis gave a sharp cry. I looked round at her. Not all of the long cilia had fallen on the floor. One of them had flipped the last six inches of its length on to her right forearm. It was already contracting, pulling her arm towards the window. She pulled back. With her other hand she tried to pick the thing off, but her fingers stuck to it as soon as they touched it. "Mike!" she cried. "Mike!"

The thing was tugging hard, looking tight as a bow-string. She had already been dragged a couple of steps towards the window before I could get after her in a kind of diving tackle. The force of my jump carried her across to the other side of the room. It did not break the thing's hold, but it did move it over so that it no longer had a direct pull through the window, and was forced to drag round a sharp corner. And drag it did. Lying on the floor now, I got the crook of my knee round a bed leg for better purchase, and hung on for all I was worth. To move Phyllis then it would have had to drag me and the bedstead, too. For a moment I thought it might. Then Phyllis screamed, and suddenly there was no more tension.

I rolled her to one side, out of line of anything else that might come in through the window. She was in a faint. A patch of skin six inches long had been torn clean away from her right forearm, and more had gone from the fingers on her left hand. The exposed flesh was just beginning to bleed.

Outside in the Square there was a pandemonium of shouting and screaming. I risked putting my head round the side of the window. The thing that had burst was no longer in the air. It was now a round body no more than a couple of feet in diameter surrounded by a radiation of cilia. It was drawing these back into itself with whatever they had caught, and the tension was keeping it a little off the ground. Some of the people it was pulling in were shouting and struggling, others were like inert bundles of clothes.

I saw poor Muriel Flynn among them. She was lying on her back, dragged across the cobbles by a tentacle caught in her red hair. She had been badly hurt by the fall when she was pulled out of her window, and was crying out with terror, too. Leslie dragged almost alongside her, but it looked as if the fall had mercifully broken his neck.

Over on the far side I saw a man rush forward and try to pull a screaming woman away, but when he touched the cilium that held her his hand became fastened to it, too, and they were dragged along together. As I watched I thanked God I had grabbed Phyllis's arm, and not the cilium itself in trying to free her.

As the circle contracted, the white cilia came closer to one another. The struggling people inevitably touched more of them and became more helplessly enmeshed than before. They struggled like flies on a flypaper. There was a relentless deliberation about it which made it seem horribly as though one watched through the eye of a slow-motion camera.

Then I noticed that another of the misshapen bubbles had wobbled into the air, and drew back hurriedly before it should burst.

Three more cilia whipped in through the window, lay for a moment like white cords on the floor, and then began to draw back. When they had vanished across the sill I leaned over to look out of the window again. In several places about the Square there were converging knots of people struggling helplessly. The first and nearest had contracted until its victims were bound together into a tight ball out of which a few arms and legs still flailed wildly. Then, as I watched, the whole compact mass tilted over and began to roll away across the Square towards the street by which the sea-tanks had come.

The machines, or whatever the things were, still lay where they had stopped, looking like huge gray slugs, each engaged in producing several of its disgusting bubbles at different stages.

I dodged back as another was cast off, but this time nothing happened to find our window. I risked leaning out for a moment to pull the casement windows shut, and got them closed just in time. Three or four more lashes smacked against the glass with such force that one of the panes was cracked.

Then I was able to attend to Phyllis, I lifted her on to the bed, and tore a strip off the sheet to bind up her arm.

Outside, the screaming and shouting and uproar was still going on, and among it the sound of a few shots.

When I had bandaged the arm I looked out again. Half a dozen objects, looking now like tight round bales were rolling over and over on their way to the street that led to the waterfront. I turned back again and tore another strip off the sheet to put round Phyllis's left hand.

While I was doing it I heard a different sound above the hubbub outside. I dropped the cotton strip, and ran back to the window in time to get a glimpse of a plane coming in low. The cannon in the wings started to twinkle, and I threw myself back, out of harm's way. There was a dull woomph! of an explosion. Simultaneously the windows blew in, the light went out, bits of something whizzed past and something else splattered all over the room.

I picked myself up. The outdoor lights down our end of the Square had gone out, too, so that it was difficult to make out much there, but up the other end I could see that one of the sea-tanks had begun to move. It was sliding back by the way it had come. Then I heard the sound of the aircraft returning, and went down on the floor again.

There was another woomph! but this time we did not catch the force of it, though there was a clatter of things falling outside.

"Mike?" said a voice, from the bed, a frightened voice.

"It's all right, darling. I'm here," I told her.

The moon was still bright, and I was able to see better now.

"What's happened?" she asked.

"They've gone. Johnny got them with the plane—at least, I suppose it was Johnny," I said. "It's all right now."

"Mike, my arms do hurt."

"I'll get a doctor as soon as I can, darling."

"What was it? It had got me, Mike. If you hadn't held on—"

"It's all over now, darling."

"I—" She broke off at the sound of the plane coming

back once more. We listened. The cannon were firing again, but this time there was no explosion.

"Mike, there's something sticky—is it blood? You're not hurt?"

"No, darling. I don't know what it is, it's all over everything."

"You're shaking, Mike."

"Sorry. I can't help it. Oh, Phyl, darling Phyl— So nearly— If you'd seen them—Muriel and the rest—it might have been—"

"There, there," she said, as if I were aged about six. "Don't cry, Micky. It's over now." She moved. "Oh, Mike, my arm does hurt."

"Lie still, darling, I'll get the doctor," I told her.

I went for the locked door with a chair, and relieved my feelings on it quite a lot.

It was a subdued remnant of the expedition that foregathered the following morning—Bocker, Ted Jarvey, and ourselves. Johnny had taken off earlier with the film and recordings, including an eyewitness account I had added later, and was on his way to Kingston with them.

Phyllis's right arm and left hand were swathed in bandages. She looked pale, but had resisted all persuasions to stay in bed. Bocker's eyes had entirely lost their customary twinkle. His wayward lock of gray hair hung forward over a face which looked more lined and older than it had on the previous evening. He limped a little, and put some of his weight on a stick. Ted and I were unscathed. He looked questioningly at Bocker. "If you can manage it, sir," he said, "I think our first move ought to be to get out of this stink."

"By all means," Bocker agreed. "A few twinges are nothing compared with this. The sooner, the better," he added, and got up to lead the way to windward.

The cobbles of the Square, the litter of metal fragments that lay about it, the houses all around, the church, everything in sight glistened with a coating of slime, and there was more of it that one did not see, splashed into almost every room that fronted on the Square. The previous night it had been simply a strong fishy, salty smell, but with the warmth of the sun at work upon it it had begun to give off an odor that was already fetid and rapidly becoming miasmic. Even a hundred yards made a great deal of difference, another hundred, and we were clear of it, among the palms which fringed the beach on the opposite side of the town from the harbor. Seldom had I known the freshness of a light breeze to smell so good.

Bocker sat down, and leaned his back against a tree. The rest of us disposed ourselves and waited for him to speak first. For a long time he did not. He sat motionless, looking blindly out to sea. Then he sighed. "Alfred," he said, "Bill, Muriel, Leslie. I brought you all here. I have shown very little imagination and consideration for your safety, I'm afraid."

Phyllis leaned forward. "You mustn't think like that, Dr. Bocker. None of us *had* to come, you know. You offered us the *chance* to come, and we took it. If—if the same thing had happened to me I don't think Michael would have felt that you were to blame, would you, Mike?"

"No," I said. I knew perfectly well whom I should have blamed—forever, and without reprieve.

"And I shouldn't, and I'm sure the others would feel the same way," she added, putting her uninjured right hand on his sleeve.

He looked down at it, blinking a little. He closed his eyes for a moment. Then he opened them, and laid his hands on hers. His gaze strayed beyond her wrist to the bandages above. "You're very good to me, my dear," he said.

He patted the hand, and then sat straight, pulling himself together. Presently, in a different tone: "We have some results," he said. "Not, perhaps, as conclusive as we had hoped, but some tangible evidence at least. Thanks to Ted the people at home will now be able to see what we are up against, and thanks to him, too, we have the first specimen."

"Specimen?" repeated Phyllis. "What of?"

"A bit of one of those tentacle things," Ted told her.

"How on earth?"

"Luck, really. You see, when the first one burst nothing came in at my particular window, but I could see what was happening in other places, so I opened my knife and put it handy on the sill, just in case. When one did come in with the next shower it fell across my shoulder, and I caught up the knife and slashed it just as it began to pull. There was about eighteen inches of it left behind. It just dropped off on the floor, wriggled a couple of times, and then curled up. We posted it off with Johnny."

"Ugh!" said Phyllis.

"In future," I said, "we, too, will carry knives."

"Make sure they're sharp. It's mighty tough stuff," Ted advised.

"If you can find another bit of one I'd like to have it for examination," said Bocker. "We decided that one had better go off to the experts. There's something very peculiar indeed about those things. The fundamental is obvious enough, it goes back to some type of sea anemone—but whether the things have been bred, or whether they have in some way been built up on the basic pattern—?" He shrugged without finishing the question. "I find several points extremely disturbing. For instance, how are they made to clutch the animate even when it is clothed, and not attach themselves to the inanimate? Also, how is it possible that they can be directed on the route back to the water instead of simply trying to reach it the nearest way?

"The first of those questions is the more significant. It implies specialized purpose. The things are *used*, you see, but not like weapons in the ordinary sense, not just to destroy, that is. They're more like snares."

We sat thinking that over for a bit.

"But—why—?" said Phyllis.

Bocker frowned. *"Why!"* he repeated. "Everybody is always asking 'why?' Why did the things come to the Deeps? Why didn't they stay at home? Why do they now come out of the Deeps on to the land? And now, why do they attack us this way and not that? How can we possibly hope to know the answers until we can find out more about the sort of creatures they are? The human view would suggest one of two motives—but that isn't to say that they don't have entirely different motives of their own."

"Two motives?" said Phyllis, meekly.

"Yes. They may be trying to exterminate us. For all we can tell they may be under the impression that we *have to* live on coastlines, and that they can gradually wipe us out in this way. You see, it is so difficult: we don't know how much they know about us, either. But I shouldn't think that is the purpose—it doesn't account for the tactics of rolling the victims back to the water—at least, not fully. The coelenterates could as easily crush them and leave them. So it looks as if the other motive might fit—simply that they find us—and perhaps other land creatures, if you recall the disappearance of goats and sheep on Saphira—good to eat. —Or even both: plenty of tribes have an old established custom of eating their enemies."

"You mean that they may have come sort of—well, sort of shrimping for us?" Phyllis asked, uneasily.

"Well, we land creatures let down trawls into the sea, and eat what they catch there. Why not a reverse process for intelligent sea creatures? But, of course, there again I am giving them a human outlook. That's what we all keep trying to do with our 'whys.' The trouble is we have all of us read too many stories where the invaders turn up behaving and thinking just like human beings, whatever their shape happens to be, and we can't shake loose from the idea that their behavior must be comprehensible to us. In fact, there is no reason why it should be, and plenty of reasons why it shouldn't."

"Shrimping," repeated Phyllis, thoughtfully. "How disgusting! But it could be."

Bocker said firmly: "We will now drop this 'why': we may, or may not, learn more about it later. The important thing now is *how: how* to stop the things, and *how* to attack them."

He paused. I must confess that I went on thinking about the "why"—and feeling that even if the purport were right, Phyllis might have chosen some pleasanter and more dignified analogy than "shrimping." Presently Bocker went on: "Ordinary rifle fire doesn't appear to trouble either the sea-tanks or these millebrachiate things—unless there are vulnerable spots that were not found. Explosive cannon shells can, however, fracture the covering. The manner in which it then disintegrates suggests that it is already under very strong stress, and not very far from breaking point. We may deduce from that that in the April Island affair there was either a lucky shot, or a grenade was used. What we saw last night certainly explains the natives' talk of whales and jellyfish. These sea-tanks might easily, at a distance, be taken for whales. And regarding the 'jellyfish' they weren't so far out—the things must almost without doubt be closely related to the coelenterates.

"As to the sea-tanks the contents seem to have been simply gelatinous masses confined under immense pressure—but it is hard to credit that this can really be so. Apart from any other consideration it would seem that there must be a mechanism of some kind to propel those immensely heavy hulls. I went to look at their trails this morning. Some of the cobblestones have been ground down and some cracked into flakes by the weight, but I couldn't find any trackmarks, or anything to show that the things dragged themselves along by grabs as I thought might be the case. I think we are stumped there for the present.

"Intelligence of a kind there undoubtedly is, though it appears not to be very high, or else not very well co-ordinated. All the same, it was good enough to lead them from the waterfront to the Square which was the best place for them to operate." ·

"I've seen army tanks carry away house corners in much the same way as they did," I observed.

"That is one possible indication of poor co-ordination," Bocker replied, somewhat crushingly. "Now have we any observations to add to those I have made?" He looked round inquiringly. "Anything else? Did anyone notice whether the shots appeared to have any effect at all on those tentacular forms?" he added.

"As far as I could see, either the shooting was lousy, or the bullets went through without bothering them," Ted told him.

"H'm," said Bocker, and lapsed into reflection for a while.

Presently I became aware of Phyllis muttering. "What?" I inquired.

"I was just saying 'millebrachiate tentacular Coelenterates,'" she explained.

"Oh," I said.

Nobody made any further comment. The four of us continued to sit on, looking out across a blandly innocent azure sea.

Among the other papers I bought at London Airport

was the current number of *The Beholder*. Though it is, I am aware, not without its merits and even well thought of in some circles, it leaves me with an abiding sense that it is more given to expressing its first prejudices than its second thoughts. Perhaps if it were to go to press a day later. However, the discovery in this issue of a leader entitled: DOCTOR BOCKER RIDES AGAIN did nothing to alter my impression. The text ran something after this fashion:

"Neither the courage of Dr. Alastair Bocker in going forth to meet a submarine dragon, nor his perspicacity in correctly deducing where the monster might be met, can be questioned. The gruesome and fantastically repulsive scenes to which the E.B.C. treated us in our homes last Tuesday evening make it more to be wondered at that any of the party should have survived than that four of its members should have lost their lives. Dr. Bocker himself is to be congratulated on his escape at the cost merely of a sprained ankle when his sock and shoe were wrenched off, and another member of the party on her even narrower escape.

"Nevertheless, horrible though this affair was, and valuable as some of the Doctor's observations may prove in suggesting countermeasures, it would be a mistake for him to assume that he has now been granted an unlimited license to readopt his former role as the world's premier scaremonger.

"It is our inclination to attribute his suggestion that we should proceed forthwith to embattle virtually the entire western coastline of the United Kingdom, to the effect of recent unnerving experiences upon a temperament which has never shunned the sensational, rather than to the conclusions of mature consideration.

"Let us consider the cause of this panic-stricken recommendation. It is this: a number of small islands, all but one of them lying within the tropics, have been raided by some marine agency of which we, as yet, know little. In the course of these raids some hundreds of people—to an estimated total no larger than that of the number of persons injured on the roads in a few days—have lost their lives. This is unfortunate and regrettable, but scarcely grounds for the suggestion that we, thousands of miles from the nearest incident of the kind, should, at the taxpayers' expense, proceed to beset our whole shoreline with weapons and guards. This is a line of argument which would have us erect shockproof buildings in London on account of an earthquake in Tokyo . . ."

And so on. There wasn't a lot left of poor Bocker by the time they had finished with him. I did not show it to him. He would find out soon enough, for *The Beholder's* readership had no use for the unique approach: it liked the popular view, custom tailored.

Presently the helicopter set us down at the terminus, and Phyllis and I slipped away while pressmen converged on Bocker.

Dr. Bocker out of sight, however, was by no means Dr. Bocker out of mind. The major part of the Press had divided into pro and anti camps, and, within a few minutes of our getting back to the flat, representatives of both sides began ringing us up to put leading questions to their own advantage. After about five of these I seized on an interval to ring the E.B.C. and tell them that as we were about to remove our receiver for a while they would probably suffer, and would they please keep a record of callers. They did. Next morning there was quite a list. Among those anxious to talk to us I noticed the name of Captain Winters, with the Admiralty number against it.

Phyllis talked to him. He had called to get from us confirmation of eyewitness reports, and to give us the latest on Bocker. It seems he had firmly put forth the theory which we had heard before, that the sea-tanks themselves didn't have intelligence, that this intelligence was in actuality somewhere in the Deeps, and directed them by some remote means of communication at present unknown. But the most trouble had been caused, apparently, by his use of the word pseudo-coelenterate. As Winters put it, "he says they are not coelenterates, not animals, and probably not in the accepted sense, living creatures at all, but that they may well be artificial organic constructions *built* for a specialized purpose. He read Bocker's statement on the subject to Phyllis over the phone.

" 'It is far from inconceivable that organic tissues might be constructed in a manner analogous to that used by chemists to produce plastics of a required molecular structure. If this were done and the resulting artifact rendered sensitive to stimuli administered chemically or physically, it could, temporarily at least, produce a behavior which would, to an unprepared observer, be scarcely distinguishable from that of a living organism.

" 'My observations lead me to suggest that this is what has been done, the coelenterate form being chosen, out of many others that might have served the purpose, for its simplicity of construction. It seems probable that the sea-tanks may be a variant of the same device. In other words, we were being attacked by organic mechanisms under remote, or predetermined, control. When this is considered in the light of the control which we ourselves are able to exercise over *in*organic materials, remotely, as with guided missiles, or predeterminedly, as with torpedoes, it should be less startling than it at first appears. Indeed, it may well be that once the technique of building up a natural form synthetically has been discovered, control of it would present less complex problems than many we have had to solve in our control of the inorganic.' "

"Oh—oh—oh!" said Phyllis painedly, to Captain Winters. "I've a good mind to go straight round and shake Dr. Bocker. He *promised* me he wouldn't say anything yet about that 'pseudo' business. He's just a kind of natural-born *enfant terrible*, it'd do him *good* to be shaken. Just wait till I get him alone."

"It does weaken his whole case," Captain Winters agreed.

"Weaken it! Somebody is going to hand this to the newspapers. They play it up hard as another Bockerism, the whole thing will become just a stunt—and that will put all the sensible people against whatever he says. —And just as he was beginning to live some of the other things down, too!"

A bad week followed. Those papers that had already adopted *The Beholder's* scornful attitude to coastal preparations pounced upon the pseudobiotic suggestions with glee. Writers of editorials filled their pens with sarcasm, a squad of scientists which had trounced Bocker before was marched out again, to grind him still smaller. Almost every cartoonist discovered simultaneously why his favorite political butts had somehow never seemed quite human.

The other part of the Press already advocating effective coastal defenses, let its imagination go on the subject of pseudo-living structures that might yet be created, and demanded still better defense against the horrific possibilities thought up by its staffs.

Then the sponsor informed E.B.C. that his fellow directors considered that their product's reputation would suffer by being associated with this new wave of notoriety and controversy that had arisen around Dr. Bocker, and proposed to cancel arrangements. Departmental Heads in E.B.C. began to tear their hair. Time-salesmen put up the old line about any kind of publicity being good publicity. The sponsor talked about dignity, and also the risk that the purchase of the product might be disregarded as tacit endorsement of the Bocker theory which, he feared, might have the effect of promoting sales resistance in the upper income brackets. E.B.C. parried with the observation that build-up publicity had already tied the names of Bocker and the product together in the public mind. Nothing would be gained from reining-in in midstream, so the firm ought to go ahead and get the best of its money's worth.

The sponsor said that his firm had attempted to make a serious contribution to knowledge and public safety by promoting a scientific expedition, not a vulgar stunt. Just the night before, for instance, one of E.B.C.'s own comedians had suggested that pseudo life might explain a long-standing mystery concerning his mother-in-law, and if this kind of thing was going to be allowed, etc., etc. E.B.C. promised that it would not contaminate their air in future, and pointed out that if the series on the expedition were dropped after the promises that had been made, a great many consumers in all income brackets were likely to feel that the sponsor's firm was unreliable . . .

Members of the B.B.C. displayed an infuriatingly courteous sympathy to any members of our staff whom they chanced to meet.

But there was still the telephone bringing suggestions and swift changes of policy. We did our best. We wrote and rewrote, trying to satisfy all parties. Two or three

hurried conferences with Bocker himself were explosive.
He spent most of the time threatening to throw the whole
thing up because E.B.C. too obviously would not trust him
near a live microphone, and was insisting on recordings.

At last, however, the scripts were finished. We were too
tired of them to argue any more. We packed hurriedly
and departed blasphemously for the peace and seclusion of
Cornwall.

The first noticeable thing as we approached Rose Cottage, 268.6 miles this time, was an innovation.

"Good heavens!" I said. "We've got a perfectly good one
indoors. If I am expected to come and sit out in a draught
there just because of a lot of your compostminded friends—"

"That," Phyllis told me, coldly, "is an arbor."

I looked at it more carefully. The architecture was
unusual. One wall gave an impression of leaning a little.

"Why do we want an arbor?" I inquired.

"Well, one of us might like to work there on a warm
day. It keeps the wind off, and stops papers blowing
about."

"Oh," I said.

With a defensive note, she added. "After all, when one is
bricklaying one has to build *something*."

It was a relief to be back. Hard to believe that such a
place as Escondida existed at all. Still harder to believe in
sea-tanks and giant coelenterates, pseudo or not. Yet,
somehow, I did not find myself able to relax as I had
hoped.

On the first morning Phyllis dug out the fragments of
the frequently neglected novel and took them off, with a
faintly defiant air, to the arbor. I pottered about wondering why the sense of peace wasn't flowing over me quite as
I had hoped. The Cornish sea still lapped immemorially at
the rocks. It was hard indeed to imagine our home sea
spawning such morbid novelties as had slid up the Caribbean beaches of Escondida. Bocker seemed, in recollection,
like an impish sprite who had had a power of hallucination. Out of his range, the world was a more sober, better
ordered place. At least, so it appeared for the moment,
though the extent to which it was not was increasingly

borne in upon me during the next few days as I emerged from our particular concern to take a more general look at it.

The national airlift was working now, though on a severe schedule of primary necessities. It had been discovered that two large air-freighters working on a rapid shuttle service could bring in only a little less than the average cargo boat could carry in the same length of time, but the cost was high, and in spite of the rationing system the cost of living had already risen by about two hundred per cent.

With trade restricted to essentials, half a dozen financial conferences were in almost permanent session. Ill feeling and tempers were rising here and there where a disposition to make the delivery of necessities conditional on the acceptance of a proportion of luxuries was perceptible. There was undoubtedly some hard bargaining going on.

A few ships could still be found in which crews, at fortune-making wages, would dare the deep water, but the insurance rate pushed the cargo prices up to a level at which only the direst need would pay.

Somebody somewhere had perceived in an enlightened moment that every vessel lost had been power driven, and there was a worldwide boom in sailing craft of every size and type. There was also a proposal to mass-produce clipper ships, but little disposition to believe that the emergency would last long enough to warrant the investment.

In the backrooms of all maritime countries the boys were still hard at work. Every week saw new devices being tried out, some with enough success for them to be put into production—though only to be taken out of it again when it was shown that they had been rendered unreliable in some way, if not actually countered. Nevertheless, that the scientists would come through with the complete answer one day was not to be doubted—and always, it might be tomorrow.

From what I had been hearing, the general faith in scientists was now somewhat greater than the scientists' faith in themselves. Their shortcomings as saviors were beginning to oppress them. Their chief difficulty was not so much infertility of invention as lack of information. They badly needed more data, and could not get it. One of them had remarked to me: "If you were going to make a ghost-trap, how would you set about it? —Particularly if you had not even a small ghost to practice on." They had become ready to grasp at any straw—which may have been the reason why it was only among a desperate section of the scientists that Bocker's theory of pseudobiotic forms received any serious consideration.

As for the sea-tanks, the more lively papers were having a great time with them, so were the newsreels. Selected parts of the Escondida films were included in our scripted accounts on E.B.C. A small footage was courteously presented to the B.B.C. for use in its newsreel, with appropriate acknowledgement. In fact the tendency to play the things up to an extent which was creating alarm puzzled me until I discovered that in certain quarters almost anything which diverted attention from the troubles at home was considered worthy of encouragement, and sea-tanks were particularly suitable for this purpose.

Their depredations, however, were becoming increasingly serious. In the short time since we had left Escondida raids had been reported from ten or eleven more places in the Carribbean area, including a township on Puerto Rico. A little further afield, only rapid action by Bermuda-based American aircraft had scotched an attack there. But this was small scale stuff compared with what was happening on the other side of the world. Accounts, apparently reliable, spoke of a series of attacks on the east coast of Japan. Raids by a dozen or more sea-tanks had taken place on Hokkaido and Honshu. Reports from further south, in the Banda Sea area, were more confused, but obviously related to a considerable number of raids upon various scales. Mindanao capped the lot by announcing that four or five of its eastern coastal towns had been raided simultaneously, an operation which must have employed at least sixty sea-tanks.

From the inhabitants of Indonesia and the Philippines, scattered upon innumerable islands set in deep seas, the outlook was very different from that which faced the British, sitting high on their continental shelf with a shallow North Sea, showing no signs of abnormality, at their backs. Among the Islands, reports and rumors skipped like a running fire until each day there were more thousands of people forsaking the coasts and fleeing inland in panic. A similar trend, though not yet on the panic scale was apparent in the West Indies.

I started to see a far larger pattern than I had ever imagined. The reports argued the existence of hundreds, perhaps thousands of these sea-tanks—numbers that indicated not simply a few raids, but a campaign.

"They must provide defenses, or else give the people the means to defend themselves," I said. "You can't preserve your economy in a place where everybody is scared stiff to go near the seaboard. You *must* somehow make it possible for people to work and live there."

"Nobody knows where they will come next, and you have to act quickly when they do," said Phyllis. "That would mean letting people have arms."

"Well, then, they should give them arms. Damn it, it isn't a function of the State to deprive its people of the means of self-protection."

"Isn't it?" said Phyllis, reflectively.

"What do you mean?"

"Doesn't it sometimes strike you as odd that all our governments who loudly claim to rule by the will of the people are willing to run almost any risk rather than let their people have arms? Isn't it almost a principle that a people should not be allowed to defend itself, but should be forced to defend its Government? The only people I know who are trusted by their Government are the Swiss, and, being land-locked, they don't come into this."

I was puzzled. The response was off her usual key. She was looking tired, too. "What's wrong, Phyl?"

She shrugged. "Nothing, except that at times I get sick of putting up with all the shams and the humbug, and pretending that the lies aren't lies, and the propaganda isn't propaganda. I'll get over it again. Don't you sometimes wish that you had been born into the Age of Reason, instead of the Age of the Ostensible Reason? I think that they are going to let thousands of people be killed by these horrible things rather than risk giving them powerful enough weapons to defend themselves. And they'll have rows of arguments why it is best so. What do a few thousands, or a few millions of people matter? Women will just go on making the loss good. But Governments are important—one mustn't risk them."

"Darling—"

"There'll be token arrangements, of course. Small garrisons in important places, perhaps. Aircraft standing-by on call—and they will come along after the worst of it has happened—when men and women have been tied into bundles and rolled away by those horrible things, and girls have been dragged over the ground by their hair, like poor Muriel, and people have been pulled apart, like that man who was caught by two of them at once—*then* the airplanes will come, and the authorities will say they were sorry to be a bit late, but there are technical difficulties in making adequate arrangements. That's the regular kind of brush-off, isn't it?"

"But, Phyl, darling—"

"I know what you are going to say, Mike, but I *am* scared. Nobody's really *doing* anything. There's no realization, no genuine attempt to change the pattern to meet it. The ships are driven off the deep seas; goodness knows how many of these sea-tank things are ready to come and snatch people away. They say: 'Dear, dear! Such a loss of trade,' and they talk and talk and talk as if it'll all come right in the end if only they can keep on talking long enough. When anybody like Bocker suggests *doing* something he's just howled down and called a sensationalist, or an alarmist. How many people do they regard as the proper wastage before they *must* do something?"

"But they are trying, you know, Phyl—"

"Are they? I think they're balancing things all the time. What is the minimum cost at which the political setup can be preserved in present conditions? How much loss of life will the people put up with before they become dangerous about it? Would it be wise or unwise to declare martial law, and at what stage? On and on, instead of admitting the size of the danger and getting to work. Oh, I could—" She stopped suddenly. Her expression changed. "Sorry, Mike. I shouldn't have gone off the handle like that. I must be tired, or something." And she took herself off with a decisive air of not wanting to be followed.

The outburst disturbed me badly. I hadn't seen her in a

state anything like that for years. Not since the baby died.

The next morning didn't do anything to reassure me. I came round the corner of the cottage and found her sitting in that ridiculous arbor. Her arms lay on the table in front of her, her head rested on them, with her hair straying over the littered pages of the novel. She was weeping forlornly, steadily.

I raised her chin, and kissed her. "Darling—darling, what is it—?"

She looked back at me with the tears still running down her cheeks. She said, miserably: "I can't do it, Mike. It won't work."

She looked mournfully at the written pages. I sat down beside her, and put an arm round her.

"Never mind, Sweet, it'll come—"

"It won't, Mike. Every time I try, other thoughts come instead. I'm frightened."

I tightened my arm. "There's nothing to be frightened about, darling."

She kept on looking at me. "You're not frightened?" she said.

"We're stale," I said. "We stewed too much over those scripts. Let's go over to the north coast, it ought to be good for surfboards today."

She dabbed at her eyes. "All right," she said, with unusual meekness.

We really needed to relax, to relieve the dreadful concentration. And so for the next six weeks we rested completely; not going near a script, cutting off the telephone and the radio, not approaching the novel.

Certainly, in six weeks I had become addicted to this life and might have continued longer had a twenty-mile thirst not happened to take me into a small pub close upon six o'clock one evening.

While I was standing at the bar with the second pint the landlord turned on the radio, the archrival's news-bulletin. The very first item shattered the ivory tower that I had been gradually building. The voice said: "The roll of those missing in the Oviedo-Santander district is still incomplete, and it is thought by the Spanish authorities that it may never be completely definitive. Official spokesmen admit that the estimate of 3,200 casualties, including men, women, and children, is conservative, and may be as much as fifteen or twenty per cent below the actual figure.

"In the House today, the Leader of the Opposition, in giving his party's support for the feelings of sympathy with the Spanish people, expressed by the Prime Minister, pointed out that the casualties in the third of this series of raids, that upon Gijon, would have been considerably more severe had the people not taken their defense into their own hands. The people, he said, were entitled to defense. It was a part of the business of government to provide them with it. If a government neglected that duty, no one could blame a people for taking steps for its self-protection. It would be much better, however, to be prepared with an organized force.

"The Prime Minister replied that the nature of the steps that would, if necessary, be taken would have to be dictated by the emergency, if one should arise. These, he said, were deep waters: there was much consolation to be found in the reflection that the British Isles lay in shallow waters."

The landlord reached over, and switched off the set.

"Cor!" he remarked, with disgust. "Makes yer sick. Always the bloody same. Treat you like a lot of bloody kids. Same during the bloody war. Bloody Home Guards all over the place waiting for bloody parachutists, and all the bloody ammunition all bloody well locked up. Like the Old Man his bloody self said one time: 'What kind of a bloody people do they think we are?'"

I offered him a drink, told him I had been away from any news for days, and asked what had been going on. Stripped of its adjectival monotony, and filled out by information I gathered later, it amounted to this: In the past weeks the scope of the raids had widened well beyond the tropics. At Bunbury, a hundred miles or so south of Fremantle in Western Australia, a contingent of fifty or more sea-tanks had come ashore and into the town before any alarm was given. A few nights later La Serena, in Chile, was taken similarly by surprise. At the same time in the Central American area the raids had ceased to be confined to islands, and there had been a number of incursions, large and small, upon both the Pacific and Gulf coasts. In the Atlantic, the Cape Verde Islands had been repeatedly raided, and the trouble spread northward to the Canaries and Madeira. There had been a few small-scale assaults, too, on the bulge of the African coast.

Europe remained an interested spectator. In the opinion of its inhabitants, it is the customary seat of stability. Hurricanes, tidal waves, serious earthquakes, et cetera, are extravagances divinely directed to occur in the more exotic and less sensible parts of the earth, all important European damage being done traditionally by man himself in periodic frenzies. It was not, therefore, to be seriously expected that the danger would come any closer than Madeira—or, possibly, Rabat or Casablanca.

Consequently when, five nights before, the sea-tanks had come crawling through the mud, across the shore, and up the slipways at Santander they had entered a city that was not only unprepared, but also largely uninformed about them.

Someone telephoned the garrison at the *cuartel* with the news that foreign submarines were invading the harbor in force; someone else followed up with the information that the submarines were landing tanks; yet another somebody contradicted that the submarines themselves were amphibious. Since something was certainly, if obscurely, amiss, the soldiery turned out to investigate.

The sea-tanks had continued their slow advance. The military, on their arrival had to force their way through throngs of praying townspeople. In each of several streets patrols came to a similar decision: if this were foreign invasion, it was their duty to repel it; if it were diabolical, the same action, even though ineffective, would put them on the side of Right. They opened fire.

In the *comisaría* of police a belated and garbled alarm gave the impression that the trouble was due to a revolt by the troops. With this endorsed by the sound of firing in several places, the police went forth to teach the military a lesson.

After that, the whole thing had become a chaos of sniping, counter-sniping, partisanship, incomprehension, and exorcism, in the middle of which the sea-tanks had settled down to exude their revolting coelenterates. Only when daylight came and the sea-tanks had withdrawn had it been possible to sort out the confusion, by which time over two thousand persons were missing.

"How did there come to be so many? Did they all stay out praying in the streets?" I asked.

The innkeeper reckoned from the newspaper accounts that the people had not realized what was happening. They were not highly literate nor greatly interested in the outer world, and until the first coelenterate sent out its cilia they had no idea what was going to happen. Then there was panic, the luckier ones ran right away, the others bolted for cover into the nearest houses.

"They ought to have been all right there," I said.

But I was, it seemed, out of date. Since we had seen them in Escondida the sea-tanks had learned a thing or two; among them, that if the bottom story of a house is pushed away the rest will come down, and once the coelenterates had cleared up those trampled in the panic, demolition had started. The people inside had had to choose between having the house come down with them, or making a bolt for safety.

The following night, watchers at several small towns and villages to the west of Santander spotted the half-egg shapes crawling ashore at mid-tide. There was time to arouse most of the inhabitants and get them away. A unit of the Spanish air force was standing-by, and went into action with flares and cannon. At San Vicente they blew up half a dozen sea-tanks with their first onslaught, and the rest stopped. Several more were destroyed on the second run; the rest started back to the sea. The fighters got the last of them when it was already a few inches submerged. At the other four places where they landed the defenses did almost as well. Not more than three or four coelenterates were released in all, and only a dozen or so villagers caught by them. It was estimated that out of fifty or so sea-tanks engaged, not more than four or five could have got safely back to deep water. It was a famous victory, and the wine flowed freely to celebrate it.

The night after there were watchers all along the coast ready to give the alarm when the first dark hump should break the water. But all night long the waves rolled steadily on to the beaches, with never an alien shape to break them. By morning it was clear that the sea-tanks, or those who sent them, had learned a painful lesson. The few that had survived were reckoned to be making for parts less alert.

During the day the wind dropped. In the afternoon a fog came up, by the evening it was thick, and visibility down to no more than a few yards. Somewhere about ten-thirty in the evening the sea-tanks came sliding up from the quietly lapping waters at Gijon, with not a sound to betray them until their metal bellies started to crunch up the stone ramps. The few small boats that were already drawn up there they pushed aside or crushed as they came. It was the cracking of the timbers that brought men out from the waterside *posadas* to investigate.

They could make out little in the fog. The first sea-tanks must have sent coelenterate bubbles wobbling into the air before the men realized what was happening, for presently all was cries, screams and confusion. The sea-tanks pressed slowly forward through the fog, crunching and scraping into the narrow streets while, behind them, still more climbed out of the water. On the waterfront there was panic. People running from one tank were as likely to run into another. Without any warning a whip-like cilium would slash out of the fog, find its victim, and begin to contract. A little later there would be a heavy splash as it rolled with its load over the quayside, back into the water.

Alarm, running back up the town, reached the *comisaría*. The officer in charge put through the emergency call. He listened, then hung up slowly. "Grounded," he said, "and wouldn't be much use in this, even if they could take off."

He gave orders to issue rifles and turn out every available man. "Not that they'll be much good, but we might be lucky. Aim carefully, and if you do find a vital spot, report at once."

He sent the men off with little hope that they could do more than offer a token resistance. Presently he heard sounds of firing. Suddenly there was a boom that rattled the windows, then another. The telephone rang. An excited voice explained that a party of dockworkers was throwing fused sticks of dynamite and gelignite under the advancing sea-tanks. Another boom rattled the windows. The officer thought quickly. "Very well. Find the leader. Authorize him from me. Put your men on to getting the people clear," he directed.

The sea-tanks were not easily discouraged this time, and it was difficult to sort out claims and reports. Estimates of the number destroyed varied between thirty and seventy; of the numbers engaged, between fifty and a hundred and fifty. Whatever the true figures, the force must have been considerable, and the pressure eased only a couple of hours before dawn.

When the sun rose to clear the last of the fog it shone upon a town battered in parts, and widely covered with slime, but also upon a citizenry which, in spite of some hundreds of casualties, felt that it had earned battle honors.

The account, as I had it first from the innkeeper, was brief, but it included the main points, and he concluded it with the observation: "They reckons as there was well over a bloody 'undred of the damn things done-in them two nights. And then there's all those that come up in other places, too—there must be bloody thousands of the bastards a-crawlin' all over the bloody sea bottom. Time something was bloody done about 'em, I say. Bu' no. 'No cause for alarm,' says the bloody Government. Huh! It'll go on being no bloody cause for bloody alarm until a few hundred poor devils somewhere 'as got their bloody selves lassooed by flying jellyfish. *Then* it'll be all emergency orders and bloody panic. You watch."

"The Bay of Biscay's pretty deep," I pointed out. "A lot deeper than anything we've got around here."

"So what?" said the innkeeper.

And when I came to think of it, it was a perfectly good question. The real sources of trouble were without doubt way down in the greater Deeps, and the first surface invasions had all taken place close to the big Deeps. But there were no grounds for assuming that sea-tanks *must* operate close to a Deep. Indeed, from a purely mechanical point of view a slowly shelving climb should be easier for them than a steep one—or should it? There was also the point that the deeper they were the less energy they had to expend in shifting their weight. Again the whole thing boiled down to the fact that we still knew too little about them to make any worthwhile prophecies at all. The inn-keeper was as likely to be right as anyone else.

I told him so, and we drank to the hope that he was not. When I left, the spell had been rudely broken. I stopped in the village to send a telegram to Phyllis, who had gone up to London for a few days, and then went back to pack my things. I left for London the following day.

To occupy the journey by catching up on the world I bought a selection of daily and weekly newspapers. The urgent topic in most of the dailies was "coast prepared-ness"—the Left demanding wholesale embattlement of the Atlantic seaboard, the Right rejecting panic-spending on a probable chimera. Beyond that, the outlook had not changed a great deal. The scientists had not yet produced a panacea (though the usual new device was to be tested), the merchantships still choked the harbors, the aircraft factories were working three shifts and threatening to strike, the Communist Party was pushing a line of Every Plane is a Vote for War.

Mr. Malenkov, interviewed by telegram, had said that although the intensified program of aircraft construction in the West was no more than a part of a bourgeois-fascist plan by warmongers that could deceive no one, yet so great was the opposition of the Russian people to any thought of war that the production of aircraft within the Soviet Union for the Defense of Peace had been tripled. Indeed, so resolutely were the Peoples of the Free Democ-racies determined to preserve Peace in spite of the new Imperialist threat, that war was not inevitable—though there was a possibility that under prolonged provocation the patience of the Soviet Peoples might become exhausted.

The first thing I noticed when I let myself into the flat was a number of envelopes on the mat, a telegram, presum-ably my own, among them. The place immediately felt forlorn.

In the bedroom were signs of hurried packing, in the kitchen sink some unwashed crockery. I looked in the desk-diary, but the last entry was three days old, and said simply: "Lamb chops."

I picked up the telephone. It was nice of Freddy Whittier to sound genuinely pleased that I was in circulation again.

After the greetings: "Look," I said, "I've been so strictly incommunicado that I seem to have lost my wife. Can you elucidate?"

"Lost your what?" said Freddy, in a startled tone.

"Wife—Phyllis," I explained.

"Oh, I thought you said 'life.' Oh, she's all right. She went off with Bocker a couple of days ago," he announced cheerfully.

"That," I told him, "is not the way to break the news. Just what do you mean by 'went off with Bocker'?"

"Spain," he said, succinctly. "They're laying bathytraps there, or something. Matter of fact, we're expecting a dispatch from her any moment."

"So she's pinching my job?"

"Keeping it warm for you—it's other people that'd like to pinch it. Good thing you're back."

The flat was depressing, so I went round to the Club and spent the evening there.

The telephone jangling by the bedside woke me up. I switched on the light. Five A.M. "Hullo," I said to the telephone, in a five A.M. voice. It was Freddy. My heart gave a nasty knock inside as I recognized him at that hour.

"Mike?" he said. "Good. Grab your hat and a recorder. There's a car on the way for you now."

My needle was still swinging a bit. "Car?" I repeated. "It's not Phyl—?"

"Phyl—? O, Lord no. She's okay. Her call came through about nine o'clock. Transcription gave her your love, on my instructions. Now get cracking, old man. That car'll be outside your place any minute."

"But look here— Anyway, there's no recorder here. She must have taken it."

"Hell, I'll try to get one to the plane in time."

"Plane—?" I said, but the line had gone dead.

I rolled out of bed, and started to dress. A ring came at the door before I had finished. It was one of E.B.C.'s regular drivers. I asked him what the hell, but all he knew was that there was a special charter job waiting at Northolt. I found my passport, and we left.

It turned out that I didn't need the passport. I discovered that when I joined a small, blear-eyed section of Fleet Street that was gathered in the waiting room drinking coffee. Bob Humbleby was there, too.

"Ah, the Other Spoken Word," said somebody. "I thought I knew my Watson."

"What," I inquired, "is all this about? Here am I routed out of a warm though solitary bed, whisked through the night—yes, thanks, a drop of that would liven it up."

The Samaritan stared at me. "Do you mean to say you've not heard?" he asked.

"Heard what?"

"Bathies. Place called Buncarragh, Donegal," he explained, telegraphically. "And very suitable, too, in my opinion. Ought to feel themselves really at home among the leprechauns and banshees. But I have no doubt that the natives will be after telling us that it's another injustice that the first place in England to have a visit from them should be Ireland, so they will."

It was queer indeed to encounter that same decaying, fishy smell in a little Irish village. Escondida had in itself been exotic and slightly improbable; but that the same thing should strike among these soft greens and misty blues, that the sea-tanks should come crawling up on this cluster of little gray cottages, and burst their sprays of tentacles here, seemed utterly preposterous.

Yet, there were the ground-down stones of the slipway in the little harbor, the grooves on the beach beside the harbor wall, four cottages demolished, distraught women who had seen their men caught in the nets of the cilia, and over all the same plastering of slime, and the same smell.

There had been six sea-tanks, they said. A prompt telephone call had brought a couple of fighters at top speed. They had wiped out three, and the rest had gone sliding back into the water—but not before half the population of the village, wrapped in tight cocoons of tentacles, had preceded them.

The next night there was a raid further south, in Galway Bay.

By the time I got back to London the campaign had begun. This is no place for a detailed survey of it. Many copies of the official report must still exist, and their accuracy will be more useful than my jumbled recollections.

Phyllis and Bocker were back from Spain, too, and she and I settled down to work. A somewhat different line of work, for day-to-day news of sea-tank raids was now Agency and local correspondent stuff. We seemed to be holding a kind of E.B.C. relations job with the Forces, and also with Bocker—at least, that was what we made of it. Telling the listening public what we could about what was being done for them.

And a lot was. The Republic of Ireland had suspended the past for the moment to borrow large numbers of mines, bazookas, and mortars, and then agreed to accept the loan of a number of men trained in the use of them, too. All along the west and south coasts of Ireland squads of men were laying mine fields above the tidelines wherever there were no protecting cliffs. In coastal towns pickets armed with bomb-firing weapons kept all-night watch. Elsewhere planes, jeeps, and armored cars waited on call.

In the southwest of England, and up the more difficult west coast of Scotland similar preparations were going on.

They did not seem greatly to deter the sea-tanks. Night after night, down the Irish coast, on the Brittany coast, up out of the Bay of Biscay, along the Portuguese seaboard they came crawling in large or small raids. But they had lost their most potent weapon, surprise. The leaders usually gave their own alarm by blowing themselves up in the mine fields; by the time a gap had been created the defenses were in action and the townspeople had fled. The sea-tanks that did get through did some damage, but found little prey, and their losses were not infrequently one hundred per cent.

Across the Atlantic serious trouble was almost confined to the Gulf of Mexico. Raids on the east coast were so effectively discouraged that few took place at all north of Charlestown; on the Pacific side there were few higher than San Diego. In general it was the two Indies, the Philippines, and Japan that continued to suffer most, but they, too, were learning ways of inflicting enormous damage for very small returns.

Bocker spent a great deal of time dashing hither and

thither trying to persuade various authorities to include traps among their defenses. He had little success. Scarcely any place was willing to contemplate the prospect of a sea-tank trapped on its foreshore, but still capable of throwing out coelenterates for an unknown length of time, nor did even Bocker have any theories on the location of traps beyond the construction of enormous numbers of them on a hit-or-miss basis. A few of the pitfall type were dug, but none ever made a catch. Nor did the more hopeful-sounding project of preserving any stalled or disabled sea-tank for examination turn out any better. In a few places the defenders were persuaded to cage them with wire netting instead of blowing them to pieces, but that was the easy part of the problem. The question what to do next was not solved. Any attempt at broaching invariably caused them to explode in geysers of slime. Very often they did so before the attempt was made—the effect, Bocker maintained, of exposure to bright sunlight. And it still could not be said that anyone knew any more about their nature than when we first encountered them on Escondida.

It was the Irish who took almost the whole weight of the north-European attack which was conducted, according to Bocker, from a base somewhere in the minor Deep, south of Rockall. They rapidly developed a skill in dealing with the things that made it a point of dishonor that even one should get away. Scotland suffered only a few minor visitations in the Outer Isles, with scarcely a casualty. England's only raids occurred in Cornwall, and they, too, were small affairs for the most part—the one exception was an incursion in Falmouth harbor where a few did succeed in advancing a little beyond hightide mark before they were destroyed, though much larger numbers, it was claimed, were smashed by depth charges before they could even reach the shore.

Then, only a few days after the Falmouth attacks, the raids ceased. They stopped quite suddenly, and, as far as the larger land masses were concerned, completely.

A week later there was no longer any doubt that what someone had nicknamed the Low Command had called the campaign off. The continental coasts had proved too tough a nut, and the attempt had flopped. The sea-tanks withdrew to less dangerous parts, but even there their percentage of losses mounted, and their returns diminished.

A fortnight after the last raid came a proclamation ending the state of emergency. A day or two later Bocker made his comments on the situation over the air: "Some of us," he said, "some of us, though not the more sensible of us, have recently been celebrating a victory. To them I suggest that when the cannibal's fire is not quite hot enough to boil the pot, the intended meal may feel some relief, but he has *not,* in the generally accepted sense of the phrase, scored a victory. In fact, if he does not do something before the cannibal has time to build a better and bigger fire, he is not going to be any better off.

"Let us, therefore, look at this 'victory.' We, a maritime people who rose to power upon shipping which plied to the furthest corners of the earth, have lost the freedom of the seas. We have been kicked out of an element that we had made our own. Our ships are only safe in coastal waters and shallow seas—and who can say how long they are going to be tolerated even there? We have been forced by a blockade, more effective than any experience in war, to depend on air transport for the very food by which we live. Even the scientists who are trying to study the sources of our troubles must put to sea in *sailing ships* to do their work! Is *this* victory?

"What the eventual purpose of these coastal raids may have been, no one can say for certain. They *may* have been trawling for us as we trawl for fish, though that is difficult to understand; there is more to be caught more cheaply in the sea than on the land. Or it may even have been part of an attempt to conquer the land—an ineffectual and ill-informed attempt, but, for all that, rather more successful than our attempts to reach the Deeps. If it was, then its instigators are now better informed about us, and therefore potentially more dangerous. They are not likely to try again in the same way with the same weapons, but I see nothing in what we have been able to do to discourage them from trying in a different way with different weapons.

"The need for us to find some way in which we can strike back at them is therefore not relaxed, but intensified.

"It may be recalled by some that when we were first made aware of activity in the Deeps I advocated that every effort should be made to establish understanding with them. That was not tried, and very likely it was never a possibility, but there can be no doubt that the situation which I had hoped we could avoid now exists—and is in the process of being resolved. Two intelligent forms of life are finding one another's existence intolerable. I have now come to believe that no attempt at *rapprochement* could have succeeded. Life in all its forms is strife; the better matched the opponents, the harder the struggle. The most powerful of all weapons is intelligence; any intelligent form dominates by, and therefore survives by, its intelligence: a rival form of intelligence must, by its very existence, threaten to dominate, and therefore threaten extinction.

"Observation has convinced me that my former view was lamentably anthropomorphic; I say now that we must attack as swiftly as we can find the means, and with the full intention of complete extermination. These things, whatever they may be, have not only succeeded in throwing us out of their element with ease, but already they have advanced to do battle with us in ours. For the moment we have pushed them back, but they will return, for the same urge drives them as drives us—the necessity to exterminate, or be exterminated. And when they come again, if we let them, they will come better equipped . . .

"Such a state of affairs, I repeat, is *not* victory . . ."

I ran across Pendell of Audio-Assessment the next morning. He gave me a gloomy look.

"We tried," I said, defensively. "We tried hard, but the Elijah mood was on him."

"Next time you see him just tell him what I think of him, will you?" Pendell suggested. "It's not that I mind his being right—it's just that I never did know a man with such a gift for being right at the wrong time, and in the wrong manner. When his name comes on our program again, if it ever does, they'll switch off in their thousands. As a bit of friendly advice, tell him to start cultivating the B.B.C."

As it happened, Phyllis and I were meeting Bocker for lunch that same day. Inevitably he wanted to hear reactions to his broadcast. I gave the first reports gently. He nodded:

"Most of the papers take that line," he said. "Why was I condemned to live in a democracy where every fool's vote is equal to a sensible man's? If all the energy that is put into getting votes could be turned to useful work, what a nation we could be! As it is, at least three national papers are agitating for a cut in 'the millions squandered on research' so that the taxpayer can buy himself another packet of cigarettes a week, which means more cargo space wasted on tobacco, which means more revenue from tax, which the government then spends on something other than research—and the ships go on rusting in the harbors. There's no sense in it. This is the biggest emergency we have ever had."

"But those things down there have taken a beating," Phyllis pointed out.

"We ourselves have a tradition of taking beatings, and then winning wars," said Bocker.

"Exactly," said Phyllis. "We have taken a beating at sea, but in the end we shall get back."

Bocker groaned, and rolled his eyes. "Logic—" he began, but I put in: "You spoke as if you thought they might actually be more intelligent than we are. Do you?"

He frowned. "I don't see how one could answer that. My impression, as I have said before, is that they think in a quite different way—along other lines from ours. If they do, no comparison would be possible, and any attempt at it misleading."

"You were quite serious about their trying again? I mean, it wasn't just propaganda to stop interest in the protection of shipping from falling off?" Phyllis asked.

"Did it sound like that?"

"No, but—"

"I meant it, all right," he said. "Consider their alternatives. Either they sit down there waiting for us to find a means to destroy them, or they come after us. Oh, yes, unless we find it very soon, they'll be here again— somehow—"

PHASE 3

Even though Bocker had been unaware of it when he gave his warning, the new method of attack had already begun, but it took six months more before it became apparent.

Had the ocean vessels been keeping their usual courses, it would have aroused general comment earlier, but with transatlantic crossings taking place only by air, the pilots' reports of unusually dense and widespread fog in the west Atlantic were simply noted. With the increased range of aircraft, too, Gander had declined in importance so that its frequently fogbound state caused little inconvenience.

Checking reports of that time in the light of later knowledge I discovered that there were reports about the same time of unusually widespread fogs in the northwestern Pacific, too. Conditions were bad off the northern Japanese island of Hokkaido, and said to be still worse off the Kurils, further north. But since it was now some time since ships had dared to cross the Deeps in those parts information was scanty, and few were interested. Nor did the abnormally foggy conditions on the South American coast, northward from Montevideo attract public attention.

The chilly mistiness of the summer in England was, indeed, frequently remarked, though more with resignation than surprise.

Fog, in fact, was scarcely noticed by the wider world-consciousness until the Russians mentioned it. A note from Moscow proclaimed the existence of an area of dense fog having its center on the meridian 130° East of Greenwich, at or about, the 85th Parallel. Soviet scientists, after research, had declared that nothing of the kind was on previous record, nor was it possible to see how the known conditions in those parts could generate such a state, let alone maintain it virtually unchanged for three months after its existence had first been observed. The Soviet Government had on several former occasions pointed out that the Arctic activities of the hirelings of capitalist warmongers might well be a menace to Peace.

The territorial rights of the U.S.S.R. in that area of the Arctic lying between the meridians 32° East, and 168° West of Greenwich were recognized by International Law. Any unauthorized incursion into that area constituted an aggression. The Soviet Government, therefore, considered itself at liberty to take any action necessary for the preservation of Peace in that region.

The note, delivered simultaneously to several countries, received its most rapid and downright reply from Washington.

The Peoples of the West, the State Department observed, would be interested by the Soviet Note. As, however, they had now had considerable experience of that technique of propaganda which had been called the prenatal *tu quoque*, they were able to recognize its implications. The Government of the United States was well aware of the territorial divisions in the Arctic—it would, indeed, remind the Soviet Government, in the interests of accuracy, that the segment mentioned in the Note was only approximate, the true figures being: 32° 04′ 35″ East of Greenwich, and 168° 49′ 30″ West of Greenwich, giving a slightly smaller segment than that claimed, but since the center of the phenomenon mentioned was well within this area the United States Government had, naturally, no cognizance of its existence until informed of it in the Note.

Recent observations had, curiously, recorded the existence of just such a feature as that described in the Note at a center also close to the 85th Parallel, but at a point 79° West of Greenwich. By coincidence this was just the target area jointly selected by the United States and Canadian Governments for tests of their latest types of long-range guided missiles. Preparations for these tests had already been completed, and the first experimental launchings would take place in a few days.

The Russians commented on the quaintness of choosing a target area where observation was not possible; the Americans, upon the Slavonic zeal for pacification of uninhabited regions. Whether both parties then proceeded to attack their respective fogs is not on public record, but the wider effect was that fogs became news, and were discovered to have been unusually dense in a surprising number of places.

Had weather ships still been at work in the Atlantic it is likely that useful data would have been gathered sooner, but they had been "temporarily" withdrawn from service, following the sinking of two of them some time before. Consequently the first report which did anything to tidy up the idle speculation came from Godthaab, in Greenland. It spoke of an increased flow of water through the

Davis Strait from Baffin Bay, with a content of broken ice quite unusual for the time of year. A few days later Nome, Alaska, reported a similar condition in the Bering Strait. Then from Spitzbergen, too, came reports of increased flow and lower temperature.

That, straightforwardly explained the fogs off Newfoundland and certain other parts. Elsewhere they could be convincingly ascribed to deep-running cold currents forced upwards into the warmer waters above by encounters with submarine mountain ranges. Everything, in fact, could be either simply or abstrusely explained, except the unusual increase in the cold flow.

Then, from Godhavn, north of Godthaab on the west Greenland coast, a message told of icebergs in unprecedented numbers and often of unusual size. Investigating expeditions were flown from American arctic bases, and confirmed the report. The sea in the north of Baffin Bay, they announced was crammed with icebergs.

"At about Latitude 77, 60 degrees West," one of the fliers wrote, "we found the most awesome sight in the world. The glaciers which run down from the high Greenland icecap were calving. I have seen icebergs formed before, but never on anything like the scale it is taking place there. In the great ice cliffs, hundreds of feet high, cracks appear suddenly. An enormous section tilts out, falling and turning slowly. When it smashes into the water the spray rises up and up in great fountains, spreading far out all around. The displaced water comes rushing back in breakers which clash together in tremendous spray while a berg as big as a small island slowly rolls and wallows and finds its balance. For a hundred miles up and down the coast we saw splashes starting up where the same thing was happening. Very often a berg had no time to float away before a new one had crashed down on top of it. The scale was so big that it was hard to realize. Only by the apparent slowness of the falls and the way the huge splashes seemed to hang in the air—the majestic pace of it all—were we able to tell the vastness of what we were seeing."

Just so did other expeditions describe the scene on the east coast of Devon Island, and on the southern tip of Ellesmere Island. In Baffin Bay the innumerable great bergs jostled slowly, grinding the flanks and shoulders from one another as they herded on the long drift southward, through the Davis Strait, and out into the Atlantic.

Away over on the other side of the Arctic Circle Nome announced that the southward flow of broken pack ice had further increased.

The public received the information in a cushionly style. People were impressed by the first magnificent photographs of icebergs in the process of creation, but, although no iceberg is quite like any other iceberg, the generic similarity is pronounced. A rather brief period of awe was succeeded by the thought that while it was really very clever of science to know all about icebergs and climate and so on, it did not seem to be much good knowing if it could not, resultantly, do something about it.

The dreary summer passed into a drearier autumn. There seemed to be nothing anybody could do about it but accept it with a grumbling philosophy.

At the other end of the world spring came. Then summer, and the whaling season started—in so far as it could be called a season at all when the owners who would risk ships were so few, and the crews ready to risk their lives fewer still. Nevertheless, some could be found ready to damn the bathies, along with all other perils of the deep, and set out. At the end of the Antarctic summer came news, via New Zealand, of glaciers in Victoria Land shedding huge quantities of bergs into the Ross Sea, and suggestions that the great Ross Ice-Barrier itself might be beginning to break up. Within a week came similar news from the Weddell Sea. The Filchner Barrier there, and the Larsen Ice-Shelf were both said to be calving bergs in fantastic numbers. A series of reconnaissance flights brought in reports which read almost exactly like those from Baffin Bay, and photographs which might have come from the same region.

The Sunday Tidings, which had for some years been pursuing a line of intellectual sensationalism, had never found it easy to maintain its supply of material. The policy was subject to lamentable gaps during which it could find nothing topical on its chosen level to disclose. It must, one fancies, have been a council of desperation over a prolonged hiatus of the kind which induced it to open its columns to Bocker.

That the Editor felt some apprehension over the result was discernible from his italicized note preceding the article in which he disclaimed, on grounds of fair-mindedness, any responsibility for what he was now printing in his own paper.

With this auspicious beginning, and under the heading: *The Devil and the Deeps,* Bocker led off: "Never, since the days when Noah was building his Ark, has there been such a well-regimented turning of blind eyes as during the last year. It cannot go on. Soon, now, the long Arctic night will be over. Observation will again be possible. Then, the eyes that should never have been shut *must* open. . . ."

That beginning I remember, but without references I can only give the gist and a few recollected phrases of the rest. "This," Bocker continued, "is the latest chapter in a long tale of futility and failure stretching back to the sinkings of the *Yatsushiro,* and the *Keweenaw,* and beyond. Failure which has already driven us from the seas, and now threatens us on the land. I repeat, *failure.*

"That is a word so little to our taste that many think it a virtue to claim that they never admit it. All about us are unrest, inflating prices, whole economic structures changing—and, therefore, a way of life that is changing. All about us, too, are people who talk about our exclusion from the high seas as though it were some temporary inconvenience, soon to be corrected. To this smugness there is a reply; it is this:

"For over five years now the best, the most agile, the most inventive brains in the world have wrestled with the problem of coming to grips with our enemy—and there is, on their present findings, nothing at all to indicate that we shall ever be able to sail the seas in peace again.

"With the word 'failure' so wry in our mouths it has apparently been policy to discourage any expression of the connection between our maritime troubles and the recent developments in the Arctic and Antarctic. It is time for this attitude of 'not before the children' to cease.

"I do not suggest that the root problem is being neglected; far from it. There have been, and are, men wearing themselves out to find some means by which we can locate and destroy the enemy in our Deeps. What I do say is that with them still unable to find a way, we now face the most serious assault yet.

"It is an assault against which we have no defenses. It is not susceptible of direct attack.

"What is this weapon to which we can oppose no counter?

"It is the melting of the Arctic ice—and a great part of the Antarctic ice, too.

"You think that fantastic? Too colossal? It is not. It is a task which we could have undertaken ourselves, had we so wished, at any time since we released the power of the atom.

"Because of the winter darkness little has been heard lately of the patches of Arctic fog. It is not generally known that though two of them existed in the Arctic spring; by the end of the Arctic summer there were eight, in widely separated areas. Now, fog is caused, as you know, by the meeting of hot and cold currents of either air or water. How does it happen that eight novel, independent warm currents can suddenly occur in the Arctic?

"And the results? Unprecedented flows of broken ice into the Bering Sea, and into the Greenland Sea. In these two areas particularly the pack ice is hundreds of miles north of its usual spring maximum. In other places, the north of Norway, for instance, it is further south. And we ourselves have had an unusually cold, wet winter.

"And the icebergs? Obviously there are a great many more icebergs than usual, but *why* should there be more icebergs?

"Everyone knows where they are coming from. Greenland is a large island—greater than nine times the size of the British Isles. But it is more than that. It is also the last great bastion of the retreating ice age.

"Several times the ice has come south, grinding and scouring, smoothing the mountains, scooping the valleys on its way until it stood in huge ramparts, dizzy cliffs of glass-green ice, vast slow-crawling glaciers, across half Europe. Then it went back, gradually, over centuries, back and back. The huge cliffs and mountains of ice dwindled away, melted, and were known no more—except in one place. Only in Greenland does that immemorial ice still tower nine thousand feet high, unconquered yet. And down its sides slide the glaciers which spawn the icebergs. They have been scattering their icebergs into the sea, season after season, since before there were men to know of it, and why, in this year, should they suddenly spawn ten, twenty times as many? There must be a reason for this. There is.

"If some means, or some several means, of melting the Arctic ice were put into operation, a little time would have to pass before its effect namely the rise of the sea level became measurable. Moreover, the effects would be progressive; first a trickle, then a gush, then a torrent.

"In this connection I draw attention to the fact that in January of this year the mean sea level at Newlyn, where it is customarily measured, was reported to have risen by two-and-one-half inches."

"Oh, dear!" said Phyllis, when she had read this. "Of all the pertinacious stickers-out-of-necks! We'd better go and see him."

It did not entirely surprise us when we telephoned the next morning to find that his number was not available. When we called, however, we were admitted. Bocker got up from a desk littered with mail, to greet us.

"No earthly good your coming here," he told us. "There isn't a sponsor that'd touch me with a forty-foot pole."

"Oh, I'd not say that, A.B." Phyllis told him. "You will very likely find yourself immensely popular with the sellers of sandbags and makers of earth-shifting machinery before long."

He took no notice of that. "You'll probably be contaminated if you associate with me. In most countries I'd be under arrest by now."

"Terribly disappointing for you. This has always been discouraging territory for ambitious martyrs. But you do try, don't you?" she responded. "Now, look, A.B." she went on, "do you really *like* to have people throwing things at you, or what is it?"

"I get impatient," explained Bocker.

"So do other people. But nobody I know has quite your gift for going just beyond what people are willing to take at any given moment. One day you'll get hurt. Not this time because, luckily you've messed it up, but one time certainly."

"If not this time, then probably not at all," he said. He bent a thoughtful, disapproving look on her. "Just what do you mean, young woman, by coming here and telling me I 'messed it up'?"

"The anticlimax. First you sounded as if you were on the point of great revelations, but then that was followed by a rather vague suggestion that somebody or something must be causing the Arctic changes—and without any specific explanation of how it could be done. And then your grand finale was that the tide is two-and-a-half inches higher."

Bocker continued to regard her. "Well, so it is. I don't see what's wrong with that. Two-and-a-half inches is a colossal amount of water when it's spread over a hundred and forty-one million square miles. If you reckon it up in tons—"

"I never do reckon water in tons—and that's part of the point. To ordinary people two-and-a-half inches just means a very slightly higher mark on a post. After your build-up it sounded like such a let-down that everyone feels annoyed with you for alarming them—those that don't just laugh, and say: 'Ha! ha! These professors!'"

Bocker waved his hand at the desk with its load of mail. "Quite a lot of people have been alarmed—or at least indignant," he said. He lit a cigarette. "That was what I wanted. You know that at every stage the great majority, and particularly the authorities have resisted the evidence as long as they could. This is a scientific age—in the more educated strata. It will therefore almost fall over backwards in disregarding the abnormal, and it has developed a deep suspicion of its own senses. Very reluctantly the existence of something in the Deeps was belatedly conceded. There has been equal reluctance to admit all the succeeding manifestations until they couldn't be dodged. And now here we are again, balking at the newest hurdle.

"We've not been altogether idle, though. The Arctic Ocean is deep, and even more difficult to get at than the others, so there was some bombing where the fog patches occurred, but the devil of it is there's no way of telling results.

"In the middle of it the Muscovite, who seems to be constitutionally incapable of understanding anything to do with the sea, started making trouble. The sea, he appeared to be arguing, was causing a great deal of inconvenience to the West; therefore it must be acting on good dialectically materialistic principles, and I have no doubt that if he could contact the Deeps he would like to make a pact with their inhabitants for a brief period of dialectical opportunism. Anyway, he led off, as you know, with accusations of aggression, and then in the back-and-forth that followed began to show such truculence that the attention of our Services became diverted from the really serious threat to the antics of this oriental clown who thinks the sea was only created to embarrass capitalists.

"Thus, we have now arrived at a situation where the 'bathies,' as they call them, far from falling down on the job as we had hoped, are going ahead fast, and all the brains and organizations that should be working full speed at planning to meet the emergency are congenially fooling around with those ills they have, and ignoring others that they would rather know not of."

"So you decided that the time had come to force their hands by—er—blowing the gaff?" I asked.

"Yes—but not alone. This time I have the company of a number of eminent and very worried men. Mine was only the opening shot at the wider public on this side of the Atlantic. My weighty companions who have not already lost their reputations over this business are working more subtly. As for the American end, well, just take a look at *Life* and *Collier's* this next week. Oh, yes, something is going to be done."

"What?" asked Phyllis.

He looked at her thoughtfully for a moment, then shook his head slightly. "That, thank God, is someone else's department—at least, it will be when the public forces them to admit the situation.

"It's going to be a very bloody business," he said seriously.

"What I want to know—" Phyllis and I began, simultaneously.

"Your turn, Mike," she offered.

"Well, mine is: how do you think the thing's being done?

Melting the Arctic seems a pretty formidable proposition."

"There've been a number of guesses. They range from an incredible operation like piping warm water up from the tropics, to tapping the Earth's central heat—which I find just about as unlikely."

"But you have your own idea?" I suggested. It seemed improbable that he had not.

"Well, I think it *might* be done this way. We know that they have some kind of device that will project a jet of water with considerable force—the bottom sediment that was washed up into surface currents in a continuous flow pretty well proved that. Well, then, a contraption of that kind, used in conjunction with a heater, say an atomic reaction pile, ought to be capable of generating a quite considerable warm current. The obvious snag there is that we don't know whether they have atomic fission or not. So far, there's been no indication that they have—unless you count our presenting them with at least one atomic bomb that didn't go off. But if they *do* have it, I think that might be an answer."

"They could get the necessary uranium?"

"Why not? After all, they have forcibly established their rights, mineral and otherwise, over more than two-thirds of the world's surface. Oh, yes, they could get it, all right, if they know about it."

"And the iceberg angle?"

"That's less difficult. In fact, there is pretty general agreement that if one has a vibratory type of weapon which their attacks on ships led us to believe they had, there ought to be no great difficulty in causing a lump of ice—even a considerable sized lump of ice—to crack."

"Suppose we can't find a way of hindering the process, how long do you think it'll take before we are in real trouble?" I asked him.

He shrugged. "I've absolutely no idea. As far as the glaciers and the icecap are concerned, it presumably depends on how hard they work at it. But directing warm currents on pack ice would presumably show only small results to begin with and then increase rapidly, very likely by a geometrical progression. Worse than useless to guess, with no data at all."

"Once this gets into people's heads, they're going to want

to know the best thing to do," Phyllis said. "What would you advise?"

"Isn't that the Government's job? It's because it's high time they thought about doing some advising that we have blown the gaff, as Mike put it. My own personal advice is too impracticable to be worth much."

"What is it?" Phyllis asked.

"Find a nice, self-sufficient hilltop, and fortify it," said Bocker, simply.

The campaign did not get off to the resounding start that Bocker had hoped. In England, it had the misfortune to be adopted by the *Nethermore Press,* and was consequently regarded as stunt territory wherein it would be unethical for other journalistic feet to trespass. In America it did not stand out greatly among the other excitements of the week. In both countries there were interests which preferred that it should seem to be no more than a stunt. France and Italy took it more seriously, but their governments' political weight in world councils was lighter. Russia ignored the content, but explained the purpose; it was yet another move by cosmopolitan-fascist warmongers to extend their influence in the Arctic.

Nevertheless, official indifference was slightly breached, Bocker assured us. A Committee on which the Services were represented had been set up to inquire and make recommendations. A similar Committee in Washington also inquired in a leisurely fashion until it was brought up sharply by the State of California.

The average Californian was not greatly worried by a rise of a couple of inches in the tide level; he had been much more delicately stricken. Something was happening to his climate. The average of his seaboard temperature had gone way down, and he was having cold, wet fogs. He disapproved of that, and a large number of Californians disapproving makes quite a noise. Oregon, and Washington, too, rallied to support their neighbor. Never within the compass of their statistical records had there been so cold and unpleasant a winter.

It was clear to all parties that the increased flow of ice and cold water pouring out of the Bering Sea was being swept eastward by the Kuroshio Current from Japan, and

obvious to at least one of the parties that the amenities of
the most important State in the Union were suffering
gravely. Something *must* be done.

In England the spur was applied when the April spring
tides overflowed the Embankment wall at Westminster.
Assurances that this had happened a number of times
before and was devoid of particular significance were
swept aside by the triumphant we-told-you-so of the
Nethermore Press. A hysterical Bomb-the-Bathies demand
sprang up on both sides of the Atlantic, and spread round
the world. (Except for the intransigent sixth.)

Foremost, as well as first, in the Bomb-the-Bathies
movement, the *Nethermore Press* inquired, morning and
evening: "WHAT IS THE BOMB FOR?"

"Billions have been spent upon this Bomb which appears
to have no other destiny but to be held up and shaken
threateningly, or, from time to time, to provide pictures
for our illustrated papers. The people of the world, having
evolved and paid for this weapon are now forbidden to use
it against a menace that has sunk our ships, closed our
oceans, snatched men and women from our very shores,
and now threatens to drown us. Procrastination and inep-
titude has from the beginning marked the attitude of the
Authorities in this affair . . ." and so on, with the earlier
bombings of the Deeps apparently forgotten by writers
and readers alike.

"Working up nicely now," said Bocker when we saw
him next.

"It seems pretty silly to me," Phyllis told him, bluntly.
"All the same old arguments against the indiscriminate
bombing of Deeps still apply."

"Oh, not that part," Bocker said. "They'll probably
drop a few bombs here and there with plenty of publicity
and no results. No, I mean the urge towards planning.
We're now in the first stage of stupid suggestions like
building immense levees of sandbags, of course; but it is
getting across that something has got to be done."

It got across still more strongly after the next spring
tides. There had been strengthening of the sea defenses
everywhere. In London the riverside walls had been rein-
forced and topped for their whole length with sandbags.
As a precaution, traffic had been diverted from the Em-

bankment, but the crowd turned out to throng it and the bridges, on foot. The police did their best to keep them moving, but they dawdled from one point to another, watching the slow rise of the water, waving to the crews of passing tugs and barges which presently were riding above the road-level. They seemed equally ready to be indignant if the water should break through, or disappointed if there were an anticlimax.

They were not disappointed. The water lapped slowly above the parapet and against the sandbags. Here and there it began to trickle through on to the pavements. Firemen, Civil Defense, and Police watched their sections anxiously, rushing bags to reinforce wherever a trickle enlarged, shoring up weak-looking spots with timber struts. The pace gradually became hotter. The bystanders began to help, dashing from one point to another as new jets started up. Presently there could be little doubt what was going to happen. Some of the watching crowd withdrew, but many of them remained, in a wavering fascination. When the breakthrough came, it occurred in a dozen places on the north bank almost simultaneously. Among the spurting jets a bag or two would begin to shift, then, suddenly, came a collapse, and a gap several yards wide through which the water poured as if over a dam.

From where we stood on top of an E.B.C. van parked on Vauxhall Bridge we were able to see three separate rivers of muddy water pouring into the streets of Westminster, filling basements and cellars as they went, and presently merging into one flood. Our commentator handed over to another, perched on a Pimlico roof. For a minute or two we switched over to the B.B.C. to find out how their crew on Westminster Bridge was faring. We got on to them just in time to hear Bob Humbleby describing the flooded Victoria Embankment with the water now rising against New Scotland Yard's own second line of defenses. The television boys didn't seem to be doing too well; there must have been a lot of bets lost on where the breakthroughs would occur, but they were putting up a struggle with the help of telephoto lenses and portable cameras.

From that point on, the thing got thick and fast. On the south bank water was breaking into the streets of Lambeth, Southwark, and Bermondsey in a number of places. Up river it was seriously flooding Chiswick, down river Limehouse was getting it badly, and more places kept on reporting breaks until we lost track of them. There was little to be done but stand by for the tide to drop, and then rush the repairs against its next rise.

The House outquestioned any quiz. The replies were more assured than assuring.

The relevant Ministries and Departments were actively taking all the steps necessary, claims should be submitted through Local Councils, priorities of men and material had already been arranged. Yes, warnings had been given, but unforseen factors had intruded upon the hydrographers' original calculations. An Order in Council would be made for the requisition of all earth-moving machinery. The public could have full confidence that there would be no repetition of the calamity; the measures already put in hand would insure against any further extension. Little could be done beyond rescue work in the Eastern Counties at present, that would of course continue, but the most urgent matter at the moment was to ensure that the water could make no further inroads at the next high tides.

The requisition of materials, machines and manpower was one thing; their apportionment, with every seaboard community and low-lying area clamoring for them simultaneously, quite another. Clerks in half a dozen Ministries grew pale and heavy-eyed in a welter of demands, allocations, adjustments, redirections, misdirections, subornments, and downright thefts. But somehow, and in some places, things began to get done. Already, there was great bitterness between those who were chosen, and those who looked like being thrown to the wolves.

Phyllis went down one afternoon to look at progress of work on the riverside. Amid great activity on both banks a superstructure of concrete blocks was arising on the existing walls. The sidewalk supervisors were out in their thousands to watch. Among them she chanced upon Bocker. Together they ascended to Waterloo Bridge, and watched the termitelike activity with a celestial eye for a while.

"Alph, the sacred river—and more than twice five miles of walls and towers," Phyllis observed.

"And there are going to be some deep but not very romantic chasms on either side, too," said Bocker. "I wonder how high they'll go before the futility comes home to them."

"It's difficult to believe that anything on such a scale as this can be really futile, but I suppose you are right," said Phyllis.

They continued to regard the medley of men and machinery down below for a time.

"Well," Bocker remarked, at length, "there must be at least one figure among the shades who is getting a hell of a good laugh out of this."

"Nice to think there's even one," Phyllis said. "Who?"

"King Canute," said Bocker.

We were having so much news of our own at that time that the effects in America found little room in newspapers already straitened by a paper shortage. Newscasts, however, told that they were having their own troubles over there. California's climate was no longer Problem Number One. In addition to the difficulties that were facing ports and seaboard cities all over the world, there was bad coastline trouble in the south of the United States. It ran almost all the way around the Gulf from Key West to the Mexican border. In Florida, owners of real estate began to suffer once again as the Everglades and the swamps spilled across more and more country. Across in Texas a large tract of land north of Brownsville was gradually disappearing beneath the water. Still worse hit were Louisiana, and the Delta. The enterprise of Tin Pan Alley considered it an appropriate time to revive the plea: "River, Stay 'Way from My Door," but the river did not —nor, over on the Atlantic coast, did other rivers, in Georgia and the Carolinas.

But it is idle to particularize. All over the world the threat was the same. The chief difference was that in the more developed countries all available earth-shifting machinery worked day and night, while in the more backward it was sweating thousands of men and women who toiled to raise great levees and walls.

But for both the task was too great. The more the level

rose, the further the defenses had to be extended to prevent outflanking. When the rivers were backed up by the incoming tides there was nowhere for the water to go but over the surrounding countryside. All the time, too, the problems of preventing flooding from the rear by water backed up in sewers and conduits became more difficult to handle. Even before the first serious inundation which followed the breaking of the Embankment wall near Blackfriars, in October, the man in the street had suspected that the battle could not be won, and the exodus of those with wisdom and the means had already started. Many of them, moreover, were finding themselves forestalled by refugees from the eastern counties and the more vulnerable coastal towns elsewhere.

Some little time before the Blackfriars breakthrough a confidential note had circulated among selected staff, and contracted personnel such as ourselves, at E.B.C. It had been decided, as a matter of policy in the interests of public morale, we learned, that, should certain emergency measures become necessary, etc., etc., and so on, for two foolscap pages, with most of the information between the lines. It would have been a lot simpler to say: "Look. The word is that this thing's going to get serious. The B.B.C. has orders to stay put, so for prestige reasons we'll have to do the same. We want volunteers to man a station here, and if you care to be one of them, we'll be glad to have you. Suitable arrangements will be made. There'll be a bonus, and you can trust us to look after you okay if anything does happen. How about it?"

Phyllis and I talked it over. If we had had any family, we decided, the necessity would have been to do the best we could by them—in so far as anyone could know what might turn out to be best. As we had not, we could please ourselves. Phyllis summed up for staying on the job.

"Apart from conscience and loyalty and all the proper things," she said, "Goodness knows what is going to happen in other places if it does get really bad. Somehow, running away seldom seems to work out well unless you have a pretty good idea of what you're running to. My vote is for sticking, and seeing what happens."

So we sent our names in, and were pleased to find that Freddy Whittier and his wife had done the same.

After that, some clever departmentalism made it seem as if nothing were happening for a while. Several weeks passed before we got wind of the fact that E.B.C. had leased the top two floors of a large department store near Marble Arch, and were working full speed to have them converted into as near a self-supporting station as was possible.

"I should have thought," said Phyllis, when we acquired this information, "that somewhere higher, like Hampstead or Highgate would have been better."

"Neither of them is quite London," I pointed out. "Besides, E.B.C. probably gets it for a nominal rent for announcing each time: 'This is the E.B.C. calling the world from Selvedge's.' Goodwill advertising during the interlude of emergency."

"Just as if the water would just go away one day," she said.

"Even if they don't think so, they lose nothing by letting E.B.C. have it," I pointed out.

By that time we were becoming highly level-conscious, and I looked the place up on the map. The seventy-five foot contour line ran down the street on the building's western side.

"How does that compare with the archrival?" wondered Phyllis, running her finger across the map.

Broadcasting House appeared to be very slightly better off. About eighty-five feet above mean sea level, we judged.

"H'm," she said. "Well, if there is any calculation behind our being on the top floors, they'll be having to do a lot of moving upstairs, too. Gosh," she added, glancing over to the left of the map. "Look at their television studios! Right down on the twenty-five foot level."

In the weeks just before the breakthrough London seemed to be living a double life. Organizations and institutions were making their preparations with as little ostentation as possible. Officials spoke in public with an affected casualness of the need to make plans "just in case," and then went back to their offices to work feverishly on the arrangements. Announcements continued to be reassuring in tone. The men employed on the jobs were for the most part cynical about their work, glad of the overtime pay, and curiously disbelieving. They seemed to regard it as a stunt which was working nicely to their benefit; imagination apparently refused to credit the threat with any reality outside working hours. Even after the first breakthrough, alarm was oddly localized with those who had suffered. The wall was hurriedly repaired, and the exodus was still not much more than a trickle of people. Real trouble came with the next spring tides.

There was plenty of warning this time in the parts likely to be most affected. The people took it stubbornly and phlegmatically. They had already had experience to learn by. The main response was to move possessions to upper stories, and grumble loudly at the inefficiency of authorities who were incapable of saving them the trouble involved. Notices were posted giving the times of high water for three days, but the suggested precautions were couched with such a fear of promoting panic that they were little heeded.

The first day passed safely. On the evening of the highest water a large part of London settled down to wait for midnight and the crisis to pass, in a sullenly bad-tempered mood. The buses were all off the streets, and the underground had ceased to run at eight in the evening. But plenty of people stayed out, and walked down to the river to see what there was to be seen from the bridges. They had their show.

The smooth, oily surface crawled slowly up the piers of the bridges and against the retaining walls. The muddy water flowed upstream with scarcely a sound, and the crowds, too, were almost silent, looking down on it apprehensively. There was no fear of it topping the walls; the estimated rise was twenty-three feet, four inches, which would leave a safety margin of four feet to the top of the new parapet. It was pressure that was the source of anxiety.

From the north end of Waterloo Bridge where we were stationed this time, one was able to look along the top of the wall, with the water running high on one side of it, and, to the other, the roadway of the Embankment, with the street lamps still burning there, but not a vehicle or a human figure to be seen upon it. Away to the west the hands on the Parliament clock tower crawled round the illuminated dial. The water rose as the big hand moved with insufferable sloth up to eleven o'clock. Over the quiet crowds the note of Big Ben striking the hour came clearly down wind.

The sound caused people to murmur to one another; then they fell silent again. The hand began to crawl down, ten-past, a quarter, twenty, twenty-five, then, just before the half-hour there was a rumble somewhere upstream; a composite, crowd-voice sound came to us on the wind. The people about us craned their necks, and murmured again. A moment later we saw the water coming. It poured along the Embankment towards us in a wide, muddy flood, sweeping rubbish and bushes with it, rushing past beneath us. A groan went up from the crowd. Suddenly there was a loud crack and a rumble of falling masonry behind us as a section of the wall, close by where the *Discovery* had formerly been moored, collapsed. The water poured through the gap, wrenching away concrete blocks so that the wall crumbled before our eyes and the water poured in a great muddy cascade on to the roadway.

Before the next tide came the Government had removed the velvet glove. Following the announcement of a State of Emergency came a Standstill Order, and the proclamation of an orderly scheme of evacuation. There is no need for me to write here of the delays and muddles in which the scheme broke down. It is difficult to believe that it can have been taken seriously even by those who launched it. An unconvincing air seemed to hang over the whole affair from the beginning. The task was impossible. Something, perhaps, might have been done had only a single city been concerned, but with more than two-thirds of the country's population anxious to move on to higher ground, only the crudest methods had any success in checking the pressure, and then not for long.

But, though it was bad here, it was still worse elsewhere. The Dutch had withdrawn in time from the danger areas, realizing that they had lost their centuries-long battle with the sea. The Rhine and the Maas had backed up in flood over square miles of country. A whole population was trekking southward into Belgium or southeast into Germany. The North German Plain itself was little better off. The Ems and the Weser had widened out, too, driving people southward from their towns and farms in an increasing horde. In Denmark every kind of boat was in use ferrying families to Sweden and the higher ground there.

For a little time we managed to follow in a general way what was happening, but when the inhabitants of the Ardennes and Westphalia turned in dismay to save themselves by fighting off the hungry, desperate invaders from the north, hard news disappeared in a morass of rumor and chaos. All over the world the same kind of thing must have been going on, differing only in its scale. At home, the flooding of the Eastern Counties had already driven people back on the Midlands. Loss of life was small, for there had been plenty of warning. Real trouble started on the Chiltern Hills where those already in possession organized themselves to prevent being swamped by the two converging streams of refugees from the east and from London.

Over the untouched parts of Central London a mood of Sunday-like indecision hung for several days. Many people, not knowing what else to do, still tried to carry-on as nearly as usual. The police continued to patrol. Though the underground was flooded plenty of people continued to turn up at their places of work, and some kinds of work did continue, seemingly through habit or momentum, then gradually lawlessness seeped inwards from the suburbs and the sense of breakdown became inescapable. Failure of the emergency electric supply one afternoon, followed by a night of darkness gave a kind of *coup de grâce* to order. The looting of shops, particularly foodshops, began, and spread on a scale which defeated both the police and the military.

We decided it was time to leave the flat and take up our residence in the new E.B.C. fortress.

From what the short waves were telling us there was little to distinguish the course of events in the low-lying cities anywhere—except that in some the law died more quickly. It is outside my scope to dwell on the details; I have no doubt that they will be described later in innumerable official histories.

E.B.C.'s part during those days consisted largely in duplicating the B.B.C. in the reading out of government instructions hopefully intended to restore a degree of order: a monotonous business of telling those whose homes were not immediately threatened to stay where they were, and directing the flooded-out to certain higher areas and away from others that were said to be already over-crowded. We may have been heard, but we could see no evidence that we were heeded. In the north there may have been some effect, but in the south the hugely disproportionate concentration of London, and the flooding of so many rails and roads, ruined all attempts at orderly dispersal. The numbers of people in motion spread alarm among those who could have waited. The feeling that unless one reached a refuge ahead of the main crowd there might be no place at all to go was catching—as also was the feeling that anyone trying to do so by car was in possession of an unfair advantage. It quickly became safer to walk wherever one was going—though not outstandingly safe at all. It was best to go out as little as possible.

The existence of numerous hotels and a reassuring elevation of some seven hundred feet above normal sea level were undoubtedly factors which influenced Parliament in choosing the town of Harrogate, in Yorkshire, as its seat. The speed with which it assembled there was very likely due to the same force as was motivating many private persons—the fear that someone else might get in first. To an outsider it seemed that a bare few hours after Westminster was flooded, the ancient institution was performing with all its usual fluency in its new home.

As for ourselves, we began to shake down into a routine. Our living quarters were on the top floor. Offices, studios, technical equipment, generators, stores, etc., on the floor beneath. A great reserve of diesel oil and petrol filled large tanks in the basement, whence it was pumped as necessary. Our aerial systems were on roofs two blocks away, reached by bridges slung high over the intervening streets. Our own roof was largely cleared to provide a helicopter landing, and to act as a rainwater catchment. As we gradually developed a technique for living there we decided it was pretty secure.

Even so, my recollection is that nearly all spare time in the first few days was spent by everyone in transferring the contents of the provision department to our own quarters before it should disappear elsewhere.

There seems to have been a basic misconception of the role we should play. As I understood it, the idea was that we were to preserve, as far as possible, the impression of business as usual, and then, as things grew more difficult, the center of E.B.C. would follow the administration by gradual stages to Yorkshire. This appears to have been founded upon the assumption that London was so cellularly constructed that as the water flowed into each cell it would be abandoned while the rest carried on much as usual. As far as we were concerned bands, speakers, and artists would all roll up to do their stuff in the ordinary way until the water lapped our doorsteps—if it should ever reach as far—by which time they would presumably have changed to the habit of rolling up to the Yorkshire station instead. The only provision on the program side that anyone had made for things not happening in this naïve fashion was the transfer of our recorded library before it became actually necessary to save it. A dwindling, rather than a breakdown, was envisaged. Curiously, quite a number of conscientious broadcasters did somehow manage to put in their appearances for a few days. After that, however, we were thrown back almost entirely upon ourselves and the records. And, presently, we began to live in a state of siege.

I don't propose to deal in detail with the year that followed. It was a drawn out story of decay. A long, cold winter during which the water lapped into the streets faster than we had expected. A time when armed bands roved the streets in search of untouched foodstores, when, at any hour of the day or night, one was apt to hear a rattle of shots as two gangs met. We ourselves had little trouble; it was as if, after a few attempts to raid us, word had gone round that we were ready to defend, and with so many other stores raidable at little or no risk we might as well be left until later.

When the warmer weather came there were noticeably fewer people to be seen. Most of them, rather than face another winter in a city by now largely plundered of food and beginning to suffer epidemics from lack of fresh water and drainage, were filtering out into the country, and the shooting that we heard was usually distant.

Our own numbers had been depleted, too. Out of the original sixty-five we were now reduced to twenty-five, the rest having gone off in parties by helicopter as the national focus became more settled in Yorkshire. From having been a center we had declined to the state of an outpost maintained for prestige.

Phyllis and I discussed whether we would apply to go, too, but from the description of conditions that we pried out of the helicopter pilot and his crew the E.B.C. headquarters sounded congested and unattractive, so we decided to stay for a while longer, at any rate. We were by no means uncomfortable where we were, and the fewer of us that were left in our London aerie, the more space and supplies each of us had.

In late spring we learned that a decree had merged us with the archrival, putting all radio communication under direct Government control. It was the Broadcasting House lot that were moved out by a swift airlift since their premises were vulnerable while ours were already in a prepared state, and the one or two B.B.C. men who stayed came over to join us.

News reached us mainly by two channels: the private link with E.B.C., which was usually moderately honest, though discreet; and broadcasts which, no matter where they came from, were puffed with patently dishonest optimism. We became very tired and cynical about them, as, I imagine, did everyone else, but they still kept on. Every country, it seemed, was meeting and rising above the disaster with a resolution which did honor to the traditions of its people.

By midsummer, and a cold midsummer it was, the town had become very quiet. The gangs had gone; only the obstinate individuals remained. They were, without doubt, quite numerous, but in twenty-thousand streets they seemed sparse, and they were not yet desperate. It was possible to go about in relative safety again, though wise to carry a gun.

The water had risen further in the time than any of the estimates had supposed. The highest tides now reached the fifty-foot level. The floodline was north of Hammersmith and included most of Kensington. It lay along the south side of Hyde Park, then to the south of Piccadilly, across

Trafalgar Square, along the Strand and Fleet Street, and then ran northeast up the west side of the Lea Valley; of the city, only the high ground about St. Paul's was still untouched. In the south it had pushed across Barnes, Battersea, Southwark, most of Deptford, and the lower part of Greenwich.

One day we walked down to Trafalgar Square. The tide was in, and the water reached nearly to the top of the wall on the northern side, below the National Gallery. We leaned on the balustrade looking at the water washing around Landseer's lions, wondering what Nelson would think of the view his statue was getting now.

Close to our feet, the edge of the flood was fringed with scum and a fascinatingly varied collection of flotsam. Further away, fountains, lampposts, traffic lights and statues thrust up here and there. On the far side, and down as much as we could see of Whitehall, the surface was as smooth as a canal. A few trees still stood, and in them sparrows chattered. Starlings had not yet deserted St. Martin's church, but the pigeons were all gone, and on many of their customary perches gulls stood, instead. We surveyed the scene and listened to the slipslop of the water in the silence for some minutes. Then I asked: "Didn't somebody or other once say: 'This is the way the world ends, not with a bang but a whimper?' "

Phyllis looked shocked. " *'Somebody or other!'* " she exclaimed. "That was Mr. Eliot!"

"Well, it certainly looks as if he had the idea that time," I said.

Presently Phyllis remarked: "I thought I was through a phase now, Mike. For such a long time it kept on seeming that something could be done to save the world we're used to—if we could only find out what. But soon I think I'll be able to feel; 'Well, that's gone. How can we make the best of what's left?'—All the same, I wouldn't say that coming to places like this does me any good."

"There aren't places like this. This is—was—one of the uniques. That's the trouble. And it's a bit more than dead, but not yet ready for a museum. Soon, perhaps, we may be able to feel, 'Lo! All our pomp of yesterday is one with Nineveh and Tyre'—soon, but not quite yet."

There was a pause. It lengthened.

"Mike," she said, suddenly. "Let's go away from here—now."

I nodded. "It might be better. We'll have to get a little tougher yet, darling, I'm afraid."

She took my arm, and we started to walk westward. Halfway to the corner of the square we paused at the sound of a motor. It seemed, improbably, to come from the south side. We waited while it drew closer. Presently, out from the Admiralty Arch swept a speedboat. It turned in a sharp arc and sped away down Whitehall, leaving the ripples of its wake slopping through the windows of august Governmental offices.

"Very pretty," I said. "There can't be many of us who have accomplished that in one of our waking moments."

Phyllis gazed along the widening ripples, and abruptly became practical again. "I think we'd better see if we can't find one of those," she said. "It might come in useful later on."

The rate of rise continued to increase. By the end of the summer the level was up another eight or nine feet. The weather was vile and even colder than it had been at the same time the previous year. More of us had applied for transfer, and by mid-September we were down to sixteen.

Even Freddy Whittier had announced that he was sick and tired of wasting his time like a shipwrecked sailor, and was going to see whether he could not find some useful work to do. When the helicopter whisked him and his wife away, they left us reconsidering our own position once more.

Our task of composing never-say-die material on the theme that we spoke from, and for, the heart of an empire bloody but still unbowed was supposed, we knew, to have a stabilizing value even now, but we doubted it. Too many people were whistling the same tune in the same dark. A night or two before the Whittiers left we had had a late party where someone, in the small hours, had tuned in a New York transmitter. A man and a woman on the Empire State Building were describing the scene. The picture they evoked of the towers of Manhattan standing like frozen sentinels in the moonlight while the glittering water lapped at their lower walls was masterly, almost lyrically beautiful—nevertheless, it failed in its purpose. In our minds we could see those shining towers—they were not sentinels, they were tombstones. It made us feel that we were even less accomplished at disguising our own tombstones; that it was time to pull out of our refuge, and find more useful work. Our last words to Freddy were that we would very likely be following him before long.

We had still, however, not reached the point of making definite application when he called us up on the link a couple of weeks later. After the greetings he said: "This isn't purely social, Mike. It is disinterested advice to those contemplating a leap from the frying pan—don't!"

"Oh," I said, "what's the trouble?"

"I'll tell you this. I'd have an application in for getting back to you right now—if only I had not made my reasons for getting out so damned convincing. I mean that. Hang on there, both of you."

"But—" I began.

"Wait a minute," he told me.

Presently his voice came again. "Okay. No monitor on this, I think. Listen, Mike, we're overcrowded, underfed, and in one hell of a mess. Supplies of all kinds are way down, so's morale. The atmosphere's like a lot of piano strings. We're living virtually in a state of siege here, and if it doesn't turn into active civil war in a few weeks it'll be a miracle. The people outside *are* worse off than we are, but seemingly nothing will convince them that we aren't living on the fat of the land. For God's sake keep this under your hat, but stay where you are, for Phyl's sake if not for your own."

I thought quickly. "If it's as bad as that, Freddy, and you're doing no good, why not get back here on the next helicopter. Either smuggle aboard—or maybe we could offer the pilot a few things he'd like?"

"All right. There certainly isn't any use for us here. I don't know why they let us come along. I'll work on that. Look for us next flight. Meanwhile good luck to you both."

"Good luck to you, Freddy, and love to Lynn—and our respects to Bocker, if he's there and nobody's slaughtered him yet."

"Oh, Bocker's here. He's now got a theory that it won't

go much over a hundred and twenty-five feet, and seems to think that's good news."

"Well, considering he's Bocker, it might be a lot worse. 'Bye. We'll be looking forward to seeing you."

We were discreet. We said no more than that we had heard the Yorkshire place was already crowded, so we were staying. A couple who had decided to leave on the next flight changed their minds, too. We waited for the helicopter to bring Freddy back. The day after it was due we were still waiting. We got through on the link. They had no news except that it had left on schedule. I asked about Freddy and Lynn. Nobody seemed to know where they were.

There never was any news of that helicopter. They said they hadn't another that they could send.

The cold summer drew into a colder autumn. A rumor reached us that the sea-tanks were appearing again for the first time since the waters had begun to rise. As the only people present who had had personal contact with them we assumed the status of experts—though almost the only advice we could give was always to wear a sharp knife, and in such a position that it could be reached for a quick slash by either hand. But the sea-tanks must have found the hunting poor in the almost deserted streets of London, for presently we heard no more of them. From the radio, however, we learned that it was not so in some other parts. There were reports soon of their reappearance in many places where not only the new shore lines, but the collapse of organization made it difficult to destroy them in effectively discouraging numbers.

Meanwhile, there was worse trouble. Overnight the combined E.B.C. and B.B.C. transmitters abandoned all pretense of calm confidence. When we looked at the message transmitted to us for radiation simultaneously with all other stations we knew that Freddy had been right. It was a call to all loyal citizens to support their legally elected Government against any attempts that might be made to overthrow it by force, and the way in which it was put left no doubt that such an attempt was already being made. The thing was a sorry mixture of exhortation, threats, and pleas, which wound up with just the wrong note of confidence—the note that had sounded in Spain and then in

France when the words must be said though speaker and listener alike knew that the end was near. The best reader in the service could not have given it the ring of conviction.

The link could not, or would not, clarify the situation for us. Firing was going on, they said. Some armed bands were attempting to break into the Administration Area. The military had the situation in hand, and would clear up the trouble shortly. The broadcast was simply to discourage exaggerated rumors and restore confidence in the government. We said that neither what they were telling us, nor the message itself inspired us personally with any confidence whatever, and we should like to know what was really going on. They went all official, curt and cold.

Twenty-four hours later, in the middle of dictating for our radiation another expression of confidence, the link broke off, abruptly. It never worked again.

Until one gets used to it, the situation of being able to hear voices from all over the world, but none which tells what is happening in one's own country, is odd. We picked up inquiries about our silence from America, Canada, Australia, Kenya. We radiated at the full power of our transmitter what little we knew, and could later hear it being relayed by foreign stations. But we ourselves were far from understanding what had happened. Even if the headquarters of both systems, in Yorkshire, had been overrun, as it would appear, there should have been stations still on the air independently in Scotland and Northern Ireland at least, even if they were no better informed than ourselves. Yet, a week went by, and still there was no sound from them. The rest of the world appeared to be too busy keeping a mask on its own troubles to bother about us any more—though one time we did hear a voice speaking with historical dispassion of *'l'écroulement de l'Angleterre.'* The word *écroulement* was not very familiar to me, but it had a horribly final sound.

The winter closed in. One noticed how few people there were to be seen in the streets now, compared with a year ago. Often it was possible to walk a mile without seeing anyone at all. How those who did remain were living we could not say. Presumably they all had caches of looted stores that supported them and their families; and obviously it was no matter for close inquiry. One noticed also how many of those one did see had taken to carrying weapons as a matter of course. We ourselves adopted the habit of carrying them—guns, not rifles—slung over our shoulders, though less with any expectation of needing them than to discourage the occasion for their need from arising. There was a kind of wary preparedness which was still some distance from instinctive hostility. Chance-met men still passed on gossip and rumors, and sometimes hard news of a local kind. It was by such means that we learned of a quite definitely hostile ring now in existence around London; how the surrounding district had somehow formed themselves into miniature independent states and forbidden entry after driving out many who had come there as refugees; how those who did try to cross the border into one of these communities were fired upon without question.

In the new year the sense of things pressing in upon us grew stronger. The high-tide mark was now close to the seventy-five foot level. The weather was abominable, and icy cold. There seemed to be scarcely a night when there was not a gale blowing from the southwest. It became rarer than ever to see anyone in the streets, though when the wind did drop for a time the view from the roof showed a surprising number of chimneys smoking. Mostly it was wood smoke, furniture and fitments burning, one supposed; for the coal stores in power stations and railway yards had all disappeared the previous winter.

From a purely practical point of view I doubt whether anyone in the country was more favored or as secure as our group. The food originally supplied, together with that acquired later, made a store which should last sixteen people for some years. There was an immense reserve of diesel oil, and petrol, too. Materially we were better off than we had been a year ago when there were more of us. But we had learned, as had many before us, about the bread-alone factor, one needed more than adequate food. The sense of desolation began to weigh more heavily still when, at the end of February, the water lapped over our doorsteps for the first time, and the building was filled with the sound of it cascading into the basements.

Some of the party grew more worried. "It *can't* come very much higher, surely. A hundred feet *is* the limit, isn't it?" they were saying.

It wasn't much good being falsely reassuring. We could do little more than to repeat what Bocker had said; that it was a guess. No one had known, within a wide limit, how much ice there was in the Antarctic. No one was quite sure how much of the northern areas that appeared to be solid land, tundra, was in fact simply a deposit on a foundation of ancient ice; we just had not known enough about it. The only consolation was that Bocker now seemed to think for some reason that it would not rise above one hundred and twenty-five feet—which should leave our aerie still intact. Nevertheless, it required fortitude to find reassurance in that thought as one lay in bed at night, listening to the echoing splash of the wavelets that the wind was driving along Oxford Street.

One bright morning in May, a sunny, though not a warm morning, I missed Phyllis. Inquiries eventually led me on to the roof in search of her. I found her in the southwest corner gazing towards the trees that dotted the lake which had been Hyde Park, and crying. I leaned on the parapet beside her, and put an arm around her. Presently she stopped crying. She dabbed her eyes and nose, and said: "I haven't been able to get tough, after all. I don't think I can stand this much longer, Mike. Take me away, please."

"Where is there to go?—if we could go," I said.

"The cottage, Mike. It wouldn't be so bad there, in the country. There'd be things growing—not everywhere dying, like this. There isn't any hope here—we might as well jump over the wall here if there is to be no hope at all."

I thought about it for some moments. "But even if we could get there, we'd have to live," I pointed out, "we'd need food and fuel and things."

"There's—" she began, and then hesitated and changed her mind. "We could find enough to keep us going for a time until we could grow things. And there'd be fish, and plenty of wreckage for fuel. We could make out somehow.

It'd be hard—but, Mike, I can't stay in this cemetery any longer—I can't.

"Look at it, Mike! Look at it! We never did anything to deserve all this. Most of us weren't very good, but we weren't bad enough for this, surely. And not to have a chance! If it had only been something we could fight—But just to be drowned and starved and forced into destroying one another to live—and by things nobody has ever seen, living in the one place we can't get at them!

"Some of us are going to get through this stage, of course—the tough ones. But what are the things down there going to do then? Sometimes I dream of them lying down in those deep dark valleys, and sometimes they look like monstrous squids or huge slugs, other times as if they were great clouds of luminous cells hanging there in rocky chasms. I don't suppose that we'll ever know what they really look like, but whatever it is, there they are all the time, thinking and plotting what they can do to finish us right off so that everything will be theirs.

"Sometimes, in spite of Bocker, I think perhaps it is the things themselves that are inside the sea-tanks, and if only we could capture one and examine it we should know how to fight them, at last. Several times I have dreamed that we have found one and managed to discover what makes it work, and nobody's believed us but Bocker, but what we have told him has given him an idea for a wonderful new weapon which has finished them all off.

"I know it all sounds very silly, but it's wonderful in the dream, and I wake up feeling as if we had saved the whole world from a nightmare—and then I hear the sound of the water slopping against the walls in the street, and I know it isn't finished; it's just going on and on and on.

"I can't stand it here any more, Mike. I shall go mad if I have to sit here doing nothing any longer while a great city dies by inches all round me. It'd be different in Cornwall, anywhere in the country. I'd rather have to work night and day to keep alive than just go on like this. I think I'd rather die trying to get away than face another winter like last."

I had not realized it was as bad as that. It wasn't a thing to be argued about. "All right, darling," I said. "We'll go."

Everything we could hear warned us against attempting to get away by normal means. We were told of belts where everything had been razed to give clear fields of fire, and there were booby traps and alarms, as well as guards. Everything beyond those belts was said to be based upon a cold calculation of the number each autonomous district could support. The natives of the districts had banded together and turned out the refugees and the useless on to lower ground where they had to shift for themselves. In each of the areas there was acute awareness that another mouth to feed would increase the shortage for all. Any stranger who did manage to sneak in could not hope to remain unnoticed for long, and his treatment was ruthless when he was discovered—survival demanded it. So it looked as though our own survival demanded that we should try some other way.

The chance by water, along inlets that must be constantly widening and reaching further, looked better, and but for the luck of our finding that sturdy little motorboat, the *Midge,* I don't know what would have happened to us. It came to us through the rather ghastly accident of the owner's being shot trying to escape from London. Ted Jarvey found it and brought it to us, knowing we had been searching futilely for weeks for just such a boat.

An uneasy feeling that some of the others might wish to get away, too, and press to come with us turned out to be baseless. Without exception they considered us crazy. Most of them contrived to take one of us aside at some time or another to point out the willful improvidence of giving up warm, comfortable quarters to make a certainly cold and probably dangerous journey to certainly worse and probably intolerable conditions. They helped to fuel and store the *Midge* until she was inches lower in the water, but not one of them could have been bribed to set out with us.

Our progress down the river was cautious and slow, for we had no intention of letting the journey be more dangerous than was necessary. Our main recurrent problem was where to lay up for the night. We were sharply conscious of our probable fate as trespassers, and also of the fact that the *Midge* with her contents was tempting booty. Our usual anchorages were in the sheltered streets of some flooded town. Several times when it was blowing hard we lay up in such places for several days. Fresh water, which we had expected to be the main problem turned out not to be difficult; one could almost always find some still in the tanks in the roof spaces of a partly submerged house. Overall, the trip which used to clock at 268.8 (or .9) by road took us slightly over a month to make.

Round the corner and into the channel the white cliffs looked so normal from the water that the flooding was hard to believe—until we looked more closely at the gaps where the towns should have been. A little later, we were right out of the normal, for we began to see our first icebergs.

We approached the end of the journey with caution. From what we had been able to observe of the coast as we came along there were often encampments of shacks on the higher ground. Where the land rose steeply there were often towns and villages where the higher houses were still occupied though the lower were submerged. What kind of conditions we might find at Penllyn in general and Rose Cottage in particular we had no idea.

I took the *Midge* carefully into the Helford River, with shotguns lying to hand. Here and there a few people on the hillsides stopped to look down at us, but they neither shot nor waved. It was only later that we found they had taken her to be one of the few local boats that still had the fuel to run.

We turned north from the main river. With the water now close on the hundred-foot level the multiplication of waterways was confusing. We lost our way half a dozen times before we rounded a corner on an entirely new inlet and found ourselves looking up a familiar steep hillside at the cottage above us.

People had been there, several lots of them, I should think, but though the disorder was considerable the damage was not great. It was evidently the consumables they had been after chiefly. The stand-bys had vanished from the larder to the last bottle of sauce and packet of pepper. The drum of oil, the candles, and the small store of coal were gone, too.

Phyllis gave a quick look over the debris, and disappeared down the cellar steps. She re-emerged in a moment and ran out to the arbor she had built in the garden. Through the window I saw her examining the floor of it carefully. Presently she came back. "That's all right, thank goodness," she said.

It did not seem a moment for great concern about arbors.

"What's all right?" I inquired.

"The food," she said. "I didn't want to tell you about it until I knew. It would have been too bitterly disappointing if it had gone."

"What food?" I asked, bewilderedly.

"You've not much intuition, have you, Mike? Did you really think that someone like me would be doing all that bricklaying just for fun? I walled-off half the cellar full of stuff, and there's a lot under the arbor, too."

I stared at her. "Do you mean to say——? But that was ages ago! Before the flooding even began."

"But not before they began sinking ships so fast. It seemed to me it would be a good thing to lay in stores before things got difficult, because it quite obviously was going to get difficult later. I thought it would be sensible to have a reserve here, just in case. Only it was no good telling you, because I knew you'd just get stuffy about it."

I sat down, and regarded her. "Stuffy?" I inquired.

"Well, there are some people who seem to think it is more ethical to pay black-market prices than to take sensible precautions."

"Oh," I said. "So you bricked it in yourself?"

"Well, I didn't want anybody local to know, so the only way was to do it myself. As it happened, the food airlift was much better organized than one could have expected, so we didn't need it, but it will come in useful now."

"How much?" I asked.

She considered. "I'm not quite sure, but there is a whole big truckload here, and then there's all the stuff we've got in the *Midge*, too."

I could see, and do see, several angles to the thing, but it would have been churlishly ungrateful to mention them just then, so I let it rest, and we busied ourselves with tidying up and moving in.

It did not take us long to understand why the cottage had been abandoned. One had only to climb to its crest to see that our hill was destined to become an island, and within a few weeks two crawling inlets joined together behind us, and made it one.

The pattern of events, we found, had been much the same here as in other parts—except that there had been no influx: the movement had been away. First there was the cautious retreat as the water began to rise, later the panicky rush to stake a claim on the higher ground while there was still the chance. Those who remain, and still remain, are a mixture of the obstinate, the tardy, and the ever-hopeful who have been saying since the beginning that tomorrow, or, maybe, the next day the water will cease to rise.

A state of feud between those who stayed and those who shifted is well established. The uplanders will allow no newcomers into their strictly-rationed territory: the lowlanders carry guns and set traps to discourage raids on their fields. It is said, though I do not know with how much truth, that conditions here are good compared with Devon and places further east, for, once the inhabitants of the lower ground had been driven out of their homes and set on the move, very many of them decided to keep on going until they should reach the lush country beyond the moors. There are fearsome tales about the defensive warfare against starving gangs that goes on in Devon, Somerset, and Dorset, but here one hears shooting only occasionally, and then on a small scale.

The completeness of our isolation has been one of the difficult things to bear. The radio set, which might have told us something of how the rest of the world, if not our own country, was faring, failed a few days after we arrived, and we have neither the means of testing it, nor of replacing parts.

Our island offers little temptation, so we have not been molested. The people about here grew enough food last summer to keep themselves going, with the help of fish, which are plentiful. Our status is not entirely that of strangers, and we have been careful to make no demands or requests. I imagine we are thought to be existing on fish and what stores we had aboard the *Midge*—and that what can be left of it now is not worth the trouble of a raid on us. It might have been different had the crops been poorer last summer.

I started this account at the beginning of November. It is now the end of January. The water continued to rise slightly, but since about Christmas there seems to have been no increase that we can measure. We are hoping that it has reached its limit. There are still icebergs out in the channel, but they are fewer now.

There are still not infrequent raids by sea-tanks, sometimes single, but more usually in fours or fives, but as a rule they are more of a nuisance than a danger. The people living close to the sea keep a rota of watchers who give the alarm. The sea-tanks apparently don't like climbing, they seldom venture more than a quarter of a mile from the water's edge, and when they find no victims they soon go away again.

By far the worst thing to face has been the cold of the winter. Even making allowance for the difference in our circumstances it has seemed a great deal colder than the last. The inlet below us has been frozen over for many weeks, and in calm weather the sea itself is frozen well out from the shore. But mostly it has not been calm weather; for days on end there have been gales when everything is covered with ice from the spray carried inland. We are lucky in being sheltered from the full force of the southwest, but it is bad enough. Heaven knows what life must be like in the encampments up on the moors when these blizzards blow.

We have decided that when the summer comes we shall try to get away. We shall aim south, in search of somewhere warmer. We could probably last out here another winter, but it would leave us less provisioned and less fit to face the journey that we shall have to make sometime. It is possible, we think, that in what is left of Plymouth or Devonport we may still be able to find some fuel for the engine, but, in any case, we shall rig a mast, and if we are warned-off, or if there is no fuel to be found, then we shall try to make it under sail.

Where to? We don't know yet. Somewhere warmer. Perhaps we shall find only bullets where we try to land, but even that will be better than slow starvation in bitter cold.

And Phyllis agrees. "We'll be taking 'a long shot, Watson; a very long shot!' " she says. "But, after all, what is the good of having been given so much luck if you don't go on using it?"

4th May.

We shall *not* be going south.

This ms. will *not* be left here in a tin box on the chance of someone finding it some day. It will go with us.

And here is why: Two days ago we sighted the first aircraft that we have seen since we came here—or for some time before that. A helicopter that came trundling along the coast, and then turned inland to pass along our own inlet.

We were down by the water, working to get the *Midge* ready for her trip. There was a distant buzzing, then this craft came bumbling along right towards us. We looked up at it, shading our eyes. It was against the sun, but I could make out the R.A.F. circle on its side, and I thought I could see someone waving from the cabin. I waved my hand. Phyllis waved her paintbrush.

We watched it plough along to our left, and then turn north. It disappeared behind our hill. We looked at one another as the sound of the engine dwindled. We did not speak. I don't know how it took Phyllis, but it made me feel a bit queer. I had never thought to find myself in a situation where the throb of an airplane engine would be a kind of nostalgic music in my ears.

Then I realized that the sound was not getting any further away. The craft reappeared, round the other side of the hill. Apparently it had been giving our island a looking over. We watched it steady up and then begin to lower towards the curve of the hill that sheltered us. I dropped my screwdriver, and Phyllis her paintbrush, and we started to run up the hill towards it.

It came down lower, but obviously it was not going to take the risk of landing among the stones and the heather. While it hung there, a door in the side opened. A bundle dropped out, and bounced on the heather, then came a rope ladder, unrolling as it fell. A figure began to climb down the ladder, negotiating it carefully. The helicopter was drifting slowly across the top of the hill, and presently the man dangling on the ladder was hidden from our sight as we panted upwards. We were still some little way from the top when the machine rose and sheered off over our heads, with the ladder being pulled up by someone inside.

We kept on struggling up the slope. Presently we reached a point from which we were able to see a darkly clad figure sitting in the heather apparently exploring itself for breakages.

"It's—" Phyllis began. "It *is!* It's *Bocker!*" she cried, and sped recklessly over the rough ground.

By the time I got there she was on her knees beside him, with both her arms twined round his neck, and crying hard. He was patting her shoulder avuncularly. He held out his other hand to me as I came up. I took it in both of mine, and felt not far from weeping, myself. He was Bocker, all right, and looking scarcely changed from the last time I had seen him. There didn't seem to be much to say for the moment except: "Are you all right? Have you hurt yourself?"

"Only a bit shaken up. Nothing broken. But there seems to be more skill in it than I'd thought," he said.

Phyllis raised her head to tell him: "You never ought to have tried it, A.B.! You might have killed yourself." Then put it back, and went on crying comfortably.

Bocker looked at the tousle of hair on his shoulder for some thoughtful seconds, and then up at me, inquiringly.

I shook my head. "Others have had to face a lot worse —but it has been lonely; and very depressing," I told him.

He nodded, and patted Phyllis's shoulder again. Presently she began to get more control of herself. Bocker waited a little longer, then he remarked: "If you, sir, would care to remove your wife just for a moment, I'd like to find out if I am still able to stand."

He could. "Nothing but a bump and a bruise or two," he announced.

"A lot luckier than you deserve," Phyllis told him severely. "It was a perfectly ridiculous thing to do at your age, A.B."

"Just what I was thinking when I was about halfway down," he agreed.

Phyllis's lips were still trembling as she looked at him. "Oh, A.B.," she said. "It's wonderful to see you again. I still can't believe it."

He put one arm round her shoulders, and linked his other into mine. "I'm hungry," he announced, practically. "Somewhere round here there's a parcel of food that we dropped."

We went down to the cottage, Phyllis chattering like mad all the way except for the pauses in which she stopped to look at Bocker and convince herself that he was really there. When we arrived, she disappeared into the kitchen. Bocker sat down, cautiously.

"There should be drinks now—but they were finished some time ago," I told him sadly.

He pulled out a large flask. He regarded a severe dent in it for a moment. "H'm," he said. "Well, let's hope it's more comfortable going up than coming down." He poured whisky into three glasses, and summoned Phyllis. "Here's to recovery," he said. We drank.

"And now," I said, "since nothing in our experience has been more unlikely than you descending from the skies on a trapeze, we'd like an explanation."

"That wasn't in the plan," he admitted. "When I found out from the London people that you had set out for Cornwall, I guessed that this was where you would be, if you had made it. So, when I was able to, I came to take a look. But the pilot didn't like your bit of terrain at all, and wouldn't risk landing his machine. So I said I'd go down, and they could buzz off to somewhere where they could land, and come back to pick me up in three hours' time."

"Oh," I said, rather flatly. Phyllis just stared at him.

"It's all very well your looking like that, but I'd have been with you before this if you'd stayed where you were. Why didn't you?"

"It got us down, A.B. We thought you'd died when the Harrogate place was overrun. The Whittiers never came back. The link went dead. The helicopter stopped coming. There wasn't a British station to be heard on the air. After a bit it looked as if things really had come to a finish. So we came away. Even rats prefer to die in the open."

Phyllis got up and started to lay the table. "I don't think you would just have quietly stayed there waiting for an inevitable end, either, A.B.," she said.

Bocker shook his head. " 'Oh ye of little faith!' This isn't Noah's world, you know. The twentieth century isn't a thing to be pushed over quite as easily as all that. The patient is still in a grave condition, he's been very, very sick indeed, and he has lost a tragic lot of blood—but he's going to recover. Oh, yes, he's going to recover all right, you'll see."

I looked out of the window at the water spread over former fields, at the new arms of the sea running back into the land, at the houses that had been homes, and now were washed through by every tide. "How?" I asked.

"It isn't going to be easy, but it's going to be done. We lost a great deal of our best land, but the water hasn't risen any more in the last six months, and we reckon that we ought to be able to grow more than enough to feed five million people, once we get organized."

"Five million?" I repeated.

"That's the rough estimate of the present population—not much more than a guess really, of course."

"But it was something like forty-six millions!" I exclaimed.

That was a side that Phyllis and I had avoided talking about, or thinking about more than we could help. In our more depressed moments I had had, I fancy, a vague idea that in the course of time there would be a few survivors living in barbarism, but I had never considered it in figures.

"How did it happen? We knew there was fighting, of course, but this—!"

"Some were killed in the fighting, and of course there were places where a lot were cut off and drowned, but that doesn't really account for more than a small percentage. No, it has been pneumonia mostly that has done the damage. Undernourishment and exposure through three bitter winters; with every dose of flu, every cold, leading to pneumonia. No medical services, no drugs, no communications; nothing to be done about it." He shrugged.

"But, A.B.," Phyllis reminded him, "we just drank to 'Recovery.' Recovery?—With nine out of ten gone?"

He looked steadily at her, and nodded. "Certainly," he said, with confidence. "Five million can still be a nation. Why, damn it, there were no more of us than that in the time of the first Elizabeth. We made ourselves count then, and, by God, we can do it again. But it'll mean working— that's why I'm here. There's a job for you two."

"Job?" said Phyllis, blankly.

"Yes, and it won't be putting across soaps and cheeses this time, it'll be selling morale. So the sooner you both start to brush up your own morale, the better."

"Just wait a minute. I can see this is going to need some explanation," said Phyllis.

She fetched the meal, and we drew our chairs up to the table. "All right, A.B.," she said. "I know you never allow mere eating to interfere with talking. Let's have it."

"Very well," said Bocker. "Now, imagine a country which is nothing but small groups and independent communities scattered all over the place. All communications gone, nearly all of them barricaded off for defense, scarcely anyone with any idea of what may be going on even a mile or two outside his area. Well now, what have you got to do to get a condition like that in to working order again? First, I think, you've got to find a way into these tight, isolated pockets so that you can break them up. To do that you have first to establish some kind of central authority, and then to let the people know that there *is* a central authority—and give them confidence in it. You want to start parties and groups who will be the local representatives of the central authority. And how do you reach them? Why, you just start talking to them and telling them—by radio.

"You find a factory, and start it working on turning out small radio receivers and batteries that you can drop from the air. When you can, you begin to follow that up with receiver-transmitter sets to give you two-way communication with the larger groups first, and then the smaller ones. You break down the isolation, and the sense of it. One group begins to hear what other groups are doing. Self-confidence begins to revive. There's a feeling of a hand at the helm again to give them hope. They begin to feel there's something to work *for*. Then one lot begins to co-operate with, and trade with, the lot next door. And then you have started something indeed. It's a job our ancestors had to do with generations of men on horseback —by radio we ought to be able to make a thundering good start on it in a couple of years. But there will have to be staff—there'll have to be people who know how to put across what might be put across. So, what do you say?"

Phyllis went on staring at her plate for some moments, then she looked, shiny-eyed, at Bocker, and put her hand on his. "A.B.," she said shakily, "have you ever thought that you were nearly dead, and then had a sudden shot of adrenalin?" She leaned across the corner of the table, and kissed him on the cheek.

"Adrenalin," I said, "doesn't take me quite the same way, but I support Phyllis. I very heartily subscribe."

"It makes me feel more drunk than alcohol ever did," said Phyllis.

"Fine," said Bocker. "Then you'd better get busy with the packing up. We'll send a bigger helicopter to take you and your baggage off in three days' time. —And don't leave any food behind; it's going to be a long time yet before we can afford to waste any of that."

He went on explaining and giving instructions, but I doubt whether either of us heard much of them. Then, somehow, he was telling us how he and a few others had escaped after the attack on Harrogate, but there was little room in our minds for that, either, just then. For myself, at any rate, quite an hour must have passed before I came out of the daze which the sudden change of prospects inspired. Then, however, I did get round to realizing that we were being a bit parochial. The operation of unfreezing the masses of locked water might have been carried to a point where it menaced us no further, but that did not mean that it would not be followed by some new, and perhaps equally devastating, form of attack. As far as we knew, the true source of all our troubles was still lurking safely out of reach in its Deeps. I put the point to Bocker.

He smiled. "I don't think I've ever been called an unbridled optimist—"

"I shouldn't think so," agreed Phyllis.

"So," Bocker went on, "I am hoping it will carry some weight when I say that to me the outlook is distinctly hopeful. There have been plenty of disappointments, of

course, and there may be more, but it does look as if, for
the present at any rate, we have got hold of something
which is too much for our xenobathetic friends."

"What, without these cautious qualifications, would it
be?" I asked.

"Ultrasonics," he proclaimed.

I stared at him. "But they've *tried* ultrasonics, half a
dozen times at least. I can distinctly remember——"

"Mike, darling, just shut up; there's a love," said my
devoted wife. She turned to Bocker. "How have they done,
A.B.?" she asked him.

"Well, it's well enough known that certain ultrasonic
waves in water will kill fish and other creatures, so there
were a lot of people who said all along that it would very
likely be the right answer to the Bathies—but obviously
not with the wave-initiator working on the surface, at a
range of five miles or so. The problem was to get the
ultrasonic emitter down there, close enough for it to do
damage. You couldn't just let it down, because its cable
would be electrified or cut—and, judging by precedent,
that would happen long before it got anywhere like deep
enough to be useful.

"But now the Japs seem to have found the answer. A
very ingenious people, the Japs; and, in their more sociable
moments, a credit to science. So far, we have only had a
general description by radio of their device, but it seems
to be a type of self-propelled sphere which cruises slowly
along, emitting ultrasonic waves of great intensity. But the
really clever thing about it is this: it not only produces
lethal waves, but it makes use of them itself, on the principle of an echo sounder, and steers by them. That is to say,
you can fix it to sheer off from any obstacle when it
receives an echo from it at a given distance.

"You see the idea? Set a flock of these things for a
clearance of, say, two hundred feet, and start 'em going at
the end of a narrow Deep. Then they'll cruise along,
keeping two hundred feet from the bottom, two hundred
feet from the sides of the Deep, two hundred feet from
any obstructions, two hundred feet clear of one another,
and turning out a lethal ultrasonic wave as they go. That's
just the simple principle of the things—the Japs' real
triumph has been not only in being able to build them, but

to have built them tough enough to stand the pressure."

"None of it sounds in the least simple to me," Phyllis told him. "The important point is, the things really do work?"

"Well, the Japs claim they do, and there'd not be much object in lying about it. They say they've cleared a couple of small Deeps already. Large masses of organic jelly came up, but they've not been able to make much of that because the pressure change had broken it up and it decomposed quickly in sunlight, but afterwards they tested with cables right down to the bottom, and nothing happened. They're working on other small Deeps now until they've got enough gear to tackle bigger ones. They've flown plans of the things over to the States, and the Americans—who've not been hit nearly as badly as we have in this small island—are going to put them into production, so that's a testimonial.

"It's bound to take some time before they can get busy on a really large scale. However, that isn't our affair for the moment—we haven't any important Deeps near us, and, anyway, it is going to be some time before we can produce anything more than immediate necessities. We were very badly overcrowded on this island, and we've paid for it heavily. We shall have to take steps to see that that doesn't happen again."

Phyllis frowned. "A.B.," she said. "I've had to tell you before about your habit of going just one step further than people are willing to follow you," she told him, severely.

Bocker grinned. "Perhaps it's lucky this one is not going to come up in my time," he admitted.

The three of us sat in Phyllis's arbor, looking out at the view that had changed so greatly in so short a time. For a while, none of us spoke. I stole a sidelong glance at Phyllis; she was looking as though she had just had a beauty treatment.

"I'm coming to life again, Mike," she said. "There's something to live for."

I felt like that, too, but as I looked out over the blue sea still set with a few glistening bergs, I added: "All the same, it isn't going to be any picnic. There's this ghastly climate; and when I think of the winters . . . !"

"Oh," A.B. said, "research is being done on that now,

and the reports indicate that the water will warm up gradually. As a matter of fact," he said, chuckling, "now the ice has gone we may have an even better climate than before, in three or four years' time."

We went on sitting there, and finally Phyllis spoke again. "I was just thinking—Nothing is really new, is it? Once upon a time there was a great plain, covered with forests and full of wild animals. I expect some of our ancestors used to live there, and hunt there, and make love there. Then, one day, the water came up and drowned it all—and there was the North Sea.

"I think we have been here before. And we got through that time."

We were silent for a while. Then Bocker looked at his watch, and said: "That machine will be coming back soon. I'd better make ready for my death-defying act."

"I wish you wouldn't, A.B.," Phyllis told him. "Can't you just let them take a message, and stay here with us until the big helicopter comes?"

He shook his head. "Can't spare the time, I'm really playing truant as it is—only I thought I'd like to be the one to give you two the news. Don't you worry, my dear. The old man's not too doddery to climb a rope ladder yet."

He was as good as his word. When the machine descended over the crest of the hill, he caught the trailing ladder adroitly, clung to it a moment, and then began to climb. Presently arms reached down to help him aboard. He turned in the doorway to wave to us. The machine speeded up, and started to climb. Quite soon it was only a speck that vanished in the distance.